That's All Right, Mama

That's All Right, Mama

A Novel
by
GERALD DUFF

BASKERVILLE
PUBLISHERS, INC.

BASKERVILLE Publishers, Inc.
7616 LBJ Freeway, Suite 220, Dallas, TX 75251-1008

Library of Congress Cataloging-in-Publication Data
Duff, Gerald.
    That's all right, Mama : a novel / by Gerald Duff.
        p. cm.
        ISBN No. 1-880909-33-2 : $20.00 ($27.00 Can.)
        1. Elvis Presley impersonators--Fiction. 2. Rock musicians-
United States--Fiction. 3. Twins--United States--Fiction.
I. Title.
PS3554.U3177T48   1995
813'.54--dc20   94-49212
                                                    CIP

Manufactured in the United States of America
Second Printing, 1995

*This book is in memory of my mother,
Dorothy Jane Irwin Duff,
who loved Elvis,*

*and for my wife,
Patricia Stephens,
who is the reason God made Alabama.*

Preface

I first encountered Mr. Lance Lee in the early phases of a research project I undertook in the latter half of the 1985-86 academic year. It was in Memphis, where I was gathering data for a study of the resurrection/false death mythology surrounding the date of the death anniversary of the singer Elvis Aron Presley.

At that point in time, the coming together of the followers of the deceased rock star had begun reaching large proportions in August of each year. A perusal of hotel, motel, recreational vehicle campground rentals and individual household leasing figures reveals a 32 percent increase over any other public event in the annual Memphis year. Interested readers may see the published results of my work on the topic in the biennial issue of the *Journal of Mass Religious Gatherings* (Vancouver, B.C.), pp. 123-129.

As part of my research, I had begun to survey the nightly performances of the many Elvis Presley imitators who had begun to gather in increasing numbers during each Death Week celebration. Not only did I visit the largest and best-known venues for such singer/actor/imitator performers (one young child of female gender and

Native-American ethnic extraction was part of that number in 1985, I remember), but I also sought out the less frequented and less prominent establishments offering such entertainment to the crowds of people fascinated enough by such to attend these events.

It was in one of these relatively unknown saloon-cum-singing establishments I found Mr. Lance Lee, or rather he found me, on the night in question. I had been guided to the Green Parrot, for such was its appellation, by a professional colleague, Professor James Lanier of Rhodes College, a scholar and specialist in the study of musical tributes to dying and resurrected deities.

Dr. Lanier and I had just ordered refreshment from the waitperson, a young woman attired in a costume designed to resemble that of a 1960s go-go entertainer/dancer, when a man hailed me from where he sat at a table just next to ours. He was taken by the fact that Dr. Lanier and I were jotting down our impressions in notebooks and that I had placed a medium-sized Japanese cassette recorder on the table before me. (I hasten to add that I had previously received permission from both the bartender and the person on stage performing a medley of Elvis Presley songs to do so.)

He announced his name, Lance Lee, informed us that the actor/singer currently onstage was not of a quality worthy of our attention or even the cost of the cassette tape in the machine, and he did so in a colorfully profane manner. Judging that the man seemed jolly enough not to cause alarm and entertained by his linguistic skills, Dr. Lanier and I asked him to join us for a beverage and a good round of conversation.

Mr. Lance Lee did so, proceeding to match us two drinks for our every one and continuously providing a running commentary on the series of performers who took the stage of the Green Parrot. We were soon caught up in the spirit he generated and, knowing as field data gatherers the importance of becoming both one with and one apart from the cultural event of investigatory interest, Dr. Lanier and I allowed ourselves to be vastly entertained by the man's manner, his encyclopedic knowledge of Elvis Presley's public history, and his insights into the career paths of imitators of the man we soon began calling the King, even as he did.

Late into that evening, after Dr. Lanier had excused himself in order to seek a moment of repose in the rear seat of my Toyota minivan, the vehicle I typically employ for fieldwork, Lance Lee and I continued to converse, swapping anecdotes and insights into contemporary popular culture in the most relaxed and convivial manner.

It was then, near four a.m., as the doors of the Green Parrot closed upon the last patrons, ourselves, I must confess, that Lance Lee made his first mention of the astounding claim developed in the body of the manuscript following these words of preface. He was, he told me, in truth and fact, the twin of Elvis Presley, and he had not died at birth as the biographers, critics, and historians assert and believe, and as documentary evidence in Tupelo, Mississippi certifies.

He had, he told me, in his possession ocular proof, and he produced from his wallet a photograph, obviously aged, faded, and lined with cracks across its surface. In the light of a streetlamp near the minivan where Dr. Lanier rested, I examined the archival item closely and admitted that the woman and child pictured thereon resembled to a remarkable degree Gladys Presley and her son Elvis at an early age, possibly four or five years.

I assured him of my belief that the photograph could be of the famous mother/child combination, but that there was no proof certainly that he, Lance Lee, was in any way involved. He pointed out to me that approximately one-third of the photograph was missing, torn down its length carefully as though by someone eager to remove the likeness of another person perhaps pictured there, and declared that the missing portion had been Elvis Aron and the remaining image of a child was indeed he himself, Jesse Garon Presley.

I clapped the clever, entertaining fellow (whom I have never seen since, search though I have for years) on the shoulder and left him there in the parking lot of the Green Parrot and departed in the Toyota minivan with the sleeping professor of Cultural Phenomenology, bound for Dr. Lanier's quarters and then my own hotel room.

The next morning when I arose, rather later than my customary hour because of fatigue from the night before, I discovered the message light blinking on the telephone next to my bed. A call to the desk revealed that someone had left me a package there, and when, in a brief space of time, I reported to claim the mysterious item, I discovered the manuscript of the work the reader of these words may find before him/her: an account, in lamentable physical condition, typed on several different machines with a myriad of interlineations on a full dozen kinds and weights of paper, of the fragmentary autobiography of a person claiming to be Jesse Garon Presley.

Is it authentic? Scholar though I attempt to be, I cannot say. Is it persuasive? Perhaps, to those who want to believe, and to those who continue to visit Graceland on an annual basis to pay homage to the King of Rock and Roll.

I myself am not finally convinced, but I must record the opinion of my esteemed colleague that night in August of 1986 in Memphis at the Green Parrot, the sober and meticulously careful critic of cultural phenomenology, Dr. James Lanier. The document so adventitiously placed in my possession is the closest we shall come, he

4

opines, to the truth about the bifurcations of the Presley personality and to the relationship between the fallen king and his maternal parent. In Lanier's words, found in his monograph on "The Shadow-Self and the Maternal Presence in the Life of Jesse Garon/Elvis Aron Presley," *Journal of Jungian Etiology*, VII, 785-1023, "what we are left to declare of Jesse Garon Presley's account of the ur-myth of his doubleness is that it is, indeed, all right, Mama."

I offer this document, changed in none but typographical and editorial detail, for what I can safely declare it to be: the luminous detritus of a late, hot, scholarly night in Memphis, Tennessee, during the Death Week of 1986. The reader is left to judge for him/herself in that light.

> Gerald Aldine Duff, Ph.D.
> Professor and Sometime Fellow
> of Cultural Phenomenology,
> St. John's College, Oxon.

1

I have never had the benefit of a mother's love. Elvis got it all.

She always made a difference between us, right back to the first things I can remember there in that little bitty house in Tupelo. We were the same, but we weren't the same. He was more himself than I was myself, and he got the big share of everything. There just wasn't enough of whatever it takes to be a person to go around for both of us. Everything that happened later on, there in Mississippi and then in Memphis and New York and Germany and Las Vegas and every damn where else came from that beginning.

When a fertilized egg divides in half and begins to multiply two by two, the same number of chromosomes and genes and whatever else it all is in there, you end up with identical twins. They are the same creature genetically. That's what science will tell you.

Science doesn't explain my voice. Oh, it's like his, and I can deliver a song. But I never could sing it like he could. Not so much that I can't make a living doing it. But I never could touch whatever it was he could with that voice.

One time the old man told me what had happened the

night we were conceived. He generally wouldn't talk about anything he thought was nasty unless he was drunk or guilt-stricken, and this time he was both. Either he had failed to get it up with one of those women he was running with after Mama died or he had had a vision or some damn thing. I forget. Whatever it was, it had got him into the Jack Daniels and into a talking mood.

"What happened that night," he said and knocked back another half-glass, "was that we had just quarreled real bad, your mama and me, about something. Not enough money, I guess. Or no job or something. I had located some busthead whiskey that morning, and I had kept it out behind the house underneath an old wash tub where one of those damn hens was setting on a bunch of eggs.

"So I'd go out every little while for a drink and run my hand up under that tub to get the bottle, and that Rhode Island Red would peck me until I nearly bled. But I finished the whole bottle off by good dark, and I set down on the back steps to watch the moon rise. It was full and red and looked almost as big a coming up as that damn wash tub.

"She came out there to see what I was doing, and when she seen that moon she just tottered and fell back against the screen door so hard she might near split it.

"What's wrong, honey?" I asked her. "Are you all right?"

"Two heads," she said. "It's two of them. Oh, Lord, no. Two in the moon."

"And then she just commenced to squalling and crying and carrying on. And I tried to hold her and quiet her down, you know, there on the back steps to the house. She never quit talking a blue streak about it being two of them and room enough for only one and not but one soul to go between them and all that kind of thing.

"'Blue moon,' she kept saying, 'blue moon.' But that didn't make no sense, because it was all red, you see, just as red as fire."

I didn't bother to explain to Vernon what a blue moon was, because it would have been like trying to explain arithmetic to a back-up drummer. I just let him go on, not that I usually listened to him at all, but this time he was talking about something that involved me directly. And that was a seldom goddamn thing, I'll tell you.

"Well," he said, "I was pretty drunk by then from all that whole bottle and damn tired from fighting that Rhode Island Red all afternoon, so I finally talked her into lying down across the bed. And I went on off to sleep.

"It must have been two or three hours later that I woke up and found out what was going on. I was on my back, and Gladys was astraddle of me, you know, and she was in full gallop. See, that kind of thing never had happened before, and it never happened after, neither, no matter how much I tried to talk her into doing it that way again."

The old man finished off his glass and poured some more into it from the quart bottle, and I stayed completely quiet so he wouldn't change his mind or lose his place or get off on something else.

"What was scary about it," he said, "was that she wasn't looking down at me. I could see up into her face, and she was looking full into that moon, and it was reflecting into her eyes like she was wearing glasses or had little mirrors instead of eyes or something like that. It wasn't red by then, since it had got higher up in the sky. But I could see it plain. Two full-size moons where her eyes were. Not shimmering or moving but just as still and cold as if they was made of two balls of ice.

"About that time I could feel it coming on, you know, starting way back, like it was moving down from my insides and going along my backbone and then taking a turn through my, you know, parts, and it was like fire or electricity moving through me in a kind of rhythm. You know, little shivers, but real regular and getting faster and faster. And then the shakes started coming too close together to keep the little electric feelings apart, and, boom, it just happened, you know, and Gladys just stopped dead still. And it was like she had taken all of me up into her there on that bed, and them two moons in her eyes got real bright and then it was like they exploded, and I blacked out and didn't know nothing until morning when I woke up with the worst pains in my head I ever felt. Last thing I could remember was them moons leaving her eyes like rockets blowing up."

2

How am I going to get back there to Tupelo, to the beginning? I have been thinking about that, and I have been wanting to tell it right, the whole story. I could come at it from several different ways, and every one of them has its points. I could back way off and generalize about everything. I could do my best to convince you that all this really happened and that it was all possible for it to happen. I thought about doing that.

Here is what I come to. There's all kinds of people have different ideas about the same thing, and there's no way to tell which one of them is the best. Who is to judge?

So what I am going to do is give the straight story by telling you little stories, as Mama used to say. Now and then I'll probably hold something back, and I may let you know when I'm doing it, and I may not. That's my business, not yours.

I look at it this way. What you're going to ask is how could it all be true. Am I real? And what I say to that is that it's not my job to convince you I'm alive. Hell, I've had enough to do to convince myself that I'm alive all these years, and I'm still working on that topic. I am alive because I'm speaking, because I'm standing up and talking back, and that's good enough for me now, and its damn sure got to be good enough for you. All right. Back to the birth place.

Mama wouldn't let us play outside in the yard at the same time those days I would come in from the country. That was way before I knew who he was and who I wasn't, of course.

It was a cold morning, back during the war sometime. I was thinking about what I'd seen the day before at the bus station when I'd gone in there with Uncle McCoy. I'd almost run back out to the pickup when I saw it up against the back wall of the waiting room of the Trailways station in Tupelo.

What it was was a shooting gallery with dolls fixed up to look like Hitler and Mussolini and Tojo, and there was a gun there that shot little pellets if you put in some money. Uncle McCoy offered to let me shoot it once during his turn, but I was too afraid to look at Hitler and Tojo long enough to aim the rifle. So I passed on that.

I was remembering that and the bad dreams I'd had all night, about those little bodies with the big heads when Uncle McCoy asked me if I wanted to ride with him over to Uncle Vernon and Aunt Gladys's.

I remember it was cold, like I said, but I don't remember the ride into Tupelo from where Uncle McCoy and Aunt Edith and I lived out in the sticks twelve miles south of town. The first thing that comes into my mind when I think back to that day is the way the smoke looked coming out of the stovepipe on Uncle Vernon and Aunt Gladys's and Elvis's house.

It was a still morning, and the smoke was thick and white, and it looked like to me it was reaching all the way to the sky and connecting things together.

"Looky yonder, Uncle McCoy," I said, "the sky is coming out of Elvis's house."

"You say some fool things, don't you, boy?"

Vernon had the door to the house opened by the time McCoy cut the engine, so I was able to run on into the front room without slowing down. I asked Aunt Gladys where was Elvis as soon as I hit the heat of the house.

"He's lying down in the bedroom resting, Jesse," she said. "He don't feel too good this morning, and I'm making him stay in bed until the sun gets good and up."

"Let me go see him," I said. "I want to tell him about Hitler and Tojo."

"No, you're not," she said. "You can't come in here and scare your cousin like that. He's got to keep his mind happy."

That kind of talk wasn't new for me, of course. I had learned that Elvis was supposed to be treated special and I had been punished plenty of times already for getting him what Aunt Gladys called "too excited."

"Please," I said, "he'll like it."

"No," she said and looked down at me so slow that her eyes seemed to be sorry to have to touch me, "you ain't going to do it. And if you do, I will wear you out myself, and I will do something else, too."

"I won't," I said, and then because I have always wanted to hear what the worst possible thing could be, I asked her what else she would do, too.

"If you get Elvis to crying and having bad dreams," she said. "I will take you outside in the yard where that little house is, and I will show you what's in there."

I knew the little house she was talking about, of course. Elvis and I had broken the lock off that structure a long time ago, and we had spent enough time inside it to know there wasn't nothing worth playing with in it, and that the two or three boxes inside had nothing in them but a few letters and papers with writing on them that we didn't care nothing about.

So I wasn't scared of what was in that little house in the back yard. What I *was* scared of, though, was the idea of having Aunt Gladys take me off by herself and making me go with her into a little room where the only people there would be us. She had a way of grabbing my hands and pulling me up close to her so she could look into my eyes for a minute or two that scared the fool out of me.

Looking into her eyes, so brown they seemed all pupil and so big I felt like I could fall into them and never come out, I would imagine myself getting smaller and smaller under her inspection until I might turn into something no bigger than a pecan and roll off across the floor and get lost under a piece of furniture or fall through a knot-hole.

When she studied me like that, she would squeeze her lips together until there was just a straight line across the bottom of her face and then she would say words to herself so low that I couldn't understand what she was saying.

"Mama," Elvis hollered from the bed, "let Jesse come in here and play with me."

"Not now, darling," she said.

"I believe it would help me to see him," Elvis said.

"All right, sugar," she said and her lips seemed to get bigger and softer as I looked at her, "just for a little while, then. I don't want Jesse giving you nothing that'll make you sicker."

"He won't never," Elvis said, and I went on in to see him, banging the door back against the wall as I went through it hard enough to make the whole house shake.

"Don't you make them loud popping noises," Uncle Vernon said. "You boys don't get started with none of that rattling and banging in there, now."

"We won't, Daddy," Elvis hollered, making a

scrunched-up face at me, and then whispering low for me to close the door.

"Guess what I found, Jesse," he said. "Something good, too. You ain't never seen nothing like it."

"What?" I asked him. "I seen Tojo and Hitler yesterday. They got big old heads and teeth like in a dog's mouth sticking out from their lips."

"Where was they? Up on the ceiling when you was trying to go to sleep?"

"No," I said. "It wasn't no dream. Really I saw them. At the bus station up against the wall, and Uncle McCoy shot at them and made them spin around every time he hit them."

"You mean some kind of a toy, then, or a game or something," Elvis said. "That ain't near what I found. I'm talking about something real and scary."

"What?" I said. "Is it a ghost's clothes?"

That was what Elvis tried to tell me he had found the last time I had come into Tupelo with Uncle McCoy. It was a thing I believed for a few minutes until he showed me what he was talking about, and I realized it wasn't nothing but a pair of women's step-ins. He finally admitted he had pulled them out of the ditch that ran along the road in the front of the house. The only thing interesting about them was the blood stains down in the crotch, which proved to Elvis that the woman had been stabbed and killed by somebody driving along the road there in East Tupelo.

I knew better than that already by then, but he didn't want to listen to me tell the truth about it. So I let him go on believing it was a murder that had happened. He always seemed to feel better when he was believing something that was an obvious lie. The woman's ghost, see, was never going to be quiet until it had its step-ins back on.

"No," he said. "It ain't no ghost clothes. It's something even you'll be scared of."

"Well, what is it, then? Is it something Aunt Gladys told you about would happen if you did something bad?"

That was pure-dee Gladys. She would just pour that stuff into him, right from the time he was able to understand what she was saying up to when she died in the hospital in Memphis. Don't do this because that will happen. Don't eat fish and drink milk at the same time or you'll die. Don't ever start something you can't finish on a Friday. Or it'll fail. Step on a crack and you break your mother's back. I tried that one out, and I know it didn't work.

"It's in the back of the house," Elvis said. "We'll have to go out there to see it. And then we can do something to it."

He got on out of the bed and we eased out the back door of the house while the grown folks were talking in the front room by the heater. I remember looking back through the door between the kitchen and the front room and seeing Aunt Gladys backed up to the wood stove with the tail of her dress hiked up to let the heat get to her. It made something low in my belly feel funny to see her like that, and I jerked my head back around so all that was before me was the yard and the cold weather outside.

Elvis was already halfway across the cleared part in back, and by the time I caught up to him we were in the patch of pines that marked the end of the Presleys' yard. Elvis looked up at the trees and counted off three of them and then kneeled down next to the fourth one beside a flat sheet of galvanized metal there in the pine straw.

"Are you ready?" he asked and looked up at me, just the way he always did later on whenever he had something to show me that he thought was dangerous and scary. You know, some new kind of pill or a high-ratio gear shift or a woman that truly liked to get oral on you.

"Yeah," I said. "Show it to me."

He pulled up the sheet of metal and propped it against the bole of the pine tree, and I leaned over to look into the hole he'd uncovered. At first it was too dark to tell what it was, there in the shade of the evergreens, and I had to bend over closer to recognize it.

"Is it a inner tube?" I said.

"Naw, Jesse. It's a snake. Biggest old snake in the world. And I'm the one that found him."

It was big. Coiled up in the bottom of that hole, the thing looked to me like it could have swallowed both of us and never slowed down.

"Is it dead?" I asked, stepping back but keeping my eyes fixed on the thing.

"It's alive. Something like that don't never die." Elvis poked it a little jab with a long stick that had been propped against the pine, and a little wave seemed to move in a slow surge all around the curves of its dark body.

"See," he said. "It can't die. It come with all this." He moved his left hand in a little circle that took in the stand of pines, the back yard, the Presley place, Tupelo, everything.

"It's always been here," he said. "And it's always going to be. Never going to die out."

"We could kill it," I told him. "Just like them chickens."

"Nuh uh," Elvis said.

"Could, too. You hit something hard enough or stick something into it deep enough, and if it's alive, it can die."

"Not this snake," he said. "Not old Tarzan Snake. I dreamed about it, and I know."

"What," I said. "After you saw it, you dreamed about it? Course you did, and you woke up a-squalling, too, and Aunt Gladys had to come put you in the bed with her."

"Naw," he said. "Before. I dreamed about it before I found it, and it told me things."

"What kind of things? Just old snake ideas?"

"It told me how to do stuff. What kind of things made stuff happen. About how poison works when you put it in something to make it die."

"Snakes don't know nothing," I said. But I remember I was starting to feel uneasy there in the pine grove looking down at that hole full of reptile. Elvis hadn't taken his eyes off of the thing since he'd pulled that sheet of metal off the hole, and it was beginning to make me feel the way it always did when he got to talking about stuff like that.

It always started down in my belly like there was something squeezing tighter together, so tight that I was going to have to run to make it ease up. It was the way I would feel the times when I thought I was late getting somewhere or that I was being left somewhere strange where I didn't know anybody. A kind of a high tight sick feeling from my breastbone on down.

"They don't," I said again. "Snakes is just like dogs. There ain't nothing in their heads. They don't even know they're a snake."

"This one does," Elvis said toward the hole at our feet. "Old Tarzan Snake knows who he is. He knows what he is, too. He told me in my dream."

"Oh, yeah, Mr. Smart Alec," I said. "What did he say he was to you in that old crybaby dream?"

"Said he was a-coming. Said he was going to live with me and look in my face when I wanted him to. Said he was going to show me how his old snake tongue worked when I was ready for him to."

"It just sticks out like the devil's tongue," I said. "It's

just forked. That's all it is."

"Tarzan Snake told me he would teach me things," Elvis said, leaning forward to rub the long stick up and down the snake's back and watching the ripples in its muscles.

"He said he would give me his voice. He said I could use it."

"Is that right?" I said. "Well, just watch this here." And I leaned forward and grabbed the stick out of Elvis's hand and jabbed the sharp end of it as hard as I could into one of the circles of the snake's body, putting all my weight into it as the point plunged through.

Elvis hollered as loud as I ever heard him and jumped on my back, knocking me on the ground just to the left of the hole and close enough to where the snake was lying that I could see the blunt end of its head not over a foot from my face. As I tried to get up from underneath Elvis, who had one arm around my neck and was hitting me on the back of the head with his fist, I saw the snake's head move and lift slowly from the coils and turn toward me. Its eyes flickered as though they saw me and the tongue moved in and out of the mouth three times, real fast, and then the whole thing began to move in a slow strong spasm. I never have forgot that.

By that time I was able to start hollering too, and I could hear the back screen door of the house fly open as somebody came running down the steps.

"Elvis," Aunt Gladys was yelling, "Honey, where are you? What's he doing to you?"

"Cover him up," Elvis said, letting go of my neck and rolling off me to reach for the sheet of metal. "Don't you tell or I'll say you was beating me up."

I didn't say anything then, watching Elvis cover the hole with the snake rolling around at the bottom of it with the broken-off stick in its side, and I didn't say anything inside the house later as Aunt Gladys held me steady by the shoulders and looked straight into my eyes. All I could think about was the dark thread of blood coming out of the hole in the snake's side, so deep red it was almost black, and the way my insides were telling me I had to run, run, run.

Elvis had one last thing to say to me as I was getting up into the pickup to ride back to the country with Uncle McCoy.

"Alive," he said, his eyes on me as blue as mine and as glassy and narrow as the snake's as he spoke, standing on the running board while Gladys hollered from the front porch.

I wanted to say "dead," but my insides wouldn't let me say anything.

"I told you," Gladys was saying, "I told you not never to go with Jesse Garon outside."

3

Several years after old Tarzan Snake I'm still living out in the country with Uncle McCoy and Aunt Edith, but I have learned a lot more about how things are and what's really going on. By this time Elvis has already won that second prize in the Mississippi-Alabama Fair for standing up in front of about fifty mothers of contestants and three judges to sing "Old Shep." I was there and saw it, but Aunt Gladys didn't know I had sneaked into the back of the building to watch.

See, I had got to go to the fair, but I wasn't supposed to be seen with Elvis there or go on any of the rides with him, and I was especially not supposed to be there when he was singing his song in that children's contest.

I never was a fool. At least about little things. I could figure things out, and I had already started to realize that the way I was kin to my cousin Elvis wasn't the way I was kin to any of the rest of the family. And, God, there was lots of them, so many it's taken me fifty years to be able to forget most of them.

But I don't want to tell about the second prize Elvis won at the fair, no matter how important all these biographers and critics see that episode to be. It wasn't that big a deal, I can tell you. I mean not at the time, of course.

What Mama did with it later is another story, and that's a large part of what I've got to explain to get this thing all told right. What I want to describe right now comes later than the first time Elvis strapped on a guitar and throwed his head back to sing in front of an audience at the fair.

We were in the fifth grade, me out in that little country school south of Tupelo and Elvis there in town. It was an afternoon early in the spring, and I remember I was out in a field full of new clover in the back of Uncle McCoy's house. I had taken me a piece of pine sapling about three feet long and peeled all the bark off of it to make a baseball bat. It was green and too heavy to swing right, but I was using it anyway to knock little rocks off into the woods that come up to the edge of the clover.

Anything hit into the woods on the fly was a homerun. Anything that bounced once was a triple, twice a double, and so on. Out was either missing one of the rocks or knocking it foul. I would do that for hours.

I had just moved a man into scoring position that day when I heard Uncle Vernon's old car come churning up into the front yard. I drove the runner on in with a double, and then I ran on around to the front of the house to see if Elvis was with him.

It was just Uncle Vernon, so I told him hello and went on back to my pine sapling and my pile of rocks.

I wasn't there but a few minutes when Uncle McCoy opened the back door to the house and hollered at me to come in they wanted to talk to me.

"Jesse Garon," said Uncle Vernon after I'd walked into the front room where they were sitting, "I'm going to ask you if you'd be willing to do something for your Aunt Gladys."

"Yes sir," I said. "What?"

Vernon looked over at McCoy, and both of them looked

away as soon as their eyes met. I could hear Aunt Edith back in the kitchen opening up the fire door to the cookstove loud enough to make the stovepipe rattle. I knew by that not to say anything else until Vernon answered.

"It's at the school house, son," he said and cleared his throat a time or two. "It's about your cousin."

"What?" I said. "Is Elvis sick?"

"Why don't you just listen, boy," said Uncle McCoy. "Maybe you'll learn something. Don't be always broadcasting when you ought to be tuning in."

"Jesse Garon," said Vernon, "what we want you to do is to go on there to the fifth grade in Tupelo for a day or two, there at Elvis's school."

"With Elvis?"

"No, son, not with Elvis," Vernon said. "That's the whole thing, see."

I remember he stopped and looked over at Uncle McCoy, and I could hear the floor creak behind me as Aunt Edith came closer to the kitchen door.

"That's the whole thing," Vernon said again. "Gladys wants you to go to the school there for a day or two and make out like you're Elvis. You know, play like you're him."

Right then I felt the way I had the time Elvis showed me Old Tarzan Snake under that sheet of metal in the backyard in Tupelo. My insides moved way down in my belly, and the room seemed like it got hot all of a sudden, and it seemed like that everything in Uncle McCoy's and Aunt Edith's house got a hard edge on it that I could literally see. I remember thinking that I bet they can't see that line going exactly around everything in the room, showing where it stopped and everything that wasn't it began.

"Won't people know it ain't him?" I said.

"Boy, you know better than that," Uncle McCoy said.

"McCoy," said Vernon. "Gladys told you about that kind of talk."

"Well, goddamn it," said Uncle McCoy.

"Both of you shut up," Aunt Edith said, in a high voice, coming up behind me from the kitchen. "Don't y'all see Jesse standing in front of you? I know he sees you two."

"Well, I just..."

"Don't you say a damn thing else, McCoy," she said, and then, looking at Vernon, "Go on and ask him and be done with it."

"I was just fixing to," said Vernon.

"Jesse Garon," he went on, "they ain't nobody won't believe you ain't Elvis. You're just like him. You know that."

I didn't know it then, and I've been trying not to know it ever since. You know, back then I thought that Elvis looked like *me* a good bit. Not just like me, of course. Nobody could look just like me, I figured, whenever I would think about it, which was seldom enough. Oh, we were alike, I knew that. But I had never had a reason to look at myself in a mirror and think of anybody but me before that afternoon in McCoy and Edith's front room.

That was what started me studying myself so much. That's what got me into this whole thing. That late afternoon in the spring, the sun setting behind the stand of pines across the dirt road in front of the house and Vernon looking first up at me, then down at the floor. I can draw a line from there to where I am right now, and there to here and there ain't a break or a curve in it.

"It's a couple of boys at school," Vernon said. "They been picking on him every day for the last several weeks."

"That ain't nothing," I said.

"Son, it ain't nothing to you, and that's the truth. That's why she came up with the idea. But it's a whole lot to

Elvis. He ain't like you in that way."

"What does he do?"

"Can't sleep. Cries. Afraid to go to school in the morning. Can't do his schoolwork."

"What do them boys pick on him about?" I said.

"Aw," said Vernon, "his lunch, you know. He has to carry biscuits and sidemeat to eat. I hadn't got the money for him to buy the plate lunch or to get that store light bread the rest of them takes."

"They make fun of that in Tupelo school?" I said.

"Well, yeah. That, and the way Elvis looks, you know."

"I'll do it," I said. "I want to."

"Are you going to get him back here by Sunday?" Aunt Edith said.

"I imagine Gladys will want him back here by then, all right," said Vernon.

"I hope she'll sew his clothes up at least."

"I'll tell her to do that," said Vernon.

"Hah," Aunt Edith said.

"The biggest one is named Leo," Elvis told me the next morning while we were drinking our coffee and eating biscuits. "He's got a big old fat face and flobber lips."

"Where does he sit?" I asked. "Next to you?"

"In that desk in front of me. His name is Leo Peeples, so that's where he sits. Alphabetical."

"You're in the back desk on the far row in the second room, then?"

"That's it. The othern's Billy Mathis, and he ain't very big, but he's always along with Leo."

"They have been so mean to your cousin, Jesse Garon," said Gladys, "that I have laid awake every night worrying about it."

She was making my lunch on the other side of the table

25

from where Elvis and me were sitting, stopping every now and then to lean across and pat him on the cheek while he told me about where things were in the schoolhouse and how to get along as him there all day.

"I'm bound to mess up some," I told him. "Since I ain't never been there before or nothing. Somebody's going to see something funny in the way that I act."

"Jesse Garon," said Elvis, laying his biscuit down in the plate and looking at me with his eyes starting to brim up with water, "there ain't nobody notices me much at school. Except Leo and Billy. Nobody won't see nothing wrong."

"Honey, honey," Gladys said and put down the sandwich she was making to come over and hold Elvis's face between both hands. "It's going to be all right, sugar."

"Yeah," I said. "They are going to notice you all right, Elvis. And it won't be long neither."

"Jesse, do you want two or three meat biscuits in your lunch sack?" Gladys asked me, never taking her eyes off Elvis as she spoke.

"Three," I said. "These here are real good, Aunt Gladys."

She walked me to the school that morning, just like she would every time I stepped in to be Elvis at school from then on. I wanted her to do it, and I didn't want her to do it, at the same time. She always walked him to school, even in Memphis, at least up to the time Elvis started high school, and that was her excuse for going along with me then and later.

I never knew what to say to her, walking along there between the ditch and the edge of the road on the way to the school house, and I always felt the whole time every time that I wasn't doing something right or that I was forgetting to say something I ought to. You know how it is when there's something just at the edge of your mind that you have just brushed up against when you're thinking about something else. And at the time you do it you tell yourself now that's really what I want to be thinking about and I'll come back to it just as soon as I finish this thing that I've already got started. But when you do get through with the first thing and try to go back and take up the thing you barely glimpsed and now have time for, it's gone. You can't get it back, and you're sorry you didn't just take it up when you first came across it instead of going on with that first thing you were onto.

That's the way I always felt with that woman. With Aunt Gladys. Hell, I'll say it. With Mama.

Anyway, that first morning I filled in for Elvis she walked me down the little dirt road from the house up to the paved highway and on down to the road the Tupelo Elementary School was on. She didn't say anything most of the way. Just held on to my left hand because that was what she always did with Elvis, she told me, although she knew I probably didn't like that kind of thing.

When we came in sight of the school house, a red brick building that back then looked to me as big as the Astrodome would look to me years later, she stopped and pulled me around so I was facing her. There was a breeze that morning, and her hair was all pushed up by it on one side so that she looked like she was mad or in a big hurry.

"Jesse Garon," she said. "You understand why I'm asking you to do this now, don't you? I mean me and your Uncle Vernon asking you. Him too."

"Yes, ma'am," I said. "Because them boys is being mean to Elvis."

"That's right. We can't let him think people can do that to him and get away with it."

"They ain't going to," I said. "I don't want nobody to bother him, neither."

"Jesse Garon," Gladys said. "I thank you. You be careful."

"Don't you worry no more about Leo and Billy. Elvis is going to take care of them boys."

"Jesse," she began and then stopped talking and turned around to go back the way she had come, never looking back a time as she walked up to the paved road and then down it until she was out of sight behind the pines.

I went on in the front door of the red brick building just as the bell was ringing and found the second class-room to the right with no trouble. I recognized it was the right one by the miniature bale of cotton that Elvis said would be sitting on the teacher's desk in front of the class. I was one of the first ones to come into the room, but by the time I had reached the last seat in the far row a whole bunch more of Elvis's fifth grade classmates had come swarming in, banging desk tops and dropping books and pushing at each other.

While they were all getting settled in their seats, I lifted up the top of my desk to see what was inside of it that I might be able to use. I remember there were a few sheets of Blue Horse notebook paper, a picture of a gospel quartet that Elvis must have torn out of a newspaper, two or three little short pencil stubs, and a metal compass. You know what I'm talking about. One of those dudes with a sharp point to stick in a piece of paper and a pencil at the other end to turn around and draw circles with. I took it out and was closing the lid on the rest of the junk when I felt the front part of my desk jolt as somebody flopped down against it.

I looked up from the compass to see who it was and could tell from the hanging mouth that it had to be Leo Peeples. He was twisted around in his seat to look over his shoulder at me, and when he saw me looking at him, he let his mouth hang open even wider to say something.

"Hey, biscuit-eater," he said. "How you this morning,

you country son of a bitch."

"Fine, Flobber Lips," I said and ran the point of the compass about an inch deep into his left arm high up on the shoulder.

He hollered loud enough to make everybody in the room quit whatever they were doing and swing around to see what was happening in that back corner of Room 102. Leo had to jerk away from me twice before the compass point came out of his arm muscle. I remember it didn't make much blood, just kind of a blue hole with one drop of red that kept popping up everytime he wiped it off.

"What's going on back there?" said the woman at the front of the room as she worked her way back to us between two rows of kids who were all leaning out of their desks to look back where Leo was squalling in his seat. "Who did what?"

"Elvis," said Leo from between those big fat flobber lips, "Elvis. He stabbed me with a knife."

In between his tears and his straining to twist around to look at the blue hole in the fat part of his arm, Leo Peeples was a busy fifth grader. He was poking at the hole, pulling at his shirt sleeve to get it up high enough to see where it was hurting him, trying to look at the teacher who was standing next to him by then, and laying his head down on his desk only to rear up again in a kind of a rolling, squirming motion.

"Did you stab him, Elvis?" said the teacher, leaning down toward me and trying to see into my face.

"No, ma'am, Miz Blackstock," I said, well-coached about names by Elvis, "It was an accident. See here."

I lifted the compass up to show her, pencil end first.

"I was just drawing some circles on a piece of paper to make a design, and when Leo sat down in his seat real hard and throwed his arm back on the top of my desk, it made the compass slip."

"Made it slip," Miss Blackstock said. "Oh."

"Yes, ma'am. And the pencil point of it must have poked him. I didn't do it on a purpose."

"Are you sorry it happened, Elvis?" she said.

"I sure am. I sure didn't mean to have nothing like that happen."

With these words, I leaned forward in my seat and put my right hand on Leo's good shoulder.

"I'm sorry, Leo. It was an accident."

"All right, Leo. Elvis has said he's sorry. You go on down to the boy's room and put some water on your arm if it's still hurting you. I'll give you an aspirin to take."

The teacher walked on back to the front of the room and told us to take out a book about American history and read from some page numbers she gave us. I forget them, of course, but what it was about was reconstruction in the South after the Civil War. We weren't that far along in the book in the country school where I was going, so I found reading it kind of interesting. About halfway through the assignment, Leo came back into the room and sat down in front of me again, looking back over his shoulder as he did, his flobber lips wet and hanging.

"Leo," I said in a whisper, "it ain't over yet, rubber mouth. I'm going to whip your ass at lunch period and send you home squalling."

Poor old Leo was too much in a state of shock to say anything back to me, and for the rest of the time before lunch recess he sat as far forward in his desk as he could, keeping a good steady distance between himself and the craziness that had settled down on Elvis.

When they let us out for the lunch recess, everybody made like hell for the side yard of the school, a piece of mud so beat down by having kids play on it that not a blade of grass or even a weed could be found anywhere.

Several of the kids came up to where I was standing by a set of monkey bars to ask what had happened to old Leo and to try to take a reading of what had got into Elvis.

"Ask old Flobber Lips what happened," I told one of the most talkative of the bunch in front of me, a short kid with eyes set so close together he looked like a fox squirrel. "He can tell you what comes of messing with me."

"You go ask him, Elvis," said the squirrel-headed kid. "There he is over yonder with Billy Travis."

"I believe I will," I said. "Y'all watch how scared old Flobber Lips is of me."

I remember the rest of the kids started yelling like a bunch of Indians in a Saturday serial at the picture show, and they all ganged in behind me as I walked directly up to Leo and Billy Travis.

It was a sight that spring morning there in the Tupelo Elementary school yard. Mud everywhere, kids running to fall in behind me, Leo and Billy up against the wire fence that ran along the back side of the school, and in the air the sounds coming from a flock of blackbirds feeding in the field across the road.

I don't know when I've felt any better, whether in Mississippi, Tennessee, or Eugene, Oregon.

As soon as I got within range, I hit old Leo with a right to the belly and then busted his lower lip when he leaned over to favor the pain in his guts. Billy Travis was backing up and trying to run, but by this time the kids had all swarmed in around us, and he couldn't find a way through all the people surrounding him. I had to hit him in the back of the head first to get him to turn around and look at me, and then I landed a shot on the left side of his face that caused him to cover up and commence squalling.

"Well," I said. "Is that enough for y'all this morning? Or am I going to have to just wear your asses out?"

"I give, Elvis," said Leo, inspecting the blood that appeared on his fingers everytime he touched them to his lower lip. "You win."

"Yeah, I do," I said. "And I am sick and tired of taking shit from you and him. And I ain't going to take no more, or it's going to be a war between us. You got that?"

"I won't do it no more," said Billy Travis. "I just want to be friends."

"What about you, Leo? You flobber-lipped ugly-looking thing."

"I done told you I give," said Leo and broke into a run off through the bunch of kids around us, looking back over his shoulder to be sure I wasn't going to follow him.

I remember for the rest of the day kids sent me notes back to Elvis's desk telling how much they liked what I'd done and how they wanted to be in Elvis's gang from now on. I gave all those little pieces of paper to Elvis later that day except for one I kept. It was from a little blonde girl with her hair twisted into ringlets who sat a row or two over from me and who kept turning back to look at me all during the rest of that time there in Room 102.

What she had done was to draw a little heart on the paper and below that she wrote, "You have the prettiest eyes in the fifth grade. You know who."

I never even asked Elvis who she was. I didn't want him to think about her. That note was mine.

That was the first time I played Elvis, that day I bought him some room in the fifth grade of Tupelo Elementary School by whipping them old boys, and everybody in the little house in East Tupelo thought it was fine when I told them what had happened.

Elvis was so damn high hearing me tell about it that he

could hardly wait for me to talk.

"And then what did I do," he'd say. "What did old Leo do then after I hit him the second time?" And on and on.

Aunt Gladys didn't want me to get too graphic about the whole thing, concerned as she always was about the dreams Elvis would have in the nights following any big excitement, so I tried to tone things down as I answered E's questions.

Oh, let me tell you, I was always alert to the environment. I knew when to soft-pedal and when to come on strong, when to speak up and when to hush, when to lay back and when to jump out into the middle of the floor.

That's the kind of stuff you learn when you're the dark twin. I've got to give her credit, Gladys was right, when she told the old man what she saw in the blue moon that night in dog-ass Mississippi. Two heads and two bodies and only one soul between them. Some heavy duty pulling and tearing coming up somewhere down the line. Bound to happen.

But at the time, sitting there in the front room of the Presley house drinking a bottle of orange soda pop that Gladys had produced from somewhere and telling Elvis what he had done to the assholes surrounding him, I felt pretty good about the day.

Hell, everybody was looking at me, they were listening and bringing me things to eat and drink, and Elvis was being told to hush up and let Jesse Garon talk.

All that was sweet music to my ears, I've got to admit. But there was something else working too, something else that had to do with the way a little queasy feeling kept kicking up right in the middle of my stomach and the bitter taste that kept coming up into my mouth with each swallow I took from that bottle of orange drink Mama had given me.

I was recounting my own story, the thing I had done that day, and they were all listening, all my audience and nobody else's, but I was listening to myself too, and what I was hearing was not all that pure to me. See, what I was reliving was a thing that had taken place in my life, something that had made people notice me and give me their full attention and all that goes with that, but I was telling it not as my own story, really, but as Elvis's.

I was only an eleven year old kid at the time, but I could tell that some strange distance was opening up in my own head and in my own life. Some kind of gap was beginning to appear between me doing something and me getting the sense I had really done it. There was a hole beginning to form right in the middle of who I was, a hole that was starting to push things away from each other that ought to be joining up instead of drifting apart.

That hole was beginning to suck the light right out of the room to down inside where all the darkness was coming from, but all the light in the world didn't seem to me to be enough to light up that gap so I could see its bottom and what might be down there waiting for me.

Sitting there sipping that bitter orange, I was trying to tell my story about what I had done, but the telling of it was giving something away that I could never get back. The more I put into my story the less it had actually happened to me.

Sometimes I felt like I was standing on an edge. I could see it and feel the pieces of dirt crumbling off its lip beneath my feet as I looked over and tried to make out what was down in that hole.

Have you ever watched yourself walk around doing things, living your life, and at the same time, as you watch, wondering what that person's doing? Who that person is? How does he know how to do the things he does?

That came to me one day on a street corner in Eugene,

Oregon, when I was living out there in disguise that time after Priscilla left us.

I was waiting for a light to change so I could cross the street to go to a hardware store to buy me something I needed at the cabin when I all of a sudden happened to look over at a man standing next to me. He was dressed in a suit and tie and polished shoes and all that, and he was looking at his watch, lifting his arm to see it. He had a folder full of papers in his left hand and when he looked at his watch, some of them slipped halfway out of the cardboard folder.

It didn't bother him. He just caught them with his right hand and went right on across the street when the light changed without showing anything at all in his face or acting the least bit upset.

That hit me like a club. How did he know to do that? Catch those papers so they wouldn't fall and then walk right on when the green light came and go to wherever he was going and never break stride and never show any hesitation.

I couldn't figure it out. And it puzzled me so much that I stood there at that intersection for over an hour before I could make up my mind to cross over to that hardware store, and I had to depend on somebody bumping into me hard enough to push me into the street before I could get started walking.

And the whole time I stood there I could taste that bitter orange that Mama gave me for helping Elvis that first time in Tupelo. A taste like metal, like something you should never have put in your mouth.

There's one more little story I have to tell from our time in Tupelo. Vernon had already changed that dollar amount on Mr. Bean's check and done his time at

Parchman for forgery, Elvis had got that first guitar and come in second at the Mississippi-Alabama Fair, like I said, for singing "Old Shep," and I had knocked maybe two tons of baseball-sized rocks off into the stand of pines at the edge of Uncle McCoy's backyard with a whole series of homemade baseball bats.

The war had come and gone, and I had looked through a hole in the side of the girls' restroom at the baseball field in Tupelo and caught a glimpse of what was going to be on my mind from then on. It was late summer of 1948.

We were thirteen years old.

All right. I was sitting on the edge of the front porch of that little house in the woods, listening to Aunt Edith making cooking noises in the kitchen and now and then leaning forward to let a drop of spit fall from my lip into a doodle bug hole there in the bare sand where water from the eaves hit when it rained. Everytime a drop would hit, the doodle bug would come out to smooth up the sides of his ant trap again, and I would wait until he was all finished before I'd let another drop fall.

Uncle McCoy was over by the well trying to tie two pieces of something together with a wire, I forget what, and it was quiet enough, even with Aunt Edith's pots and pans and stove lids, to hear the sound of a car coming from way up the dirt road in our direction.

I gave the doodle bug one last gob to contend with and walked out to the middle of the road to see what was coming. By the time I got there, I could see the cloud of dust the car was raising before I could see the car itself, and in a minute or two I could pick out the shape of the machine. It was a black Plymouth, a '37 model, humpbacked and narrow nosed, and as it got within range I saw that Uncle Vernon was driving it.

He raised a hand when he saw me there in the road,

revved up the engine and shifted down, and just as he got close to Uncle McCoy's place, jerked the wheel hard to the right, stood on the brakes, and the Plymouth slid sideways up into the yard.

Something was wrong with the gas feed because the engine kept revving higher and higher while he sat there messing with the dashboard, and it seemed like a full minute before he got the ignition turned off. When he did, the car backfired twice like a shotgun going off, and two perfect smoke rings rose up from the exhaust and took off for the treetops. I can still see them, one chasing the other in perfect time as they widened and rose straight up, one a little bigger than the other, both off-white.

"Looks like you got yourself a buzz-bomb, Vernon," said Uncle McCoy, coming up to the car from where he had been working on whatever it was that wouldn't stay together. "Looks like it can do tricks, too."

"It's a '37," said Vernon.

"I see that. How did you learn it to blow smoke rings?"

"It's this damn foot-feed. Thing gets stuck and lets too much gas in there, and when you cut her off, she backfires."

"Damn near blows up, you mean."

"It's a good engine in it," said Vernon and crawled out from behind the wheel after reaching through the window to open the outside door latch. "Runs just like a sewing machine."

"Takes big stitches too, I reckon," said McCoy. "What you pay for her?"

"Nothing yet. Traded some stuff."

"You did?" said Uncle McCoy and reached out to pull me off the running board by the back of my shirt. "Don't go getting too close to that thing, Jesse. We ain't sure it's turned off yet."

"It's all right," said Vernon. "Get on in there behind

the steering wheel, Jesse. See how it feels."

I was doing just that when I heard McCoy ask Vernon if he had come all the way out Morning Glory Road to give us all a ride in his new car. Sitting in the driver's seat, I could see Vernon look off toward the woods across the road as though he had spotted something wild moving in the trees. I remember he stood that way long enough to cause McCoy to look up at him from whatever that gadget was in his hands and for me to stop moving the steering wheel back and forth like I was driving.

"No," Vernon finally said. "Well, yeah, I reckon so. One of you."

He was talking to whatever he was seeing moving through the pines. Then he turned back to look at me through the cracks in the Plymouth's windshield.

"Jesse," he said, nodding his head once at the driver's seat. "Come to get him."

"Where are you planning on taking Jesse Garon?" asked McCoy, looking back toward the house where Edith was fixing the meal.

"Memphis."

"Memphis? What you going to do in Memphis?"

"It's work up there," said Vernon.

"You know that for a fact?"

"It's got to be. It's bound to be better than Tupelo."

"Huh," said McCoy. "You just going to take off then?"

"I got to. They done found out."

Uncle McCoy looked back down at his gadget. I have always wanted to remember what it was, for some reason. But try as I can I never can see what's in his hands, though the rest of that scene there on Morning Glory Road in September of 1948 is as clear to me as last night's first drink.

McCoy turned the thing in his hand over and over and spoke again. "So you taking him? Why? Why now?"

"Elvis he told Gladys he wouldn't go without Jesse Garon."

"She is about to twist them off of you, ain't she?"

"I come to get him," said Vernon. "That's all I know."

"Edith ain't going to like that," McCoy said. "Hell, *I* ain't going to like it."

"She said it would be better for him. More of a chance."

"Better for Jesse?"

"Well," said Vernon. "For Elvis, you know. Up yonder in Memphis."

"Where did that idea come from? Where did she get it?"

"Well," said Vernon and coughed gently. "The moon, she says. It done told her."

"Shit," said McCoy. "I'll tell Edith to get him his stuff."

We left in the middle of the night. Thinking back to it now, I can see all kinds of reasons why that was exactly the right timing for the farewell to Tupelo. The moon put us into the middle of that part of North Mississippi, and it was the moon that took us out. As interpreted by Gladys, that is. A woman spoken to by the moon and by raw milk and by dropped dish cloths and by nose itches and magic numbers and by every damn thing else but common sense or a brain.

Don't ask me how she got all those messages. They just come to her. Sometimes it would be in the night, Vernon said, when she'd wake him up by rearing up in the bed to slap at the air around her like it was full of yellow-jacket wasps coming to sting her.

"She'd holler out and say things," Vernon said to me once in one of his talkative moods, "she'd even cuss at the things that was trying to come in at her ears and work on into her brain. Call them every kind of a goddamn son of a bitch and worse than that. Lord, the language she would use. She'd say she didn't want to learn what they was going to tell her and make her know."

"What would these things say?" I asked him. "What did she say they looked like?"

"Oh, hell, Jesse, that was the worst part. I never could see nothing flying around her head. And she would just squall and beg me to tell her I saw something, too, and at first I would say I did. But then that seemed to make it all get worse, so I got to where I just made out like I was still asleep, and I wouldn't have raised up if a bolt of lightning had struck that damn iron bedstead."

"Never saw a thing, huh?"

"No, but God she did. And she'd talk to them, too, after awhile when she'd get kindly calmed down some. And that was the worst part of them night fits."

"Worse than her slapping and cussing at whatever she saw?"

"Aw, yeah, lots worse. Let me ask you how you'd like it if your wife could rouse up about once a month in the middle of the night, dead hours of midnight, and just talk to things in some kind of a foreign language for up to an hour at a stretch sometimes. And the only word you could understand in the whole damn conversation was Elvis, Elvis, Elvis."

"I ain't got no wife," I said, and that shut Vernon up.

It was dark by the time we got back over to Green Street in Tupelo that night after throwing my stuff in a tote sack there at Uncle McCoy and Aunt Edith's. Neither one of them said much as I got the things together to load in the Plymouth, and it wasn't until both Vernon and me were in the car with the engine running that Edith said the first word to him.

"Vernon," I remember her saying, leaning in at the window on the passenger's side where I was sitting to look over at him, "this is the last."

"I know it," he said. "Don't think we don't appreciate what y'all..."

"Don't never ask nothing again," she cut him off, "about this boy."

"I'd pay you if I could," Vernon said and tapped at the accelerator.

"You're going to pay all right," said Edith, "but it ain't going to be me collecting that bill."

She stepped back from the car and looked in at me. "I hope you get to play you some baseball, Jesse," she said.

And then the Plymouth's foot-feed stuck wide open, and Vernon popped the clutch, and we left that place on Morning Glory Road with the back wheels spinning and kicking rocks and clods out behind us as though we were racing in one of those stock cars on the dirt track in Tupelo on a Saturday.

I didn't look back.

Leaving town late that night for Memphis we left every light in the house blazing. Whoever it was who had found out whatever it was that was making Tupelo too hot for Vernon would be fooled by all them lights being on and wouldn't know we were gone until it was too late.

That was the thinking, if you want to call it that.

You might have read what people claim to know about the reason the Presleys left for Memphis that night. Elvis told somebody, I believe it was a reporter from *Rolling Stone*, that Vernon took off for Memphis because there was work up there. I heard Vernon tell McCoy that himself that evening he came to pick me up in the Plymouth. Another fool writer says the Tupelo police found out Vernon was peddling moonshine and they gave him two weeks to get out of town.

There was moonshine at the bottom of it, all right. But

it wasn't the kind you make in a car radiator and swig out of a Mason jar. The moonshine that sent us to Memphis was the natural thing, as seen and read by Gladys Presley.

The beams that sent us North came from that big piece of rock flying around the earth every day. They came in the window of a rent house in Mississippi, fell on the eyelids of a woman who knew more asleep than she did awake, and they put both me and Elvis into an orbit turning around each other that hasn't ended yet.

Vernon didn't cut on the ignition until we had rolled almost all the way to the bottom of that hill which Green Street climbed, and he kept the Plymouth's headlights off even after the engine cranked.

Nobody was saying anything all the way to the bottom of the hill, so that when Vernon turned the key and let in the clutch the roar the engine made starting up made all of us jump and tense up.

I was riding in front with him, cramped up at his elbow with some boxes on the other side between me and the door. I was there for a reason, to reach down and pull that foot feed up when it got stuck and keep the engine from revving so high. Vernon couldn't steer and shift and watch out for what was coming and make the whole thing go all at the same time. I had to do that.

Elvis and Gladys were in the back seat, clothes and dishes and kitchen utensils stacked all around them and Elvis's guitar propped up between the seats so that the loose ends of the strings kept jabbing me in the back of the neck when I'd set up straight for some relief from operating the accelerator by hand.

"Cut it down some, Jesse," said Vernon, shifting to a higher gear and fighting the wheel to steer around something lying in the road. "It's too much gas getting to it."

"Y'all make it quiet on down," said Gladys from the

back seat. "It's making my ears ring and pop."

"I'll help make your ears feel better, Mama," Elvis said and leaned forward to pluck at the strings of the guitar jammed against the back of the front seat.

"Some sweet morning," he began to sing, "when this life is o'er, I'll fly away."

"In the morning," chimed in Vernon, and then a beat or two later Gladys herself.

"I'll fly away, O Glory, I'll fly away. In the morning. When I die, hallelujah, by and by, I'll fly away."

They all kept singing, all the way to the big highway turning North to Memphis, out past the saw mill and the radio station tower, one hymn after the other, louder and louder.

And I just kept working the foot feed.

4

Sam Phillips said more than he knew that summer of '54 when he made his famous rock and roll pronouncement. "If I can find me a white boy that can sing like a nigger, I can make me a millon dollars," Sam is supposed to have said to one of the blues freaks or radio deejays or some of that bunch that hung around the Sun Studio there on Union in those days.

See, that is supposed to have been a prophetic statement about what all was going to bust loose when Elvis came on the scene. Like one of those Old Testament dudes forecasting the stud horse times to come whenever Jesus would show up in the next chapter in the New Testament.

All that hindsight was designed to make Sam look like some kind of a genius with intentions, a man that knew what he was doing and what he was looking for all the time, right up to and including Elvis and the rest of them. Jerry Lee, Johnny Cash, Orbison, all of them.

I have to laugh when I think about what all these music writers have said about stuff like that. All the hints of things to come they are able to find in every damn thing that happened before the whole real thing hit the Sun.

I'll tell you the best prophet, the one that said it first

and the one that was so profound she was invisible. Gladys Presley. My mama. And his.

It was in that 1937 Plymouth, heading up 78 toward Memphis that September night in 1948, boxes full of all kinds of sorry household goods all around her and her unacknowledged offspring working the gas pedal by hand, when Gladys gave tongue to the fundamental truth about what was ahead for us all.

"What's it going to be like in Memphis, Mama?" Elvis had said to her loud enough for me to hear him from where I was half-crouched in the floorboard.

Elvis sounded scared, like he did lots of times back then, his voice crawling higher up in his throat as he spoke.

"I done dreamed it, honey," Gladys said. "It's done come to me about Memphis, what all it's going to mean up yonder. Don't you worry none about it."

"Well, what is it then?" he said.

"It's sounds."

"Sounds? What kinds of sounds?"

"It's two kinds, mainly," said Gladys. "They are mixed up together, wound around each other so they can't be heard apart. But you can tell it's two of them making up one between them when they coil up together like they do. Wrapped around like."

"Is it like a bunch of car horns blowing at the same time?"

"No. It's people. It's people's voices. Two people's voices coming together to make one. One of them's black, and the other one's white, and they ain't never going to be separated away from each other again."

"Are they talking words?" said Elvis in that scared sounding way.

"Yes, but it's music in the words and the words can't live on their own without the music inside of them."

"Are they talking to us?"

Gladys didn't say anything back to him for a good space of time, and when she finally spoke she sounded the way she did when she would go into one of her fits of talking with her eyes closed and her head throwed back as if she was trying to look through her slitted eyes at something she was afraid to see.

"The sound is talking to two people. But only one of them can hear the full sound, but he can't say the words back. The other one can say the words back just like they come to him, but he can't hear what the truth is that the words are saying."

You tell me if Sam Phillips or a critic or any rock historian can figure that prophecy out, that one that come in First Plymouth, 1937 on 78 heading toward the City of Memphis in the last days of '48. There's blood to lose over trying to figure scripture.

We're living in Memphis, up close to downtown where the city meets the river, and we have already moved a time or two.

Of course. Poor people are always moving. They're like rich people that way. It's only these pitiful mortgaged suckers that squat in one place for a long time. They remind me of a poor old sorry black and tan hound I saw once in Mississippi. He had eaten something that he shouldn't have, too hungry not to, and it was working on him strong. Something foreign. He was bowed up with his hind legs spread, trying to get a purchase to expel whatever it was that was griping his guts, but he wasn't having any luck. He'd strain and whine and throw his head back and howl and there wasn't anything good going on for him squatted where he was on the gravel shoulder of the road.

But he was fixed in one place. The whole time I watched

him, and it must have been five minutes, and he was still there when I came back by three or four hours later, that poor black and tan never strayed two feet from that one spot. He was in hell, he was dying, he was trying to get something out that acted like it had become part of him, but he had found his spot. And that spot was good to him and he wasn't going nowhere, no matter how staying there was killing him.

Vernon Presley wasn't no hound dog. He had learned to move, to spread his pain around, or at least to transport it to a new location.

I found me a job the third day we were in Memphis in that first downstairs apartment in an old house with brick siding. It was working for a man that owned a junkyard about eight blocks from where we lived, and it involved me crawling through, around, and over wrecked Fords, Chevrolets, Hudsons, and you name it, with a wrench in one hand and a ball-peen hammer in the other, cannibalizing parts.

Don't ask about school. That word was never mentioned to me after we hit Memphis and I sure wasn't going to bring it up. I was satisfied to bang on car bodies and engine blocks to take home that fifteen dollars that Mr. Jordan paid me every Saturday and put it in Gladys's hand, and to walk over as much of the city as my feet would take me every chance I got.

Vernon was unloading boxes full of cans of paint every day over at the paint company dock, Gladys was listening to voices that only she could hear, and Elvis was starting in at Humes High School.

I had me a pallet on the living room floor, lots of things in Memphis to look at, and no reading assignments or arithmetic problems to do.

47

It was beating the pure shit out of Tupelo.

One day early in the spring right before Vernon moved us all into the Lauderdale Courts I knocked off work early and got to the house at the same time Elvis did coming home from school. Mr. Jordan wasn't moving any carburetors from Chryslers or connecting rods from '39 Fords that day and had sent me off to avoid paying for an afternoon's work, and I was feeling pissed about not getting the time in. Thinking back to it, I can't imagine why that would bother me. I never saw but a dollar or two of the money every week anyway, but Lord back then I was earnest. I purely wanted to work, not just spend the money I got for it.

What I used to like about the whole thing of working was this. You did something that somebody told you to do, and it wasn't really anything you would have done on your own. That was the pain of it. Then he gave you something for the pain, and if it was enough then everything equalled out. You could reason out how much it hurt to do what you didn't want to, look down at what he had put in your hand, and then you could figure out exactly if everything was in a balance.

It was later on, of course, that everything got out of kilter, and I couldn't see any more connection between what I was holding in my hand and what I had done to get it. Or not done. Or should have done.

But that came later on. Train, train, sixteen coaches long. Gone, gone, gone, as the man sang. Took my baby and it's gone.

I was about to walk across the yard up to the house when I saw Elvis coming toward me from the direction of Humes High. I remember he was wearing a red shirt with a big old floppy collar that Gladys had hustled up from somewhere, and he was in a big hurry.

"That looks like a shirt made for a girl," I told him as

he came up.

"It don't neither," he said. "It's real pretty on me, Mama thinks."

"Like I said."

"At least it ain't got car grease all over it."

"I like lubrication," I said. "I like the way it smells on a car part. And the way it makes everything slide real easy."

"Jesse," Elvis said and then stopped for a minute to lean over and rub out a spot on one of his shoes. "Tell me something. And be true now."

"What?"

"Do I look to you like I'm a, you know, a sissy?"

He looked up at me, and from the way he was leaning, it looked like he was a full head shorter than I was. He was looking straight at me, a thing he didn't do much back in those early days in Memphis, and I could see directly into his eyes.

"No," I said and looked off toward a big old stone urn that sat on one side of the steps going up to the rent house. I guess it used to have flowers in it back when the house was new and only one family lived in it. Before they made it into those four apartments and let the country folks move in.

"You look fine," I said. "Just like anybody else. Pretty much."

"Well," he said. "All right."

I looked toward the other side of the steps to see if there was another stone urn on that side, but there wasn't one. Somebody had taken it off a long time ago, I guess.

"You know who's coming to the auditorium tonight and tomorrow?" Elvis said and didn't wait for me to answer. "The Blackwood Brothers, that's who. And you know who else? The Singing Sons of Gospel."

"Over at the Ellis Auditorium? Let's go tonight."

"You think Mama will let me go?"

"Yeah," I said, "that or else we can sneak out."

"I ain't got the money."

"I'll let you borrow fifty cents," I said. "That'll make eight dollars and fifty cents you owe me."

"I'll pay you back," Elvis said. "I done told you I would. Don't say nothing to Mama. Let's just sneak on out."

Let me tell you how that crowd looked, coming to the singing convention to hear the Blackwoods work it on out, praising the Master through song, like the posters said on the outside of the auditorium underneath the pictures of the quartet itself. There was a steady swarm of them coming in through all those doors across the front of the building by the time we got there, and they were ready to jump.

It was family groups, mainly, like always at a gospel singing, but it was Friday night, so here and there you see a couple of girls paired off together and small packs of boys running side by side like we were doing. The girls were eyeing the boys and the boys were eyeing the girls and each other, and the old folks were just trying to get to a seat, the men in khakis and the women in flowered dresses.

Most everybody there would have said they were from Memphis, if you asked them, but hardly a family was long off the farm or out of the equivalent of Tupelo, whether back home was in Tennessee or Arkansas or north Mississippi. They were all like me and Elvis in one main way. They were losing Jesus, or whatever it was they thought having him meant at one point, and they needed to hear the sounds the Blackwoods put out to make them believe they still had that thing that used to make them feel like they knew where they were in the world.

When you're in Tupelo or Marked Tree, Arkansas or

Bells, Tennessee, you forevermore know you're there. No chance of waking up one morning puzzled about your whereabouts or lying wide-eyed in the middle of the night trying to make out what those shadows mean outside the window or what that noise was that brought you up out of your coma. That's city sleep.

Don't get me wrong. Memphis ain't no world capital. It's not much more than Jackson, Tennessee written in big letters, but you couldn't have told that to me and Elvis in 1949 or to that crowd of people pushing into the Ellis Auditorium that Friday night to let the Blackwood Brothers lull them back to sleep and into a closer relationship with Jesus Christ. Memphis was plenty big enough to cause country folks to need that music.

The ticket I had paid for with my dollar bill let us into the general admission section, but that didn't satisfy Elvis. He worked his way along the edge of the crowd of people milling around the front bunch of seats, and by the time I had followed him to where he found a place he wanted to stop we were right up close to the stage, near enough to the drummer to count the hairs in his pencil line mustache and to judge the color of the drink he had in the glass sitting next to his bass.

"That's Arnold Merry," Elvis said, nodding at the drummer who was polishing his sticks with a piece of white cloth. "You can hear every lick he hits them drums in all of them songs if you listen for him."

"You never heard the Blackwoods before," I said.

"On the radio I have."

"How can you hear just the drums when everything else is going on?"

"You just listen for the drums by themselves. I can pick out anything just by itself and listen to just it, whenever I want to. Just the lead guitar or the man singing tenor or the bass or any of it."

"Huh," I said just as Arnold Merry dropped his white cloth and hit the snare drum a double lick.

That sound started a commotion loud enough to keep me from saying anything back to Elvis to dispute his word, and that left me unsatisfied. Even as early as those first few months in Memphis he was already getting loud-mouthed about himself and music, what he could do with it and hear in it and what couldn't be done by most any-body else with it. I remember one time we were listening to something on the radio, one of those silly pieces of junk that later on got to be called "novelty tunes" by deejays and folks in the business. Maybe it was "Rag Mop" or "Open the Door, Richard" or some such trash, but whatever it was Elvis had reached up and clicked off the radio in the middle of it.

Then he turned to me and said something like hey, Jesse, can you remember how many times they repeat such and such. No, I had told him and neither can you because they do it too fast and it ain't the same every time any-way.

I remember his exact count. "Eight," he said and turned the radio back on in time to hear that part of the song again and count whatever the damn word was while the singer said it over and over.

"See," Elvis said, "I got an ear."

"You also got a asshole," I told him.

But when old Arnold Merry dropped the flag on that first song by the Blackwoods, all the folks in Ellis Audi-torium let out a big sound, one you could hear down in your belly and in your navel and in your balls.

What that sound was there at the Ellis in 1949 when the Blackwoods cranked up the machine after Arnold Merry hit the starter button was a long heavy sigh. It came from deep in the lungs of mechanics and warehouse clerks and city maintenance men, and it came from women who had stood over an ironing board for two hours smoothing out the wrinkles in a short-sleeved shirt and a pair of khakis, and a couple of blouses and skirts for the girls and the clothes for the boys and finally the flowered dress for her before they all left the rent place on Manassas Street to get over to the hall before the singing started.

And that sigh came up through the throats of men who'd shaved close and put on strong lotion and women who'd powdered their cheeks to hide what the Memphis sun had done and from half-grown boys and girls who couldn't keep their fingers off their faces where all those hot juices were throwing up those pimples day after day.

That sound that went up when Arnold Merry's drumsticks went down didn't come from relaxed folks out for a pleasant evening of music, movement, and mood. It came from pork fat and red beans, from thin-soled shoes and busted-out underwear, and it forevermore put more warmed-up air in that hall than it could safely hold.

I looked over at Elvis just as the tenor of the Blackwoods hit the first note of "Have a Little Talk with Jesus," and he was standing straight up against the wall, where we'd both been leaning, in the posture of somebody who'd just been shown his first picture of a full grown naked female or who'd just learned through a lightning flash that what he'd always wanted he had always had. I don't know how else to put it exactly when I try to describe the way that first sight of a big name gospel quartet affected Elvis that night way back there in Memphis.

It wasn't just the sight of the Blackwoods that was working, of course. The sound was the large part of it, I could see then and I realize now, but the way Elvis stood up against that wall like he'd been hit in the back of the head with a wood maul made it look like he was sucking everything in by sight.

It was like his eyes, open as wide as they were and not

blinking once all the time I watched him, were able some-how to see the sounds that the Blackwoods were making, the tenor and the bass and the lead baritone and all the notes from the instruments that went along with the sing-ing.

It got to me. I was getting more and more pissed off as I stood there watching him take everything in through the same damn eyes I had, no more conscious of what was going on around him than if he'd been the only one in the audience in the Ellis Auditorium that night.

It was like that time in the backyard with the sheet of metal covering up old Tarzan Snake there in Tupelo. Elvis looking at something like he owned it and was the only one able to have any kind of appreciation of what it re-ally meant. Where was my part of it? What was I going to get out of the thing after Elvis had sucked it all up through his eyes into his head and locked it away for just himself?

I remember at the time thinking that it wasn't such a real big deal, the Blackwoods singing on stage right in front of us. It wasn't the first time Elvis had seen people whose names were known to people outside of their own folks, neither. He used to sneak on across the highway there in Tupelo when him and Vernon and Gladys were living in the Shakerag section of town and go into the WELO radio station building to look at the Harmonaires sing in front of the microphone on Saturday mornings. He had told me about that, and one time when Uncle McCoy had let me ride to town with him I had gone with Elvis myself to the WELO building and watched a little blind girl sing seven or eight gospel tunes into the live microphone.

I remember her singing name well, Mary Dell, the Blind Girl of Bessemer, and the way her mother kept reaching up to point the mike straighter at Mary Dell's mouth while she was singing "Higher Ground" and "Bringing in the Sheaves."

So there in the Ellis Auditorium, listening to the Blackwoods doing a job on "Have a Little Talk with Jesus" and watching Elvis just seeming to hog it all for himself somehow, I got a mite impatient.

"They ain't all that perfect," I said, leaning over to speak into Elvis' ear, "I just heard the tenor mess up twice."

It was like I hadn't said a word, of course, like I didn't exist, so I leaned into his shoulder with mine to jostle him a little from that damn trance he was in. All he did was twist the upper part of his body so I stumbled a little bit when my shoulder slipped off of his, and I had to catch myself to keep from tumbling up against a man in front of me. I remember that man had his arms crossed over his chest, and I could see tattoos all over him wherever his shirt sleeves didn't cover.

"What's the matter with you?" I said to Elvis. "You gone stone deaf from standing this close to the drummer? I said the tenor's done messed up a word."

At that, Elvis turned his head around toward me like it was on a mechanical swivel and looked right into my eyes. His pupils were almost as big as his entire eye. There was just a little thin line of blue circling around the black part of the eyes, and when I looked into the center of that I felt like I was about to fall into something that I'd never be able to get out of once I slipped. That nothingness pulled at me. And I wanted to go.

I jerked my head back around and fixed my eyes on Arnold Merry's flashing white drum sticks, and for the rest of that performance by the Blackwoods and the Sons of Gospel Song I tried to keep count of Arnold Merry's licks on the snare, the drum that was lit by the brightest spot coming high up in the ceiling.

I wanted the light, and I wanted the white color, and I wanted to count something as close to perfect as I could get it.

The Blackwoods hammered on, and I tried to keep up with Arnold Merry's double and triple licks on the snare, and I never looked back at Elvis standing there against the wall, straight up and not blinking or saying a word.

5

The long summer before Elvis's last year at Humes High we were living in the Lauderdale Courts. I had moved up in the business world after finding me a job at a Sinclair Station on Jackson Avenue, and I was hauling in close to thirty dollars a week. And that was after deductions, let me remind you.

Everything smelled like grease and burnt engine oil to me back then, even the plates of cold cooked-down turnip greens and crowder peas Gladys left on the back of the stove for me to eat after I'd come in at midnight from the late shift, but that smell seemed like a small price to pay for the money in my pants pocket. Lord, I was a fool.

Whenever I'd get in, Gladys and Vernon would be already asleep, of course, but Elvis would be lying on the sofa in the front room with the radio tuned in and turned low and set close to his head. I had bought that Philco after one of my first paydays, and he hadn't let it get out of his hearing range since.

"Jesse," he'd say, "lie down on the floor and put your head up against this song. It's a hot one."

Generally I'd do that, being careful not to make any noise that would wake Gladys up, and I'd go on off to sleep most of the time in a few minutes, the voice of some black blues singer hollering quietly in my ear or a harmonica humming to me.

Elvis didn't. That was the summer he hardly ever slept at night, as far as I could tell, because if I ever did rouse up there in the dark, I could always tell he was still awake. He'd say something like, "Listen to this one, Jesse," or "You're lucky you woke up while he's singing." Or if he didn't say anything I could tell by the way he was lying there on the sofa that he wasn't passed out. He'd either be breathing like a person that's awake or I'd think that I could see his eyes on me as I lay there on my pallet by the radio. It was too dark to tell, really, but I believed I could see a glitter. And that was always enough for me to stay still and pretend I was asleep whether I felt wide awake or not.

One night sometime that summer I came in a little later than usual. I forget why. Maybe I had a couple of extra flats to fix or it might have been a night when the midnight shift man showed up late at the station. I don't know. But when I got to the Lauderdale Courts there wasn't a light on in a single building. Even the bulb that burned all night in the entrance hall was out, stolen probably by somebody in the building who didn't want to waste money on buying one themselves, so I had to feel my way up the stairs and down the corridor to the Presley apartment.

Time I got to the door and eased it open and stepped inside, my eyes had pretty well adjusted to the dark, and I could see the bulk of Elvis as he lay on the sofa with the radio playing low beside him. He didn't move as I walked across the room to get to the kitchen and the plateful of Glady's cold cooking, so I could tell that he had dropped off to sleep for a change.

I didn't turn on the light in the kitchen, just ate the beans and squash mainly by feel as I stood there by the stove and listened to the song coming over the radio. I remember it was playing "The Wayward Wind," and just as old Gogi Grant got to that last big section where everything swells up and the music lifts and she sings the part about "and he was born the next of kin, the next of kin to the wayward wind," all hell broke loose in the living room.

I put my plate down so hard it broke into two pieces on the top of the stove, and by the time I got the light switch turned on in the living room, I could hear Gladys and Vernon rumbling around in their bedroom as they crawled out of sleep to see what was going on.

Elvis was in the middle of the floor bent over in a crouch with his fists out in front of him, and he was steadily but slowly backing up toward the door, jabbing, dodging, and weaving the whole way, and now and then letting go with a big swinging right hand and alternating that with a left hook. His left foot was all snarled up in the extension cord he had used to plug in the radio, and just as I came into the room he kicked out to the side at whatever it was he thought had him by the leg, and ended Gogi's song before she had a chance to.

"Elvis," I said, "what's wrong?" just as Gladys got the door to the bedroom open and came bursting through it in a nightgown so old and ragged it made you want to cry to look at it.

"Honey," she said, "sugar, sugar," and reached out toward her only child with her right hand as though she was going to touch him on the head to smooth his hair back. Elvis bobbed, weaved, slipped Gladys' right, and then came up with a short blow that caught her under her left arm in the ribs. As Gladys stumbled back from that exchange he ripped a left toward her head that would have put her lights out if he hadn't gotten snagged in the radio wire and lost his balance, falling to one knee and instantly beginning to scramble back up.

I was on him by then and had both arms throwed around the top part of his chest so he couldn't swing again, and by the time Vernon got into the room to join the crowd I had Elvis wrestled on down to the floor on top of the extension cord and the radio and the pair of shoes he had taken off to lie down on the sofa.

Let me tell you it was a struggle. He didn't quit rolling and twisting and trying to get his hands free until Vernon had got on down there with us and given me some help holding him. Gladys, of course, was squalling and hollering during all this scene, holding one hand to her side where Elvis had got in the body blow and saying over and over again, "Don't you hurt him, don't you hurt my baby."

Elvis still hadn't said nothing up to this point, and when I finally got a chance to look up from where I had been fighting to hold his arms down, I could see he had his jaw set so hard I could hear his teeth grinding together.

"Elvis," I said, "Elvis, look at me. It's Jesse. What's wrong? What you doing?"

His eyes were open, but they were fixed in his head like he was looking at something far off and having a hard time making it out. He kept bringing his eyelids together and then relaxing them, over and over, like you will when you're trying to focus on something you want to see that's somehow just out of range. And as me and the old man held Elvis down, he kept struggling to get an arm loose or a leg or even just a foot or a hand judging from the way he was squirming and straining there on that linoleum floor.

It wasn't until Gladys had leaned over and put her hands on each side of his face that he seemed to stop looking so hard for whatever it was he was trying to see, and after I had asked him a couple of times more what he was doing he suddenly spoke for the first time during the whole scene.

"Where are they?" he said. "Where they gone?"

"Who, honey?" said Gladys. "Where's who?"

"They was in here," he said. "Four or five of them. More than I could tell. They had some more out there waiting in the hall."

"They ain't nobody here but us," said Vernon. "Look around this here room. You can see there ain't nobody but me and your mama and him."

That was me he was talking about. Jesse Garon, the cousin from the country. Him.

"Elvis," I said. "What you talking about? Was it something on the radio you was hearing? Was it you dreaming somebody else was in here?"

"They was here," Elvis said and jumped up from the floor where we'd been holding him. "All around me. I couldn't see their faces because they kept them in the dark. They were putting their hands all over me and trying to get something from me."

"What did they want, sugar?" said Gladys, still rubbing her side where Elvis had connected with the right.

"It was men," Elvis said, "wanting what I got. I was having to fight them to keep it."

"It wasn't nothing but a damn dream," I said and leaned over to pick up the radio to see if it still worked.

"Don't you come in here with that kind of talk," Gladys said in that voice of hers. "Trying out them words you heard from them tacky people at that filling station."

"It just slipped out," I said. "I meant to say 'dern.' That's all."

The knobs on the Philco still turned, and the dial lighted up when I plugged the extension cord in the wall and in about a half a minute, after it had time to warm up, the speaker started letting the sound of a guitar being worked on by some black dude come pouring into the room.

"Turn that thing off, boy," said Vernon. "Don't you

61

know it's the middle of the night? It sounds like a nigger honky tonk in here with that thing a going."

"No," said Elvis, sounding like he had some sense for the first time that night, "let that one play on out. It's Leadbelly on that record."

"Couldn't you see it was me when I turned that light on?" I said. "You had your eyes wide open."

"I did? Well, sometimes my eyes don't work right."

"Oh, darling," said Gladys. "Do you need you some glasses to see better?"

"No, ma'am," Elvis said to our dear old mama. "It ain't glasses that will help me. Glasses won't do me no good."

The best I can remember it must have been another hour before everybody got bedded on down again that night. Gladys had had to get her some Goody's Headache Powders for her side where Elvis had caught her with the looping right, and then he and her had had to sit down beside each other on the sofa to cry together and kiss and make-up about what had happened. Vernon, of course, had stumbled on off to bed after threatening to make anybody else rue the day they broke into his sleep any more with dreams about fighting men who weren't there but were trying to get something that couldn't be identified away from somebody who should have been asleep with the radio off in the first place.

Finally when the room cleared and the getting-back-to-bed noises from Vernon and Gladys had died out, Elvis leaned over from the sofa and clicked the radio back on, and I stretched out on my pallet. A commercial for Royal Crown Hairdressing came on the Philco, and after we had finished listening to that, I looked up at the dark bulk of Elvis lying down again and could tell he was watching me.

"Why don't you close your damn eyes and go to sleep?" I said.

"Can't," he said. "Scared to."

"Why? What are you scared of here in this housing project? Roaches or bedbugs?"

"There ain't no bedbugs in this apartment. She keeps it clean in here."

"It's roaches, all right," I said. "Fly up in my face when I came in the kitchen after work. Turns my damn stomach so I can't eat nothing."

"You can't get rid of them. Can't kill them and they won't go away. It don't make no difference how clean you live. They still going to come in on you."

He got quiet for a while after saying that, but I could tell by the way he was lying on that sofa that he wasn't about to doze off. I tried to nuzzle on down into my pallet and start up the picture show in my head that after a few minutes would generally lead to me passing out. It was the best way I had found up to then to get things to cut off and let me slip on out of the pallet on the floor, away from Lauderdale Courts and out of Memphis, Tennessee. This was all way before dope, you understand.

What I would think about to get the show going on behind my eyelids was the portholes on the side of a Buick Roadmaster. It didn't have to be any certain color itself, the car I mean, but I would mostly make it a red one or one of those deep blue colors. It would be new, no marks or scratches on it, and it would be sitting on a white street, made out of cement, I guess, and wouldn't have anything else around it.

The eyes behind my eyelids, not the real ones, but the eyes you have when you close the ones you actually see out of, would act like a movie camera starting far enough back from the Roadmaster to see the whole car and then slowly coming in closer and closer, what the Hollywood boys would later call a tight shot, and the scene at the beginning of my movie would end up with just these three portholes on the left side of the car filling up the screen.

When that was all that I could see with my closed eyes, just those three perfectly round silver holes in the middle of that dark blue or red metallic background, then I had to make a choice of the one I would be going into. My eyes never would let me look first into one and then another and then the other before making things final, though, so whichever one of the silver circles I picked was the one I had to live with in that whole movie. And all the time I would be dealing with what the choice had brought me, I would be knowing that something else was going on in the other two portholes, the silver circles opening up to other movies besides the one I had picked.

But after my eyes had made that first decision to slide on into whichever porthole they picked that time, it didn't bother me to know that I could have taken one of the other ones and seen a whole different movie happen, and I never felt restless with the one I ended up with. In fact that really was what helped put me to sleep, let me slide on off that pallet and float on somewhere else, that feeling that there was a lot more going on than I could ever deal with all by myself, just being one person, somebody's cousin lying on a floor in Memphis hoping to pass out as fast as I could make it happen.

When I think back to those Roadmaster dreams, those movies I made up myself according to which silver circle I let myself float through, I never can really remember any sharp details of the stories that would always take me up into a kind of a cloud full of dim lights with music coming from people singing and playing far off somewhere.

The movies would have colors, real sharp and bright, and people walking around fixing to do things with me and always just about to say something to me as the silver porthole got bigger and bigger on that screen as I passed through it into the story going on inside, there where the engine would have been if it had been a real Buick.

Just as I reached a point inside the silver circle of the porthole somebody in the story would be turning to see me coming close to them, and they'd be pretty if it was a woman, dressed real expensive and classy, and friendly and handsome if it was a man. They'd look glad to see me, like they knew I was coming and they had been waiting for me to get there, and they'd be turning toward me like you will toward somebody you want to see be there, and then just before they'd talk, say whatever it was they were going to, maybe about the story they were in or just hello, I would go on off to sleep there on the pallet, deep enough for all of it to dim out and slip away, and I wouldn't wake up until other people's noises brought me out of it in the morning.

I have always been glad of learning that way to trick myself into sleeping, but I can't tell you how many times I regretted not being able to hear what those people in those stories inside those silver circles were about to say to me.

"Jesse," Elvis whispered from the sofa, "you asleep? Listen to old Arthur Crudup sing this one. You got to listen real close to get all the words right."

That's the way that summer before Elvis's last year at Humes High went on day after day, night after night. Vernon unloaded thousands of gallons of paint down at the truck dock, to hear him tell it, I pumped gas and washed off windshields, fixed flats and checked air in tires and ate cold grease at midnight, Gladys cleaned and cooked and gained weight and worried about her leading man, and Elvis laid across the sofa with the Philco tuned in wherever the airwaves led him, fighting off sleep and the nightmares that came with it.

It would give me the red ass those nights I would come in late, dirty as a hog from all the grease and oil from those old burned out wrecks I had to tend to at Al Seay's Sinclair and tired enough to be able to sleep like a baby on a linoleum floor. I mean to see Elvis lying there across the only soft thing in the front room, the radio pouring music into his head while he looked into a little pocket mirror he had got from Glady's purse and combed his hair into different arrangements.

He had let it get long by then and with the help of Royal Crown Hairdressing he could make it do just about any trick he wanted to. It would swoop up from both sides and meet in the middle at the top and flop forward across his forehead in what he called a waterfall. In the back it was a ducktail, of course, with a square cut across the bottom and the back of his neck shaved to give it a clean look.

Or sometimes he would comb it just straight back all over so it would look real slick and polished like one of those 1930s movie stars you could see in the Suzore No. Two, the picture show close to the Courts. That wasn't the look he wanted very often, though. Mainly it was the ducktail.

You'll read all kinds of stuff about how Elvis grew sideburns real early on. To look like a truckdriver, they always say. Let me get the sideburns issue laid to rest, for once and for all. He did let his side hair on his head grow long so it would come down his cheeks and look like sideburns. With the help of Royal Crown, that is. But they weren't real sideburns until he was nineteen or twenty years old. Neither him nor me could grow much of a beard until late in our teens. It would just be a sprinkling of reddish whiskers every inch or so on either one of our faces before then. What I'm saying is that Elvis's famous damn sideburns were self-manufactured all through those early years, thanks to careful combing and the staying power of Royal Crown Hairdressing. Anyway, like I said, I'd be kind of mad and jumpy, seeing Elvis like that all summer before that last year in school, listening and combing and staying awake all night. Not that I could let anybody in the house know how I felt about it, of course. I knew better than to try that.

I also know that while I was at work in that hot Memphis sun all day, Elvis would rise up from his bed of ease and go see the girl that lived upstairs with her folks, I forget her name, and play his guitar for her and buy her Cokes and take her to the picture show. That preyed on my mind some.

Not that I cared anything about her in particular myself, you understand. It was just that I looked upon that as easier work than what I was doing and would have preferred some of that kind of action myself. And it also wasn't the case that I hadn't had the chance to get close to a girl or two myself by then, neither. It was just that it wasn't a leisurely procedure for me like it was for Elvis during that summer, having to work everything I wanted to do in between long sessions of stuff that I wasn't especially glad to be involved in.

Try sticking your head down inside the hood of an overheated Plymouth so you can see to replace a frayed belt before the whole thing snaps apart and the water pump red hot, and you'll see what I mean. Oh yeah, and let it be August in Memphis and 103 degrees and four flats waiting on you to fix them.

Everything finally cooled off, though, like it always will, and September came, and it rained every day for two weeks, and Elvis got on into his senior year at Humes.

It was late that month when the next thing I want to talk about came up.

I was getting ready to leave for the filling station, late afternoon and the sun sinking across the Mississippi into Arkansas, and Elvis was in the front room with all his shirts and pants laid across the sofa.

"Looky here, Jesse," he called to me back in the kitchen where I was looking out the back window in a kind of low level dread of the nightful of gas pumps and oil cans to come. "Come here and look at something for me."

"What is it?" I said, walking on into the front room. "You get some Mum stains on the underarms of your shirts?"

"Come on," he said. "I'm serious now. Which one looks the best? This one or the red one?"

He had two shirts on hangers in his hand, a short-sleeved blue one and a red one with sleeves and black trim around the edges of the pockets.

"What's it for?" I said. "To wear to school? It don't make no difference."

"Yeah, it does, too. It's for that talent show tomorrow. Now, look here. The blue one's short-sleeved and it's still hot enough to need that, but it ain't nearly as pretty as this red one, is it?

"Ain't that cloth thick on that red one? It'll burn your ass up wearing that thing all day."

"Not if I don't move around much. I mean until the talent show's over with."

"Suit yourself," I said. "It won't be me frying in that brick building all day."

I watched him stand there for what seemed like another five minutes trying to decide which shirt he was going to wear, laying first one then the other down on the arm of the sofa and then walking across the room to get a better look from long distance at the effect. He finally hung the hanger the red one was on from the edge of the door facing and went all the way back to the kitchen to look at it from there.

"That's it," Elvis said. "When you get this far from it you can't tell that's heavy cloth and the long sleeves give it a lot better look than the little old blue one's got."

"Talent show, huh?" I said. "What are you going to be doing, Elvis? Acting in a play or something?"

"Aw, hell no, Jesse. I'm going to be playing my guitar and singing. It's a talent show, not no play."

"What song are you going to do, then? One of them ones you sing to these little old girls around here? Billy or what's her name?"

I knew that would get to him since we'd both agreed several times before that none of the girls in the courts looked like much. But, of course, Elvis had never let that kind of thing bother him. He was always able to look into any female's eyes and sing to her like his heart was breaking for love. It wasn't until years later that I was able to figure out the trick. What he was seeing in those women's eyes was the reflection of himself so he was always singing his soul's burden directly into the best receiver he ever was to have. I mean the actual reflection of his own face in those thousands of eyeballs and millions of camera lenses. When you're singing to the thing you're just crazy about, you're bound to look love-struck and pussy-charmed.

Anyway, when I said that to him, it got Elvis's attention a little bit off his wardrobe plans and onto his ideas for the show itself, and he walked over to the front window to look out at the cars passing by and think about what I'd asked him.

"Well, Jesse," he said, "I've been going over and over it in my mind trying to figure out what would be exactly right."

"What kind of a thing is this? Just everybody singing different songs?"

"No, Jesse Garon, it's a talent show. You know, where different ones get up and show what they can do. Miriam Banks is going to play the piano again, I reckon, and an old fat boy named Jerry Wayne will act like he's Bob Hope and tell some jokes. You know, like that."

"I'm glad I ain't going to be there, then," I said. "I'd probably get a heart attack from getting too worked up over it. Who got you into that mess?"

"Miss Scrivener," he said,"my teacher that's heard me sing. You got to be there, Jesse."

"Nuh uh," I said. "You ain't getting me back into no school even on a visit. Where did she hear you sing?"

"At the homeroom picnic in Overton Park. I need for you to be there tomorrow, Jesse."

"Why? What you scared of that's going to happen?"

"Nothing," Elvis said. "I ain't scared of nothing that's liable to happen. I just need you to be there when I'm up on that stage singing. You can sit way in the back or just stand back yonder in the door. You ain't got to be at work until night anyway."

"What if some teacher or somebody asks me what I'm doing there? They don't want no strangers hanging around a Humes High School talent show."

"They won't take no notice of you" he said. "Look, there goes a black '50 Ford. It's got spinners on the hub-caps too. You just dress like you always do and won't nobody make the connection."

"I don't know," I said. "I'll have to think about it for a while. I might have myself some plans for about that same time of day."

Elvis didn't say anything after that for a long time, taking instead a deep interest in whatever cars passed by in front of the Lauderdale Courts and leaning all the way into the window with his forehead jammed up against the screen to watch one or two of them carry on down the street as far as he could keep seeing them. Finally, when there was a lull and nothing in hearing range from either direction, he turned back to face me, the marks of the screen wire making a pattern on one side of his head right above his eye.

"Don't you want to help me?" he said. "Didn't you hear me say I needed for you to?"

"I heard you all right," I said. "But I don't know nobody over there. They all going to look at me funny. Maybe say things, you know, about me to each other so I can hear it."

"I'll do something for you, if you'll just be with me this time."

"What?" I asked. "What'll you do for me that'll do me some good?"

"I can't do nothing right now," Elvis said, and that was sure God's truth, "but later on I'll be able to."

"How many songs are you going to sing?"

"One," he said. "Two if I win it. I get to do an encore, Miss Scrivener says. That's what the winner gets."

"More of the same, huh?" I said. "Are you going to sing something fast? Something by Hank Williams? 'Hey, Hey, Good Lookin'?'"

"No," Elvis said, as though he'd reached a decision after he'd been thinking about it for a long time.

"I'm going with 'Old Shep' again. Just like when we was just kids together that first time back there in Tupelo. When I came in second at the Alabama-Mississippi Fair."

6

I had planned my arrival at the front door of Humes High School so all the kids would be in class inside the building and there wouldn't be any of them able to watch me walk up. I had had the experience before of walking by a bunch of kids that knew each other and didn't know me, and I knew what they were capable of doing to a person alone, or at least saying to him and looking that way at him. I didn't need any of that shit, thank you. I have always had what baseball players call rabbit ears anyhow.

And so did Elvis. Why do you think he sealed himself into the tomb alive like he did for all those years? Even to put up sheets of aluminum foil over the windows of hotels and hospital rooms he was in. That kind of behavior doesn't come from welcoming the close attention of your fellow man with open arms and a smile on your face. But I know, as they say, where he was coming from, and I had that feeling of dread that morning when I walked up to the red brick front of Humes High.

I went back a couple of years ago, and I was surprised at how little the building really is. I expected to be seeing it different as a grown man than from the times before when I was a teenager living in the neighborhood. But even prepared for the difference, I was still knocked over by the way my memory didn't fit with the way it really is.

It was during one of the Death Weeks, probably on a Friday or Saturday, when I drove over to see old Humes, and I got there at the same time a Grayline bus was discharging a whole herd of Japanese tourists, Nikkon cameras, portable video outfits, tape recorders, running shoes, eyeglasses and all, onto the sidewalk.

I followed the crowd of them up the front steps of the building, the steps where I had been relieved that there wasn't any students hanging around that September in the '50s, and we all crowded on into the front lobby where the principal's office was. Two little black kids, wearing white sashes across their chest with the words *Humes Guide* on them, directed us all to stand in a circle while they gave us a lecture. Humes is a junior high school now, and the guides didn't look to be over twelve years old. They were cute. Had on matching clothes and serious looks, and they had a well-memorized spiel to deliver to us foreigners.

While they told the Japanese visitors about the historical significance of where they were standing, I looked around at the fresh paint and the computer terminal I could see through the glass partition of one of the offices and remembered how it felt when I opened that big door to walk inside Humes High and look for the auditorium where Elvis was going to be in the talent show his senior year.

Nobody was there as I let the door close slowly behind me so it wouldn't make any noise, but I could hear the high heels of some woman walking off down the hall to the left. It smelled like school in that lobby, something which came from the sweeping compound they used on the floors, I guess, and that odor of kids the same age all bunched up together, and the other part of it which couldn't be identified according to source, but which always hangs in the air in a place like that. Maybe it's the smell that comes from being nervous or uneasy or like I always was in school, never sure what the hell was coming next but certain I wasn't going to like it.

Whatever it was it was enough to make me walk close to the wall that morning feeling like every step I took away from that door was just that much further from safety.

I walked to the right down the hall, the other direction from the one that woman's high heels had taken, and it turned out to be the way I should have gone because in a few seconds I could hear the sound of a piano coming from a room up ahead that had double doors to it. It was the auditorium all right, and the Humes High Talent Show was already in progress.

There was a seat open on the end of the last row right by the door, and I can't tell you how good that location made me feel. I eased into it and slid down as low as I could reach, keeping my eyes straight ahead the whole time. I had already learned that if you don't let people catch your eyes on them they don't really believe you exist, most of the time, and they're a lot more apt to leave you alone. So I collapsed myself as low as I could get in the seat, propped my knees on the back of the one in front of me, and started watching a little dark-haired girl up on stage facing a baby grand piano like it was a German shepherd fixing to snap.

She was sitting as far back from the keyboard as she could get and still touch it, and she was picking out some tune a note at a time as though she was stealing something from the shepherd and was being careful not to let it notice what it was losing a little bit at the time. That piano wasn't a fool, though, and it was giving up those notes only after a struggle.

"Old Emma Alice always plays that same song every time," said a low voice to my right. "Don't she?"

It was coming from an old boy with a burr haircut, a new one I could tell from that strip of white skin along the edge of where the hair started. It was cut close enough to let you count the small scars on his head and check out every direction his hair grew in. That was several.

"Ain't that right?" he said and then as Emma Alice stole a whole bunch of notes all at once from the German shepherd, he craned forward to get a better look at me. "I thought you was going to be up there. Where's your guitar?"

"No," I said. "Not me. I'm not going to be up there."

"Elvis," the burrhead said out of the side of his mouth so he wouldn't be seen talking by the teacher roving up and down the aisles, "Where's that red shirt? You done changed it since this morning?"

I didn't say anything, but he wouldn't leave it alone, and after the teacher had moved on past us up the aisle toward the stage, the old boy spoke up again.

"Hey," he said. "Didn't you have on a red shirt this morning, and where's your damn guitar?"

"That ain't me," I said. "I ain't him who you said. I ain't Elvis."

He leaned forward in his seat and twisted around to look directly at me, and as he did, the girl at the piano finally stole one last note, stood up and nodded toward the audience and left the stage in almost a dead run. People started clapping a lot louder and lot longer than what she deserved for the little damage she had done, and the burrhead joined in, leaning back in his seat.

"I see you're not Elvis now," he said. "Your hair ain't right. It lacks about a pound of grease. Who are you? His twin brother?"

"No," I said feeling all of a sudden like he'd said something I had to answer to, "I'm not. I'm his cousin, that's all."

"Well, you hillbillies sure do breed true," he said. "You look just like you both came out of the same old country woman's pussy."

"I'm going to want to see you a little later on," I said to the burr haircut. "I want to explain something to you so you can understand what you been dying to know."

About then, a woman came onto the stage from behind the curtains and the applause got a lot louder and then began to die down when she made a motion with both hands as though she was flicking water off her fingers toward the front row of seats.

"Yea, Miz Scrivener," somebody a couple of rows up and over to the left yelled out, and most of the Humes High students laughed like they'd just seen somebody fall out of a third-story window. The fool beside me kicked the back of the seat in front of him with as much strength as he could muster in that confined place, and the girl sitting in it jerked around to glare back over her shoulder at him.

"You quit that, Bill Avery," she said, "or I'll tell Mr. Strickland on you."

I put his name away so well I still remember it after all these years of tiptoeing along that edge I've been telling you about, and I never saw him again after that day.

"Boys and girls," Mrs. Scrivener said, "let's welcome our next contestant in this year's Humes High talent contest. He's going to sing and accompany himself on the guitar. He is a senior. Elvis Presley."

And here came Bubba onto his first stage in Memphis.

He hadn't been outside the house in the daytime all that summer, like I said, and his skin looked so pale against that red shirt that I thought for a minute he was about to pass out. He gave one little quick look at the audience on his way to the middle of the stage and then dropped his head again as though he needed to see where every step was going to fall lest he was to trip over something and never rise again. A few people were clapping, and just as Elvis stopped at the mark he seemed to be looking for on the floor of the stage, several more joined in and he had to wait until the noise died down before he did anything.

While he stood there with his mouth halfway open, fixing to say the name of the song he was going to do, he looked to me about as scared as I had ever seen him, even more than the time the two kids had him spooked back in Tupelo Elementary School or the first day he had to go off to Humes High alone after we had moved to Memphis.

Something happened to me then, sitting on the last row in the seat closest to the door in that Humes High auditorium, seeing him up there in front of all those people with that look on his face. The way Elvis's eyes were jerking back and forth from one side of that big room full of people to the other made something get tighter and tighter in the middle of my chest and then break apart and begin to move up through my throat, all of a sudden until it came out through my mouth in words. Words that I didn't think to say or have any idea were there at all, much less about to be shouted out in that room.

"Elvis," my voice said in a yell as I sat there and listened to it, just as surprised and curious as the people in front of me who were beginning to turn to look back for the source of the sound, "Elvis Presley, sing it, sing that thing."

He heard me, lifted his gaze up to look toward the back of the room, and hit a chord on the guitar.

"I'm going to do 'Old Shep' for you," he said, his voice clear and loud as it cut through the last smattering of whispers from the younger kids in the first few rows.

With that, he hit the guitar another lick and got into the song itself, and I still have to admit he did it better than I had ever heard him do it before, either back in the apartment or sitting on the front steps or looking up at Billy as she stood on the porch and listened to him sing it to her.

"What did he say he was singing?" said Bill Avery in a low voice, "'Old Shit'?"

"Hush up, asshole," I told him. "I'll explain it to you note by note after school today."

The whole crowd got quieter as Elvis sang about the boy and the dog, and by the time he was halfway through, even teachers who had been walking guard duty had stopped where they were to look toward the stage and listen to him. When he hit that last note on the guitar, that little plink, plink, plink that gets slower and slower and higher and higher as the song ends, he let the last word swell up and then trail out in a kind of quiet moan, like he was holding back tears, but just barely.

That last sound died, and he was standing with his head back and his eyes closed, and the whole auditorium was completely still for the first time since I had walked into it. The surface of the guitar was picking up a sunbeam from a window to the left and reflecting it up into Elvis's face so a shadow was thrown across his eyes and forehead. It looked like what Gladys would have called God's spotlight, hitting him like it did just at that moment.

The applause began with a single person clapping somewhere at the front of the room, and then it broke out all over the crowd at the same time like fire hitting gasoline, and it got so loud you could hear it vibrating in the wood of the seats, a background hum behind the sound of hands clapping and people hollering up toward the stage where Elvis stood for a few seconds before going off toward the wing. He was carrying his guitar in front of him as he left, held up chest-high like he was about to offer it to somebody that none of us in the audience could see.

After he left the stage the noise got louder and louder, now with the sound of the seatbacks being beat on by some of the students and it didn't drop in level until Mrs. Scrivener came back on the stage and held up her hands again to quiet things down. She went ahead and asked for them to vote for the other people in the talent show by clapping, but it was clear what they were all waiting for, those girls wearing big full skirts and little white blouses and scarves tied tight around their necks and that gang of burrheaded boys in blue jeans. It was Elvis they wanted, Elvis and that damn song about a dying dog and a squalling kid.

He was the one that got to do the encore, of course, and he sang "Old Shep" over again, naturally, and as I sat there almost to the end of it before I climbed out of that last seat and sneaked out the door to the empty hall outside, I could hear one of the phrases running through my head over and over. You know how it is when part of a song gets stuck in your mind and keeps repeating itself no matter how much you try to put something else in its place, no matter how you try to change the thing just a little so it'll go away.

What that phrase was from "Old Shep" that wouldn't leave me, that followed me back to the Lauderdale Courts that day and that still comes up even these days at times I can't sleep, say, or when I'm driving somewhere on the highway by myself, is this here. It comes from the very end and why it was that part that stuck and wouldn't ever let me go I never have figured out. And I have tried to understand it for over thirty years now. Here it is then.

...has a wonderful home. That's it. That's all of it right there. Just that part over and over, and yes I know, the first part of it is the name "Old Shep." So the phrase

would be a whole sentence. If I remembered that. But that's not what stuck that day in Humes High Auditorium when Elvis sang his song on his first Memphis stage. Just the part that comes after the damn dog's name is what sank into my mind like oil sludge in a 1947 Plymouth's cylinders and with the same kind of movement and sticking power.

In fact, years later, on that day with the Japanese tourists from the Grayline tour, it came into my head as soon as the Humes Guide opened the door to the auditorium and told us to walk in and see where Elvis won the talent contest in 1952. The little short yellow people all tumbled through the door and down the aisle to take thirty-five-millimeter shots of the stage, and I waited until they had all cleared the door before I stepped inside.

They had changed things in the auditorium since that day, of course. The seats were now like you'd find in a movie house at a shopping mall, upholstered in some kind of cloth and plastic, and there seemed to be fewer rows of them. But when I looked down at where I had sat back on that September day, I could tell from what began crawling up in the back of my head that I was in the right spot.

...*has a wonderful home* said Elvis from somewhere inside my head, and then he played that little plink, plink, plink that goes higher and higher and slower and slower until it stops. And then Bubba was nice enough to do the whole phrase all over again for me as I stood there in the back of the auditorium and looked toward the stage where Mrs. Scrivener had just walked off to the wings to tell him to come back and do his encore because he had won, they all loved him and wanted to hear more, had to hear more and couldn't hear enough of him ever again.

I left the tour at that point of it, passing up the chance to see a school room that had been restored to what it looked like when Elvis used to sit in it and do his grammar exercises in English class, and I went back to the car and pointed it toward Elvis Presley Boulevard and a place called the Throw Down Lounge where at about two o'clock the next morning my twin stopped singing to me about a wonderful home, and I was able to check into the Teddy Bear Motel next door and pass out across the bed to the thrumming of magic fingers.

"Wasn't you scared, Honey, walking out there in front of all them people?"

"Naw, Mama," Elvis said to Gladys as she worked on the round steak she was fixing to chicken-fry for him that night. "Well, yeah, some. But that's all part of performing, see. You're scared, you understand, but that's good because it makes you do a better job singing."

"My throat would just close up," she said and flopped a piece of floured meat into the grease, "but that's just the difference between you and me. I'm just so proud of you for winning that talent contest. I wish I could have got off work to see it."

"I know it," Elvis said and moved over to the stove to lay his hand on the back of Gladys's neck. "I wish you could have seen me too. You'd have loved it. Someday you will."

"Well," Gladys said in a voice soft enough to use for a pillow. "We'll see."

They could go on like that for an hour, and would too, while Vernon and I sat waiting for the meat to fry or the beans to cook. One thing you got to say for the old man. He could take it. He'd sit there in the middle of that kind of thing until it was over and hardly ever show a sign of getting sick of it or wanting to hear a different subject discussed for a while. I don't know where he was in his head.

Me, hell, I'd stand it for as long as I could, generally

right up to the first caress or hug or the first word or two of baby talk, and then I'd have to leave the country. The next room, the hall, the porch, the street, anywhere else would start looking so good to me that I'd almost run to get to it. I couldn't bear that stuff between them, to see them together like that.

I don't exactly know how to describe it, my reaction I mean, but it wasn't exactly anything in particular I'd start to thinking in those situations and there weren't any words that would come to mind that I'd want to say or think that ought to be said. It was just a feeling in the tops of my legs, right above my knees, a kind of weakness that told me I had to move quick or I'd never be able to move again. It felt like my muscles were getting loose and slack without my telling them to, and that if I didn't flex them right then they'd relax completely and leave me stranded forever in that spot, able to hear and touch and see but never to be in control again of things no more than a piece of furniture in the room might be, or a plate on the table or the food on the plate itself.

Well, that night after the talent show was a bad one for getting that feeling. Or a good one, whichever way you want to look at it. My legs told me. They said move.

"Jesse," said Elvis as I began to ease out of the kitchen toward the front room and the door leading to the out-side, "wait a minute. Ain't you going to eat supper?"

"I got to go to work. I don't want to be late or old man Seay will jump on me."

"Listen," he said. "I want to talk to you some before you leave. Ask you about something."

"Sweetheart," said Gladys from the stove, "don't you go off now. This here chicken-fried steak is about done. Let Jesse go on, now. He's got things to do."

"Yes, ma'am. Just a minute. I ain't going to leave the building."

Elvis followed me on out into the hall and made sure the door to the apartment was closed behind us.

"Hey, Jesse," he said, looking over his shoulder and up the stairs, "let's do something tonight when you get back in. Let's go somewhere."

"What kind of thing you want to do? You got something in mind?"

"No," he said. "Something fun, you know. Something to follow up on this thing today."

"All right. I'll take your guitar-playing ass to Beale Street tonight. See what we can scare up. Little poon maybe."

"That's what I want," Elvis said. "That's the ticket." Something flared up in his eyes and then narrowed down to a thing that was smaller and brighter as he looked at me there in the hall of the Lauderdale Courts.

"Say," he said. "Jesse, were you there today when I was singing in the talent show?"

"No," I said. "I never made it."

"I thought I heard you say my name when I was up on the stage. There at the start of it."

"Nuh uh. Wasn't me that said nothing."

"I asked you to come be there. I told you I needed you there."

"You didn't need nobody," I said. "You done all right by yourself."

"Yeah," he said. "I done just fine. But I thought you was there with me."

"Naw," I said. "Old Shep has gone where the good doggie goes. You be ready at midnight when I get back."

"All right," Elvis said and put both hands up to his head to make sure his hair was still holding out. "We going to ramble on Beale Street tonight."

I could hear him start singing it again before I got all the way to the street, and it followed me all the way to Seay's Sinclair Station, even though nobody but me could hear it.

7

After that redneck convict killed Martin Luther King, all the white folks in Memphis got scared to death of black folks even more than they had been before, so they just tore downtown all to shit. Then all the whites moved out to the east and built houses and told the poor folks to stay put and don't say nothing else. These days when tourists come to Graceland and then go on down to Beale Street they might as well be in Disney World.

These little styrofoam honky tonks they got built now on Beale for people to look into and listen to some of the worst done blues ever sung have got no more relation to the Beale Street me and Elvis knew in 1952 than Elvis's latter-day karate kicks did to dancing. If you've ever seen it, you know what I mean. They've even got a daiquiri factory on Beale now where you can get goddamn fruit drinks to have with your chocolate chip cookies you just bought next door at Famous Amos.

The only chocolate we saw on Beale that night after Elvis won the Humes talent contest was in the complexions of the cats and chicks roaming up and down the street. And they weren't sipping fruit drinks with little umbrellas in them, neither.

It was almost one in the morning by the time we got

there. It was a good long way from the Courts, and we had to walk it, of course, afraid to take the chance of borrowing Vernon's old Ford. He would have heard it crank up even if he was in a coma, and the last thing we wanted was for Gladys to know Elvis was out of the apartment past midnight.

Anywhere else in Memphis besides Beale was closed up tighter than a snaredrum by one o'clock, but the places on that street were wide open and roaring at that time on a Friday night. The doors were open to most of the juke joints and the catfish places because of the heat and the smoke and noise being generated by the people inside, so it was like coming up to the midway of the Mid South Fair when we walked down that first block. Lights, grease, and music.

We counted three different bands playing in places on one side of the same block, and across the street two more were blowing and going next door to each other. One of them had a tenor lead with a voice that cut so deep and true that we could pick him out above all the others just like he was singing alone.

"I told you I love you, honest I do," he was wailing as me and Elvis walked up close to the door of the place he was in.

"I ain't never put no one above you," Elvis sang right along with the tenor in the next line, throwing his head back like a wolf howling at the moon.

"Let's go on in, Mr. Blues Singer," I said to him and opened the screen door to the place. "See if you got the guts to sing inside the house."

"All right," he said, "Jesse, stick close to me."

"You stick close to me," I said. "I got better things to do than watch out for your ass."

I remember the place was packed with people, standing all along the bar that ran down one side of the room and crammed together in the space between that and the dance floor which wasn't no bigger than a good-sized kitchen. The band was up against the far wall, and the lead singer was out in front, working almost in the middle of the dance floor to give himself enough room to maneuver. And he needed that.

We had to squeeze up into a little space right up against the bar and behind a man that must have weighed three hundred pounds easy and smelled like he had been wallowing in a vat of rose perfume and barbecue sauce. He must have felt Elvis come in behind him because he lurched forward a little and then swung around to look back at us, straining to get his head around far enough to see what was approaching.

"White boys," he said and took a big slug from a quart bottle of Pabst Blue Ribbon he was holding, "what y'all want in here?"

"We come to listen to some music," I said and threw my arm around Elvis's shoulders, "and eat some ribs."

"Move on in here, then," he said. "You done come to the right place."

"Lord," said a woman I hadn't noticed before because she seemed to be standing in the shade of the fat man, "ain't they pretty boys? Two of them too."

I grinned at her and nodded, and she tipped me a wink. When she grinned back, I could see that she had designs inlaid in gold in two of her front teeth and a narrow little tongue that looked blood red in the light.

"Hey," said a man from behind the bar and jerked his head up at me and then cut his eyes over at Elvis. "What y'all drinking?"

"Sloe gin and Coke," I said.

"Same for me," Elvis said in a real offhand tone.

I laughed out loud standing there to hear him say that. Elvis and alcohol is one of the things that's always been amusing to me ever since those early times. Later on that night Elvis was going to throw up everything he could get loose. Chicken fried steak, butterbeans, biscuits, ribs from that Beale Street tonk, probably part of his own damn liver. And all because of two paper cups full of Coca-Cola and about a finger and a half of sloe gin.

I gave him shit about it all the way back home from Beale that night, too. "I don't know why they call it slow gin, do you, Elvis?" I remember saying several times to him. "It sure seems to work fast enough, don't it?"

But the thing about Elvis and alcohol you always see in books and magazines and hear all these so-called side-kicks say is that Elvis wouldn't take a drink. Wouldn't do that and wouldn't smoke either, like he was acting according to some kind of a damn moral code in connection with those things. The fact is he loved the taste of all those damn sweet cocktails you find at places like Caesar's Palace or Caballero's in L.A. or even, maybe *especially*, in a fern bar in Memphis. You know what I'm talking about if you've got any experience at all with nightlife. Harvey Wallbangers, MaiTais, frozen goddamn daiquiris, Purple Passions, you name it.

It wasn't that Elvis didn't like the stuff or had promised our sweet Mama he would never dirty his lips with it or anything like that. It just all made him puke his guts out if he had more than a couple of swigs of it. One thing he didn't inherit from the male side of the parentage was the ability to drink anything that had the least acquaintance with alcohol and hold it down, come hell or high water, until it had done its appointed work.

But back there in the Blue Light Cafe on Beale in 1952, where presently you can buy canned panties, chocolate covered pretzels and the like in a little shop called "Just Things," real life started getting on down as I drank my sloe gin cocktail and Elvis sipped at his.

A little surge in the crowd when some folks left allowed us to work our way up closer to the dance floor and the band, and the music was working and the heat was on.

The band didn't waste any time between numbers, and the beat of one song was hardly gone before the next one started up. The dancers weren't leaving the floor until they just had to, either for a hit of something or to catch a little rest, the ribs were coming over the counter at a steady rate, and the Blue Light clientele was firing on every cylinder, hands clapping, feet stomping and tongues giving voice.

What few people had taken notice of me and Elvis when we came in had stopped doing that, and I was well into my second sloe gin Coke, and Elvis had moved off to one side to get a better look at the chording the lead guitar was doing. The number ended, that old one about big-legged women, and I let out a yelp or two, and the woman standing next to me reached over and pulled at my shirt collar. It was a big floppy creation almost as big as a damn hood, as I remember, and at the time I thought it looked like a million dollars.

"Hey, pretty thing," she said. "You want to dance a little dance?"

"I want to dance," I said to her and knocked back the rest of my drink, "and I want to sing. I want to dance to the music and I want to sing the blues."

"Well, come on, my man, and let's see what you got."

She moved away and by the time she hit the dance floor she was shaking like a woman with bad fever chills, both feet as solid on the floor as if they were nailed to it and everything from the knees up going ninety miles an hour in every direction at once. I jumped on in and did what I could to catch up to her, and after a few beats I was there, running dead even with her and after a minute or two, increasing the pace. She matched it, kept the tempo stroke for stroke to show she could do it, then spun around so her back was to me, moving from side to side at the same rate and straight ahead at the same time in a gradual glide. She had one of these high jacked-up rear ends like you will see on black women sometimes, not near often enough for my taste, and like I have never seen on a white woman. You know the kind I'm talking about, if you're interested in that realm of experience at all. The kind of ass you could sit a plate on top of and not worry about it falling off even while you ate a four course meal. If you could get your jaws to work, that is.

What she had was a fine example of the species, and I moved on in close enough to smell that heavy perfume and funk she was broadcasting, and I was moving with every little twitch of that thing, up, down, down, up, every which away, let it go. The drummer was into the beat so deep I was afraid the poor boy was going to drown before he came up for air, the guitar was crying and chattering like a crazy man in a small, empty room, and the tenor lead sounded like he was about to eat the microphone.

I was dancing, she was dancing, and I was following that high-set ass like it was a sacred signal leading me through the jungle to a lost city of gold. I was Tarzan, she was the savage jungle queen, and our secret trip was well under way and was bound to succeed and get us there.

She jerked and moved and wound it up and let it go, and I caught it before it hit the ground and threw it back up into the air so the light could hit it and make it shine. She reached the temple steps, hopped over a whole stack of vines and creepers, nearly lost the beat and then nailed it again just as she spun across the platform where they make human sacrifice to the stone gods with jewels in their eyes. I jumped, I kicked, I faltered, and I almost fell, but I caught my balance just in time to end up behind her as the sounds of the wind and the bells and the chants came together into one last sound I could see in front of me, purple mixed with red and gold and blue.

And then I was back in the Blue Light Cafe, watching that black-skinned woman look over her shoulder at me and smile.

"You can shake it up, pretty white boy," she said. "You come about as close to getting it as I ever seen one of you boys come."

"You're a dancer," I said. "Real modern."

When I found Elvis, standing over by the drummer with another drink in his hand he looked at me with that little twist to his lip he'd always get when he thought something was out of his range or that somebody had said something to put him down and he hadn't understood it.

"Damn, Jesse," he said. "Are you crazy? You trying to get us razor cut?"

"What you talking about, white boy?"

"You know what I mean. It looked like you was fixing to hump her from behind every minute y'all was dancing out there. One of these guys is liable to get pissed off."

"It's just an act, Elvis," I said. "Dancing ain't real life. It just acts like it is. It's like singing that way."

"Singing's real," said Elvis. "It feels more real than talking or even just being alive does. You don't know how it feels to really sing something."

"You don't know how it feels to really dance something then," I said. "Let your backbone slip."

"I can dance," he said. "I can dance up a storm."

"Go prove it with that one yonder, then. That one with the high-set rear end, the one I just danced into the floor."

"I can't dance with nobody like you did. It has to be by myself. You know that's just the way I have to do it."

Elvis was right about that. You think back if you ever saw him in one of those movies dancing with a woman or on any of those specials on television, and you'll come up with nothing. When he moved to the music, he was all by himself and there wasn't any room for another person on that floor. What was happening was going on inside, and the partner he was circling around and sliding up to and away from couldn't be seen by anybody but him.

She was there, all right. I could look into his eyes or at the way he was holding his head and smiling, and I could tell he was moving in time to the beat with a woman out there who was a perfect match for his every move, who never had to be given any directions or any lead, and who was lined up so exact and absolute according to what Elvis needed to see that she couldn't even cast a shadow, much less occupy space.

I even asked him one time if he ever saw anybody there with him when he was in the middle of the music and the song and his moving around inside all that, and he looked at me funny, jerking his head to the side and then back like he would do when something surprised him, and said how did I know. That's all he ever said about it to me, though, and I never brought the subject up again because I knew he thought if anybody knew he had ideas like that, an invisible person with him that nobody but him could see, that would make him seem different from ordinary folks in a strange and dangerous way.

And he never wanted to be different from anybody else, at least sixty percent of the time. The rest of it, of course, he was working every angle not to be like anybody else he'd ever met or seen or imagined. And he was always doing his best to get people to notice either one or the other, that he was just like one of them only dressed in snappier clothes and driving a better car, or then again that the only fit companion for him was somebody like Jesus or Richard Nixon or Ann-Margret or Kang Rhee, the karate master.

It'd be him either saying something like "the only thing different about me is that I like my eggs fried real hard," or else "Jesse, do you suppose some kind of a space ship from another world set us down back there in Tupelo to live among the earth people?" And meaning it.

My dancing that night there on Beale in the Blue Light Cafe with the black woman with that jungle ass had set Elvis a challenge, and he couldn't have rested until he did something about it. I could tell he was in a deep brood by the way he was keeping his eyes fixed on the pair of black hands picking out the lead notes on the guitar and by the fact that he had already finished that first sloe gin and was working on the second.

I was feeling up. Standing there on the edge of the dance floor, jiggling from side to side and now and then letting out a yell when a good lick was hit by the band or when the tenor lead sang something real righteous. Elvis stood me as long as he could and then he knocked back the rest of the sloe gin and Coke, crushed the paper cup and threw it against the wall of the Blue Light Cafe, and stepped up to the lead singer and put his hand on the old "stand-up" microphone.

He said something to the singer, a little short dude with a part cut into his hair down one side of his head, and the man took a step back, looked up into Elvis's face and nodded. He smiled big, and his teeth looked the size and color of silver dollars against all that black surrounding them.

"Ladies and gentlemen," he said, pulling the mike up close to his mouth, "cats and chicks. We have done got us a guest singer at the Blue Light. Says he wants to do a little number for us, sing us a little blues."

The little dude took a half step back and leaned toward Elvis to ask him something, and after Elvis had said something back, he spoke into the microphone again.

"Cats and chicks, patrons of the Blue Light, the boy says his name is er, uh *Eat This Pretzel*. Say he going to do it now."

He pushed the microphone towards Elvis and lit out for the bar, and a few of the people in the place looked over at the band, but most of them kept on doing whatever they were doing. Nuzzling each other's necks, taking drinks out of cups and bottles, rubbing up against whatever was closest to them, and putting their hands wherever they could get away with it.

I took a big slug of my sloe gin and coke, wishing for something stronger, and got ready to listen to one more round of "Old Shep," I figured. Maybe he'll do it quick, I remember thinking, and be through at the same time the tenor lead finishes his drink and before the crowd has time to hear what's really going on and gets restless and starts hollering. Maybe they won't even notice he's singing until it's all over with and the goddamn dog finally has that wonderful home. Plink, plink, plink.

I looked up at Elvis from where I was standing about six feet away from him, and he caught my eyes with his for about two beats. Then he shook his shoulders like a man trying to shrug off a coat without using his hands, grabbed the mike stand with his left hand and pointing directly at the lead guitarist with his right, jammed his mouth right up against the microphone.

"You're like a picture on the wall," he wailed so loud, prolonged and sudden that the speaker made a high popping noise, "please don't fall."

By the time he got to the next line, after wringing the pure shit out of that first one, the guitar had joined in and caught up and was crying like a man whose woman was just fresh gone, the drummer was pounding a low back bass that was the sound of the abandoned man's heart breaking, and the crowd was swinging around from whatever its separate parts had been doing to join in looking at the white boy on the far side of the room and listening to him tell about what had happened wrong in his life.

"It's my life I'm thinking of," Elvis sang in a kind of crouch that began low behind the mike and then began to come slowly uncoiled as he worked his way up to a standing position to scream the next words directly into the long gone woman's ear and right between the eyes of everybody in the main room of the Blue Light Cafe. "Darling, please, please accept my love."

The rest of it went on that slow painful sweet way like when you're locked up with somebody in love and feel the thing coming apart and there ain't nothing you can do about it but feel it slide. It's that way your mind gets when you're with a woman, inside her, and you know you got to hold on or it's going to be lost and gone before it does her the good you need it to do, so you've got to put yourself somewhere else or else you can't be right there where you're dying to stay. Because if you let yourself stay in that spot you're in, that place that's become all the world to you, you won't be able to stay there. You've got to put your mind somewhere else where you really don't want it to be so that you can partway be where all of you is dying to be. Understand what I'm saying?

It's a bitch. And that's the way Elvis sang it that night in the Blue Light Cafe when he got his teeth into that mournful wail. And that's why both of us ended up getting our first taste of what it's like to have a woman. And that first time for both of us was off Beale in the alley that ran behind that building. And it was in the front and back seats of a big old hump-backed Packard. The doors were locked and the lights were off, and the women were so dark I couldn't even see mine there on that seat where we were lying together.

But she called me her pretty dancing white boy, and she took me inside, and it was sweet, sweet, sweet where she took me.

8

They have changed the sign on the front of that little sliced-off building there on Union Avenue. Changed it again, I mean, from what they had hanging on it for so long from sometime in the '60s right up to a year ago. People are always trying to get back to the original look of something, and they always end up missing it, of course. It reminds me of something Priscilla used to say a lot from a book the nuns had made her read in class there at the Immaculate Conception High School on Central.

"You can't go home again," she would say whenever something came up about the way things used to be. And then she'd frown and get that little straight line between her eyebrows that made her look like she was at least twenty years old instead of the eighteen or nineteen she really was at the time. That would always knock me out, that little line and her saying that so serious.

What she said applies to a lot of things, that sign on the building being one of them, and what they were trying to do when they took off the big one and went back to just the little plain white neon ones in the windows on each side of the front door of Sam Phillips' place.

The big one painted across the entire top of the building had said something like "The Legendary Sun Studio" and it had a picture of the logo that Sam had put in the middle of the records that came out of there in the '50s. You're bound to have seen it. It's as famous as that damn green apple with one bite taken out that popped up a few years later. Sam's had a red rooster profiled and crowing in front of a rising sun. It always put me in mind of the Japanese flag and Tojo getting shot by Uncle McCoy, but Sam didn't mean for none of that to be in there.

The little neon signs in the windows that I passed by every day driving up and down Union in the tow truck didn't say nothing fancy in 1954. "Memphis Recording Service" was what the glass spelled out, and that was it, so little you could hardly read it if you didn't have to stop for the light there at the corner.

You probably know the popular opinion about how it all began there on Union in that little room with the loose wires and the bad echo. How Elvis was supposed to have stopped in one day, stealing a few minutes from his busy schedule with the Crown Electric truck, and made a recording for his mama for her birthday and then thought no more about it but went on his electric company truck-driving way. And how, lo, Sam Phillips was spoken to by Marion Keisker and she sayeth how this boy is a good ballad singer, and Sam Phillips, being convicted in his soul for the need to searcheth for a white boy who can sing like an Ethiopian, sendeth forth for the strange youth to cometh to Memphis Recording Services and singeth into the mike.

And behold, he did, and the youth came forth and sang, and yea, his voice was that of the Ethiopian, and riches followed and the walls came tumbling down, even in Memphis, New York, Las Vegas, and throughout the land.

Like I said, that's the way the scripture about the Sun revelation reads, and that's the way folks want to and need to believe it all happened back there at the beginning. People dearly love to see a design in what's already past, and if they can't see one, well by God they are going to make one fit on in there or bust a gut trying.

And the days at the Sun are the richest soil these folks can find, the ones that are plowing the Elvis plantation and hoping for a bumper crop come picking time. They figure there's got to be that thread, that divine order behind the things that took place in 1953 and 1954, and if they turn the thing so the light hits it just exactly at the right angle the whole pattern will stand out as plain and clear as the ribs in a chest x-ray.

And, of course, the biggest believer in the x-ray theory of the King's career was Elvis himself. By the time it all ended up there in Graceland in the latter days, he had studied his own life so close, turning the events of it every which way and inside out, that he couldn't really remember what took place at the launch site on Union Avenue at the start. He told every kind of crazy story about it and believed every one of them while he was telling it.

So it's up to me to straighten that whole mess out, and that's one story I most particularly want to chase down, hem up in a corner and brand. Once I get that one taken care of, maybe, I'll feel like in my own mind that I've got a little more space to get a separate breath in for myself.

All right, then. Here is what took place at the Sun Studio at the sign of the rooster in the years of 1953 and 1954.

At that time, like I said, I was driving a tow truck for old man Seay, having graduated from pumping gas and checking the air in slick tires. He liked the way I would get to a wreck fast and the fact that I would work any hour, no matter how late or early. Anytime of the day or night on the road beat the hell out of lying around the apartment for me, listening to Vernon complain about how his feet hurt and how his back was acting up, or hearing Gladys read signs and make predictions.

She had got into heavy prophesying by then, sitting in a big rocker that Elvis had drug up from somewhere for her and leaning forward to let her hair fall across her forehead and eyes. She'd rear back in the chair, let it tilt forward on the rocker runners and back again until it reached the rhythm she wanted, and then she'd start speaking in a low flat voice to anybody who was in the room with her.

"Seems like to me something's coming," she'd say, "something's out there behind a kind of cloud, and it's making sounds and letting out flashes of light."

"What kind of sounds, Aunt Gladys?" I asked her one afternoon when I was between runs with the tow truck.

"Is it like bombs going off? Or guns or something like that?"

"It's like music," she said. "But it's different from what I've heard before. No man knows it for what it is."

"Uh huh," I said and sat there for a while, watching her surge back and forth in the rocking chair, her hair falling forward and rising up as her head moved in a steady two-foot arc.

"Does it sound good," I said. "The music you're hearing, I mean?"

"Carrying stuff with it. Different colors, heavy things, things moving and leaving, coming and going, all of it staying together in a big wad coming towards me."

With that, she suddenly stopped the rocker by planting her feet flat on the floor and pointed with her right hand toward the wall behind me. I looked over my shoulder at it with the little hairs rising up on the back of my neck, but all I could see was a water stain on the flowered wall paper that was in the shape of nothing I had ever seen before.

"There," Gladys said, "there. And it's got Elvis inside of it, and he's pushing it and moving it and trying to get outside of it so he can catch his breath."

She stopped talking and kept staring at the wall as if her eyes were boring through it like wood augers, and then she gradually relaxed her legs until the rocker fell back into a motion, slower now than it was before, and she said one more thing before I got up to leave for the tow truck and whatever wreck I could find on some street in Memphis.

"It's sweet," Gladys said. "But it's hurtful, and it's coming soon, like a freight train."

Now that was just one session with Gladys in the rocker, and it was about par for the course there those last few months of 1953. There was something in the air for her then, working steady and building up, and keeping Vernon in a coma and me on the road and Elvis close to a fit.

He had caught on at Crown Electric by then and was driving a delivery truck for them and was singing on Friday and Saturday, when they'd let him, between shows of the country band that was regular at the Eagle's Nest. I had heard him a couple of times, stopping by between runs to drink a beer and listen to Elvis do his Dean Martin imitation. I knew I could do better than that myself, even if I didn't have the words to "Old Shep" engraved on my heart, so that was what really gave me the idea to stop off one afternoon at Memphis Recording Services on Union.

When I walked into the front part of the building, I found myself in a room about the size of Gladys's kitchen back in that apartment on Alabama Avenue. It had a desk off to one side and a door that led to the studio itself on the other, and the only person in the room was a woman somewhere in her forties, writing down numbers in a book. It was Marion Keisker, of course, one-half of the pair that has carried on the famous feud for thirty years about who really discovered Elvis Presley. Marion claims she took the first sure notice of what was going to come, and her boss, Sam Phillips, claims naturally that she didn't know anything about talent and that he was the man who saw the answer to his prayers standing in front of him when Elvis walked in off the street dragging a guitar.

Sam's famous prediction, reported a thousand times, has undergone some cleaning up over the years since he was supposed to have given voice to it.

"If I can find me a white boy that can sing like a nigger, I'll make a million dollars," declared Sam, according to the historians.

He claims now he never said "nigger" and besides, that was different times. But both him and Marion claim they recognized the answer first, and it was wearing a Crown Electric shirt, sideburns and size nine workshoes.

Uh huh. Let me tell you what really happened that afternoon in that rock and roll delivery room in Memphis, Tennessee.

I walked over close to Marion Keisker's desk and stood there watching her write her numbers in a row for almost a half minute before she looked up at me. She had the look of somebody having trouble adding things up, and her glasses had slipped all the way to the end of her nose.

"Well," she said. "It don't make sense. Can I help you?"

"Is this where y'all make records?"

"It sure is. Do you want us to come out and record something for you? A wedding or a funeral or something?"

"No, Ma'am" I said. "I want to do one here. See how I sound singing on a record, you know."

"Sure," Marion Keisker said. "It'll cost you four dollars."

Let me tell you, she underestimated that final bill by a little. Like about thirty-one years and still counting. That debt is still being paid, and I don't see any end to the installments lined up ahead of me. That bill is forevermore still outstanding and overdue.

But it was different times back then, like Sam Phillips likes to say, so I just followed her on back into the studio part of the building, picked up a guitar lying on a chair, launched into an old Ink Spots song, and gave history a kick in the ass to get it started.

After Marion finished messing with the dials, adjusting cutting depth and checking microphone levels, I did it all again and got both sides of the record cut with the sound vibrations from the voice of Jesse Garon Presley accompanied by the man himself on that borrowed guitar. She put the results in my hands back in the front room, took my four dollars and asked me what my name was.

"Presley," I said. "Jesse Garon."

"Is that with one s or two?" she asked, writing down the last name on a little piece of paper about the size of a toilet paper square.

"One."

"All right," Marion said. "Give me your telephone number too if you got one. We might give you a call to sing for us sometime. You got a voice might be good for ballads. I taped that last one, 'My Happiness.'"

"It's the number for the folks upstairs," I said. "He's a Jewish rabbi, but he'll take a call for me."

"We'll see," she said and stuck the little toilet paper square in the drawer of her desk.

I took that record with no label on it out to the truck with me, and it wasn't until 1968 that I slung it off the Golden Gate Bridge into San Francisco Bay. And it sailed like a frisbee, rising up first before it took that last long dive into the water, catching light and sparking all the way until it hit and sank in all that blue.

So who at Memphis Recording Services discovered Elvis Presley late of a Saturday afternoon in 1953, getting on toward evening? That question's not one that Marion Keisker or Sam Phillips can answer, as I think you know by now. Because neither one of them nor nobody else saw Elvis that day or recorded that couple of Ink Spots songs as sung by him.

That was me, Jesse Garon, and I wasn't wearing sideburns or a Crown Electric shirt, and I wasn't carrying my own guitar with me. I was in blue jeans and a brown checked shirt, and my hair was cut in one of those old-fashioned white sidewalls styles with a part on the right where my cowlick used to fall.

But that's the truth, and the truth ain't had much of a chance where the history of Elvis Presley is concerned. It just gets in the way and makes people uncomfortable and mad.

I remember once years later at a big party in Vegas where Elvis had got me to stand in for him, the subject of that first appearance at Memphis Recording came up. The gin was flowing, I was mad and about half-drunk although I was supposed never to drink alcohol when I was doing Bubba, and I was just fixing to say "uh huh" to a young thing that was dying to get into Elvis's pants. Up comes Sam Phillips to me with a couple of guys in tow that looked like Eastern promoters or editors of the *National Enquirer*. It was in the late '60s or early '70s, I forget which, and Sam was sporting long hair, a beard, gold necklaces and an open shirt front, and he was flying high and showing out.

"Elvis," he said, "you're looking good. Meet such and such and such and such. I was just telling them about that day you came in off the street wanting to pay me to record you singing."

He stopped at that point to let everybody laugh, and then he shook his hair to keep the fluff up and began talking again, describing how I'd looked in the Crown Electric outfit and the kind of guitar I was carrying and all that other tired horseshit about that magic day in rock and roll history. I let him go on, nodding now and then to give him his cues and sucking at my gin and ice, right up to the point where he asked me to witness for him.

"Remember," he said, "I didn't let you know I was taping that first little session to save for later while I was cutting the acetate on that record? And how it surprised you so damn much when I asked how to get in touch with you later on?" At that, he turned his head to speak to the promoters, but he kept his eyes on me while he talked. "This little guy didn't even have a telephone. He couldn't hardly even remember what his address was. Little country dude."

"That's right, Sam," I said. "You were the first big time music man I ever run into. You could run them tapes, twist them knobs, spot that talent." I turned toward the guys Sam was working so hard to impress. "It didn't take him but nine months to call me back. He was that fast to recognize what he had got a hold of. And later on, shit, he just held RCA up for robbery when he sold me to them. He got thirty-five thousand dollars for my contract, cash money on the line." Then I looked back at Phillips. "Didn't you, Mr. Phillips?"

That was the truth and Sam Phillips, and it just caused him to walk off and leave me with that sweet thing who was wanting to climb on Elvis. I think I might have let her do it, too. But I don't know right now.

That telephone call did come nine months after I had sung for Marion Keisker, though, there in the studio. And it came to the rabbi's wife and she came downstairs and knocked on the door and talked to Gladys and told her some woman was on the phone for the Presley boy who sang. And Gladys closed the door to the apartment without making any noise which might wake me up where I was sleeping on a pallet in the front room and tiptoed out to the street where Elvis was washing the hubcaps on Vernon's car.

"Honey," she must have said, "It's starting up. Get your guitar and go down to the Sun where all the sounds and lights are mixed up together in a big wad coming at us."

And then he would have jumped up from his knees and thrown down the cloth he was holding and started for the house, and she would have held her finger up to her lips for him to be quiet about it. And it would have all happened while I was dreaming there on the floor of the house on Alabama Street in Memphis on the river.

And Gladys stood there in the yard after they had kissed and hugged and whispered in each other's ears and watched him out of sight as Elvis half-ran up the street carrying his guitar toward my appointment at the Sun, answering that call I never got and never will.

9

By the time I heard about the telephone call that had come to the rabbi asking for the boy who had sung for Marion Keisker last year, Elvis had already begun practicing with Scotty Moore and Bill Black so they could go into the Sun studio on July 6 and get famous. That's when I almost left Gladys's love nest on Alabama Street, and I ought to have done it then and gone out and had me a life of my own.

And I tried it, but I couldn't. I went so far as to buy me a suitcase made out of cardboard and tin and fill it up with all my clothes and the letters from Aunt Edith and the record of me singing "My Happiness." But somehow I couldn't pick it up. It seemed as heavy as so much lead as I stood there in the front room of that apartment on Alabama Street trying to lift it off the floor. There wasn't anybody in the house but me that morning, and I could hear the voices of children out in the street walking to school and I could smell the bacon grease left from Gladys's cooking at breakfast. And I was the only one there, and I was all by myself.

It was like I was in a dream, trying to wake up like you will when something in your own head has scared you and you can feel your muscles trying to work and failing you. I must have stood there for half an hour, that damn suitcase handle in my hand and my body not doing what my mind was telling it to, before I finally let loose of everything and walked on out to the street.

The sun didn't look right, it was pale and the light it put on things seemed to be making them hazy instead of clear, the flowers that the rabbi's wife kept in some pots on the front porch, the edges of the steps down to the sidewalk, the cars parked out in front and across the street. I had to put my feet down hard, each one of them a separate thought, to make them stick to the porch and the steps and the ground. It was like they wanted to fly up and push away from things instead of settling solid on them, and I had to catch at the stair railing to keep from falling off to the side and slipping to the ground. I knew if I ever did that, I wouldn't be able to get up again, so I was careful, careful to let myself ease down the steps until I could get to the front yard and sit down on the grass with my back propped against the single tree growing there, a dogwood in bloom.

I went to sleep sitting like that, and I didn't wake up until Vernon shook me by the shoulder some time that afternoon when he was coming home from work.

"Jesse," he said, moving his head from side to side to look into my eyes, "ain't you going to work? You going to be late."

"I'm already late," I said. "I have been late for a long time, and I'm going downtown to see if I can't catch up some."

So all those months Elvis was learning how to sing with a band and how to take advantage of a guitar and a bass and put his voice ahead, behind, and on top of anything around it, Jesse Garon was learning Beale Street and South Main and black women and his first white ones and how to drink all night, puke in the morning and go to work and not miss a lick.

I bleached my hair out platinum blond, I got the fraction 1/2 tattooed high up on my left shoulder where you can hardly see it if you don't know it's there, I bought me a '49 Ford and turned the gear shift around to the left side of the steering wheel so I could hold on to a woman with my right arm with no hindrance, and I did my best never to be home when Elvis was there or when Gladys was awake.

I did a good job of all of that, and it wasn't until the day after Elvis and the boys taped "That's All Right, Mama" that he caught up with me just as I was leaving the house to get into the Ford and head for the Thicket Bar and Grill across the bridge in Arkansas.

"Jesse Garon," he said, waving at me from the sidewalk, "wait a minute. I want to tell you about what we done last night over at the studio. Me and Scotty and Bill."

"Hurry on up then," I said. "I got something waiting for me in Arkansas. I got to jump."

"What?" said Elvis. "Ain't this Memphis stuff hot enough for you? You got to cross the Mississippi to find some that'll suit you?"

"You got to talk too much to it over here in Memphis. Rattle a feed bucket in Arkansas they come a-running."

"What it was," he said, "was we was singing all kinds of stuff, trying to get something to suit old Sam Phillips, and it wasn't nothing doing it for him. He always keeps on saying make it different, but then he doesn't know what he wants to sound different or how to make it sound that way. You got me?"

"Yeah," I said, "you got real problems, don't you?"

"So we was taking a break, and Sam was gone out to buy him some more cigarettes, and he left the tape machine going not on purpose. We found that out later.

Scotty was messing with his guitar, and I started singing that old Arthur Crudup song I listened to all last summer. Remember it? 'That's All Right, Mama'?"

"Yeah, I heard it. About a thousand times."

"I started cutting up. Going real high, letting it tumble, going real fast, seeing how quick I could say stuff and it still be words. Sam came on back with his cigarettes, and when he wound that tape back up and listened to it, he said that was it, I had done made it different. Then we worked on it until morning, and Jesse, we got it right."

Elvis was standing there at the bottom of those steps, wearing his Crown Electric clothes and jiggling around while he talked like he had fever. The sun was low behind him, and it kept getting in my eyes, and maybe that was part of the reason why I could hardly stand to look at him. But let me tell the truth, it wasn't all. Not by a long shot.

I stood it as long as I could, listening to him tell about the recording session, and which songs seemed to work and which ones didn't and why, and finally I broke into the middle of something he was saying about how it was all finally rhythm and timing and knowing when to cut it off and let it go and when to raise it and when to draw it down.

"That telephone call was for me, you bastard," I said. "And nobody never let me know anything about it."

Elvis stopped talking and looked back at me for a full minute, his eyes narrowed into slits as he stared, the blue of them the same blue as mine. Neither one of us blinked or looked off until he finally spoke.

"I know that," he said. "I knew at the time. But you couldn't never have finished up what you started over there at the Sun Studio. That was for me to do. I was the one."

"What makes you figure it that way? Who told you

that you're so damn special only you could finish what I got started?"

"You know who it was. It was Mama. She's always known that about me and you. It comes to her out of things around her and in the air, things that you can't understand and I can't understand. But they're real, and they're pointers to what has to be and what's going to come."

"I did it first," I said, thinking one word at a time so I could get them all out in the right order. "I thought to put my voice on a record, and I went to the studio by myself to sing it alone. And I did it."

"Yeah, but you know, Jesse Garon," Elvis said and put his eyes back on me again with the look he had used that time back in Tupelo after he had showed me the snake coiled in that hole, "you know that wherever you go and whatever you do some of me is with you. Always, always with you. I'm there when you are."

And then he stopped talking for a few seconds and moved his head a little to the side so that the sun hit him at just the right angle to make his features vanish and just his outline stand out against the light. It was then he said one more word before he moved past me and walked up the steps into the house.

"Brother," he said. And I have heard the sound of that word coming from him and following me from that time there in Memphis right up to now. And it has stayed in my head, asleep or awake, like those rings and circles of snake under that sheet of metal behind that little house in Tupelo, that snake I tried to kill and that Elvis said would always be alive.

Nobody has ever accused Elvis of being real smart, but that was one time he was right and I was wrong. That thing was alive, no matter how much I wanted it dead, and it has stayed alive all these years.

Everybody knows the rest of that scene at the Sun Studio, and I'm not here to tell that part of Elvis's story one more time. How Dewey Phillips played "That's All Right, Mama" and "Blue Moon of Kentucky" over and over that first night on WHBQ until it just drove every kid in Memphis crazy, how he interviewed Elvis on the radio without letting him know the mike was on, how that Sun record just took off on the hillbilly chart even though everybody was scared the singer might be a nigger after all, no matter what the deejays said about his graduating from a white high school in Memphis and driving a truck.

What I'm interested in is what I was doing in my life or in as much of one as I could claw out for myself, and during those days at Sun I was keeping as much distance as I could while hanging on to wherever I could grab a hold. I didn't take part in any of that first stuff, in other words, since if I had let myself be pulled into trying to, I believe at the time it would have purely killed me or set me crazier than I already was.

It wasn't until well into the period when Elvis and that bunch were driving all over Arkansas, Texas, Alabama, and other points south in used Cadillacs, that I finally got back into it with the Big E, and it came about because of marital discord between Scotty Moore and his little lady. I never knew the details and didn't want to, but somehow Scotty had received the word that he wasn't going with the boys on the next trip, this one down to several towns in East and North Texas, and Elvis came to me where I was living in a boarding house on Manassas after finally moving out of Vernon and Gladys's happy home.

I had done that at some cost, let me tell you. You would have been surprised to see how much Gladys carried on about wanting me to stay and about my betrayal of her and Elvis by leaving, after what all you've learned about

111

me and her so far. But it was true. She told me many times and in many different ways how much Elvis needed his cousin Jesse Garon now that he was making his name known and singing his songs in auditoriums and fairgrounds and off the backs of flatbed trucks all over the South and that if I was to pull out and not be there for him that he was liable to go into a sinking spell that might ruin everything for the whole family.

But I scuttled. I had to. It was that or die. And one difference between me and my brother, in case you haven't noticed yet, is that I ain't dead and I never have given myself up to yearning for the big final stretch-out. That's not the way the dark twin's constructed. Even then I saw what I had to do to survive, and I did it.

So I was there that evening in my room on Manassas lying across the bed, listening to the radio and waiting for it to be time to crank up the Ford and head for the honky tonks when my door opened and Elvis walked in. He was wearing highwaisted black pants with enough material in them to make a suit for a middle-aged man and a pink sport coat with black stitching all down the lapels. When he turned to close the door, I could see that a pink stripe ran up the leg seam of the peg pants too. His shirt was made out of that old crinkly nylon stuff that you don't ever see anymore, and it was sky blue and fastened up to the neck where he had a little thin tie knotted close and tight.

"What color are your socks?" I asked him.

"Pink and black plaid," he said and lifted one foot to show his shoes to me too. "You're supposed to use black lacquer on the edges of the soles and just brush the tops of them with a soft rag. Won't never need polishing. They are supposed to look dull, all except for that sole edge."

"That's a piss-cutter, then, ain't it? They sell you any boxer shorts to go underneath all them threads?"

"Naw," Elvis said and gave me that crooked lip smile, "they'd just get in the way."

"Uh huh," I said. "You just come by to show me your new suit of clothes? Or do you want some advice about chording a guitar?"

I remember Elvis looked around the room at the stuff I had lying around in there for about two minutes before he said anything. When he did, he wasn't looking at me but at a pack of Pall Malls he had picked up off the top of my chest of drawers.

"Why do you smoke these things?" he said. "It'll make your teeth look yellow." He put the cigarettes back down but kept looking at them. "Jesse Garon," he said. "I need you to go to Texas with me."

"Hell, son," I said, "you got everything you need right now. You sure don't need nothing I could come up with. What could a tow-truck driver that lives in one room on Manassas Street have that Elvis Presley would want? I'm plumb out of pink and black suspenders. You want a Pall Mall, you can have one. I see you're awful interested in that pack."

"Are you through carrying on?"

"No," I told him. "I sure as hell ain't." Then I sang a little bit of one of his Sun songs to him, a verse from "Baby, Let's Play House," and I put in every damn hiccup too.

"That's good," Elvis said when I stopped. "That's real good, Jesse. And that's just why I come over to ask you to go with me on this Texas thing. I need somebody who can play that guitar and knows the stuff I do the way I do it."

"If that's all you're here for, forget it," I said. "Run it up your round brown. There's all kinds of guitar players in Memphis. You could have your pick of any damn one of them, too, and you know it, Mr. Elvis Presley."

"I wish you wouldn't stay so mad about all this thing. You know things happen the way they will and to a pattern that's got to be. It's all lined up already."

"I don't know no such of a goddamn thing, Elvis," I told him. "You know I don't buy that stuff."

That was Gladys talking through him, of course, and to hear that excuse for what had happened just royally burned my ass. Elvis could see that, and thinking back to it now, I can see that he realized he'd have to try a different line. At least I think it was just a line, another way of trying to get the twin to fall into place and fill out the empty half that was now in need somehow of what only that other self could add. But naturally I wasn't sure, and that's the way it always was between us, me wanting to believe what Elvis was telling me and him wanting to tell me what he knew I wanted to believe.

You see what I'm talking about? You see how tight and crazy and separate and together at the same time it always was, having to try to get a breath of my own that wasn't borrowed from him?

"All right," Elvis said. "I know I could get plenty of other people to play and sing in Texas with me. That really ain't why I'm asking you to do it. You know why it is."

"Well, why is it then? You say it."

"I need you, Jesse," he said. "I can't never make it for long at a time without you being with me to make things feel they're coming together like they ought to."

"How come?" I said, pushing him to make him say something that would give me the excuse I needed to be able to say yes to him.

"Think back," he said. "When we were little, growing up in Tupelo and later on here in Memphis. I always depended on you more than anybody else. Even Mama, but don't you tell her I said it."

I remember I looked out of the window next to my bed at that point and saw the limb of that pine tree I had studied so long and so well every afternoon while I was lying across my bed waiting for it to be time to go get in the tow truck and take calls to go haul in wrecks. The pine needles on it were always green, and the cluster of three pine cones at the end of that limb was always there as brown and compact as ever. I looked at them for fully a minute before I said anything to him, and when I did I didn't take my eyes off the pine framed through the window casing.

"All right," I said. "I'll go to Texas with you just this one time."

"Well, that's good news," Elvis said and turned for the door. "I'll pick you up about midnight. And listen here, you're going to enjoy this thing. The pussy hound you are, you are going to have trouble knowing which way to jump."

And that's how I ended up on the stage of the Civic Building in Marshall, Texas two days later standing a few steps behind Elvis and picking at a guitar while he spun, did splits, fell to his knees, crawled on the floor, humped the microphone stand, and sang all those first ones from Sun. I played every piece like a machine, no more life to it than you can find in a can of English peas, but nobody noticed it but me.

Bill Black was off in that world where bass players live, you know where everything goes *whum whum whum*, I wasn't anybody to him but Elvis's tow-truck driving cousin, and the crowd sure as hell wasn't listening for the fine points of musical accompaniment. What they were doing was coming apart at the seams as Elvis worked them like a dose of Epsom salts going through a colicky cow.

I just stood back and strummed and watched, most of

the time not even able to hear the lead guitar myself during the numbers. I could feel the bass down in my belly and my fingers tingled from the strings I was hitting, but the dominant sound in my ears was the voice of the crowd as it talked back to the songs he was doing. And that sound was high and low, and it was shrill and deep, and it had female hysterics written all over it.

Elvis wasn't worth a damn, really, on a guitar, and he couldn't do more than just peck at a piano keyboard. And I've seen him work away at an instrument for hour on end, at least back at the beginning, and not sound one bit better at the end than when he sat down at it. But he could play that one thing. The people out front.

And that's the hardest damn instrument of all.

This was back, of course, before they had begun to use security people between the stage and the first row of people in the crowd, so after the first couple of numbers people were crammed all up against the edge of the stage from one end of it to the other. By the time Elvis had broken a good sweat, fallen to his knees and crawled from where he had been standing up to the edge of the platform there must have been two hundred girls and women leaning forward and reaching out for him.

That was the first time I noticed that look in their eyes when he was singing, and the first one I noticed with the mark was a sixteen or seventeen year-old little Texan who had maneuvered her way up to a point on the edge of the stage just a little to the right of center. I remember she was wearing a white shirt and a blood-red scarf tied around her neck, and she had her right arm stretched out about far enough to let her touch the toe of Elvis's shoe. She gave a little final lunge and did it, and then she looked up along Elvis's leg past his crotch and his belt buckle and his thin tie into his face as he squalled his way through "Mystery Train."

As she stood there with her fingertips just touching that lacquered shoe sole, I got my first real glimpse of that look I was to see for the rest of my time whenever Elvis sang in front of a woman. Don't get me wrong, it was an expression I had seen before plenty of times already by then, but never on the face of a stranger. That was the difference. What I was looking at when I studied the face of that teenaged kid in Marshall, Texas was Gladys Presley purified. There were the wide eyes, opened more than you would have thought possible, and the full mouth, lips parted just like they were fixing to frame the word *yes* or maybe *you,* and it was the expression of a woman seeing something she had always heard about but had been afraid to believe really lived in her very world. And now there was the living proof right in front of her, and she could finally believe what every bit of her had been dying to be able to believe for the longest time. It was finally possible all her dreams might really come true. The closest I ever came to a woman looking at me that way, when she wasn't thinking I was Elvis, that is, was a girl in Eugene, Oregon the time I was living there those three years in the '60s. She didn't have any more notion of me being somebody other than who was right before her than Gladys ever did looking at Elvis. That was the part that counted.

This woman was named Gail and she was married to an old boy I had run into working in the logging woods during that time. He was all right, but she didn't love him really. I mean not in the way you have to to be able to stand living your life with somebody else's life there all tangled up with it, and we got into a little thing pretty quick after I met her.

The time she gave me that look that Elvis got all his damn life from Gladys and all the rest of the female world was one time when we were in bed together. We had already made love once, and she had come but I hadn't yet, so I was lying there beside her with still a hard on, watching the red splotches on her chest fade. Then she looked into my eyes and showed me that look, and it was just for me, that Gladys-purified expression I saw back in Marshall, Texas in 1954 on that little girl with her fingers on the toe of Elvis's shoe.

I stopped going to see Gail right after then, and I haven't seen that look since, not when it was just for me, for Jesse Garon himself and no mistake about it. It doesn't pay me to think about that, and I try not to.

Elvis went on for over an hour that night, singing everything he'd put on Sam Phillips's records there at the sign of the rooster and the rising sun, and by the time he'd finished with that crowd he had wore both them and himself plumb out. From where I was standing behind him I could see that the back of his sport coat was sopping wet wherever it had touched him and then some, and the sweat was rolling from his hair, soaking into his collar, and making his skin shine in the light like it had a fluorescent bulb inside it.

He finished the last song, I believe it was "I Want to Play House With You," turned and pointed toward me, and I hit the guitar a lick that broke one string and stretched another, and the set was over in Marshall, Texas.

"Ladies and gentlemen," Elvis said into the microphone, "thank you. Boys, I ain't got nothing to say to you. Girls, meet me out behind the barn."

They squalled like they all had simultaneously had a fingernail jerked out with pliers, and we broke and ran for the dressing room, carrying our instruments chest high as shields and trying our best not to stumble or slip down before we got behind a door we could lock.

One old girl almost stopped us all before we could get to safety. She had gotten a lead on the rest of the crowd somehow and was waiting in the hall there by the drinking fountain with her purse in one hand and a poster announcing the coming of the Hillbilly Cat in the other. She must have torn it off a telephone pole or the side of a fence somehow, I remember thinking, because you could see where the staples had ripped out all along both edges of it.

When she saw us coming, Elvis in front and me and Bill Black right behind him, she dropped into a kind of a three point stance like a halfback and released just as we got there. Elvis took the full force of her charge so he was throwed back into me and I half fell into Black and had to catch myself on the water fountain to save the whole bunch from falling to the floor. I got to give her credit. She could have made some college teams, judging from the effect of her charge there in the hall, and every damn high school team I ever saw.

And she didn't do it in deadly silence, neither. She let out a squall when she came up from that floor that threw Bill Black into a blind panic, and it didn't make me any too damn comfortable, neither, to tell the truth about it.

"Elvis," she hollered, "Oh, God, Elvis, it's you. Please just write your name on this here poster."

The rumble of feet behind me was getting louder, doors were being slammed open and shut, and high-pitched screams and hollers were getting close by the time I got us all three straightened up and through the dressing room door, the female halfback tumbling in along with the bunch. When I got the door latched and looked around I could see that she was a lot littler than I thought she was at first, a dark-haired girl with close-set eyes and lips painted up as red as the inside of a ripe watermelon. She looked real worked on.

"I can't believe it," she said, "I'm in here with Elvis Presley. God, God."

119

"That's right, sugar," said the Hillbilly Cat, "what was it you wanted me to sign?"

"I need a drink," I said to the room, and Bill Black produced a pint of bourbon in about ten seconds which I bubbled twice before I took it down from my face.

The voices in the hall got louder, but none of us noticed it much until some fool in the bunch outside got all of them to yelling Elvis's name at the same time, and that turned out to be an attention-getting device.

The little dark-haired girl was running around the room like she was on roller skates, me and Bill was killing the pint between us, and Elvis was propped up against a table in the corner with the sweat still dripping off his nose and chin.

"Honey," he yelled above the sound of his own name coming in waves from the other side of the dressing room door, "I want you to do something for me."

"Oh, Elvis," she said in a voice so soft and melted that she could barely get the words past her lips, "What? What do you want me to do? You pretty thing."

"Go out yonder," he said, wiping his face on the tail of a shirt he'd just pulled out of a suitcase, "and get about four or five other girls just as good looking as you and meet us at the East Texas Motor Court in about an hour. What room is it, Jesse?"

"I forget," I said.

"It's one-ten," said Bill.

"We'll have us a little party," Elvis said through the cloth of the shirt as he wiped off some more sweat. "What's your name, cute thing?"

"Earline Trousdale," she said and took her poster out into the hall as Elvis opened the door. "We'll be there."

"Hot, ain't it?" he said as he relocked the latch and looked at me. "I'm soaking wet."

"I want some more whiskey," I said.

"I need me some pussy," Elvis said. "I'm still just as hard as a hoe-handle from all that singing."

He pointed down at the front of his peg pants. "Looky there."

"These little Texas girls will shrink it up for you," said Bill. "Give them half a chance."

"I'm going to give them the full chance," Elvis said. "Just like old Jesse's going to do, huh, cousin?"

"Let old Tarzan Snake loose," I said. "See can he wiggle."

"You got it," Elvis said. "Now you're talking, Jesse."

I don't have to talk about what went on in that dark room in the motor court out on the highway. It was five of them showed up, counting Earline, and wasn't but one of them not above average in looks. And what that one didn't have in the way of a face she made up for in enthusiasm.

Everybody had a good time, and nobody got hurt. Don't get me wrong about that, nor about what usually took place on the road in those early days when Elvis travelled what you might call surface. Before he got up off the ground and passed above things instead of passing through and among them, close up and at eye level.

There was a lot of movement, a lot of shifting around, a whole bunch of trying things one way, then another. There was two here, three there, then another two yonder, and all that was subject to change at any time. People drove up the highway, then down, took the long way around and then the short-cut, made detours and went right on through barriers, blockades and all. Everybody got where they were going, most of the time, and them that didn't, didn't miss out by not trying or misreading the roadmaps. There wasn't many rest stops, and they didn't last long when they came. The road kept calling everybody, and everybody came.

121

Only person bothered ever during that recess in Marshall, Texas was one Jesse Garon Presley, I believe, and that was when he was riding high and pumping hard and about to get to where he was dying to go but not just yet, please Lord, and he happened to notice that the long-legged blonde he was joined to was straining to look back over her shoulder to watch Elvis drive that sharp-faced one down the backstretch into the last lap and across the finish line.

Seeing that made me slow things down and almost slip away, but I caught it again at the last minute and ground on through, a different pace and a new rhythm, something out of a harmonica on Beale Street and a bad rainy night in Arkansas across the river, an old song I made new enough to tease the blonde back to the dark twin and finish the tune together in synch, beat for beat, note for note and field holler for field holler right up to the last drum tap.

Everybody left at once. They always, always did. Sometimes that was sad, and the room seemed emptier than it really was, if you counted the bodies that were still around, and the quiet settled down so quick and heavy you could smell it pressing into your nostrils and mouth, moving on in further and further until it reached your belly where it coiled in the dark insides you never see if you're planning on staying alive.

10

After Elvis had started hitting it real big, kicking ass up north as well as down home, getting "Heartbreak Hotel" to the top of all three charts at the same time and touring all over the place with the Colonel latched on like a land terrapin, it was high, fast times, and Bubba was running like a Japanese watch, up all night and up all day and not missing a tick.

I was cut loose from most of it at that point, staying to myself and keeping a wide space between me and my famous cousin. Mainly I was trying to drive enough trucks long enough and drink enough whiskey often enough and bird-dog enough women close enough to be able to keep my mind permanently disengaged. If my brain was a flywheel, then the way I was living was supposed to work so as to let the clutch float free. Let it spin, spin, spin and don't let the gears come together and make something happen in a straight line. That was my motto, and that was the way I was trying to make it there on Manassas, down at the end of lonely street.

I was lying up in bed that afternoon the phone rang, waiting for the aspirins to take hold and let me go out to the car and head out somewhere. It was the first time I had lived somewhere with a telephone actually in the same place where I slept and ate, and I felt like I was making a statement with it. So it was a new enough experience that hungover or not I was still glad to hear it ring, and I was glad to pick it up.

"Jesse Garon," she said. "This is your Aunt Gladys talking. How have you been?"

"Fine," I said. "You calling from your new house?"

"Yes, it's real nice. I don't know why you won't come out here and see us in it."

"Busy, you know. Like y'all are now. Of course, I ain't going to nowhere but West Memphis and Dyersburg, but it's been real steady."

"Uh huh," she said. "Working hard, are you? Listen, did you see Elvis on TV the other night?"

"No, ma'am," I said. "I had to go out to a big wreck on Poplar and missed it. I hear it was the thing."

That was a lie I told her. I watched Elvis on that first Sullivan show just like I had watched him everytime he was on TV before. All of them, the Dorsey brothers, Milton Berle, even Steve Allen where they dressed him up in a tuxedo and made him sing to that damn dog. I didn't miss a one, but I wasn't going to give Gladys the satisfaction of knowing it.

"Well," she said, "I wished you had. You'd have been proud of your cousin if you could've seen him up there."

"Yeah, I imagine I would."

Gladys didn't say anything for a few seconds, long enough to let me know she had something she wanted me to do and was trying to find a way to get into talking about it. But, hell, I knew that already. Why would she have called me, otherwise? I couldn't remember a single time before that she didn't have a motive when she showed an interest in me.

I figured that out when I was fourteen years old. I mean the definition of love. What real love is is an interest without a motive in it. And, hoss, you don't find much of that commodity around. When somebody says they love you, most of the time you better start checking out your belongings because one of them has just caught some interest from somebody other than you.

"Jesse Garon," Gladys said, "I'm worried about Elvis. Purely worried, son. Purely worried."

"Why's that, Aunt Gladys? He's on top of the world now. Singing them songs, making all that money. Everybody just crazy to see him and give him stuff. He's doing fine."

"I don't mean all that part. That's all good, I know it. It's just other things that's part of all that that's got me so worried about him I can't even sleep right."

At that point I knew to keep quiet. I could tell from the sound of her voice that Gladys was fixing to go into one of her one-sided conversations and that all I could do was to hold on to the telephone and wait for my ear to go dead. I just hoped it wouldn't turn into the subject of religion and lead her off into speaking in tongues.

"I don't trust *him*," she said. "He talks like sugar wouldn't melt in his mouth and he looks you straight in the eye the whole time he's saying something to you. But I can tell he's always thinking about two other things at the same time he's talking to me. Vernon just loves him, thinks he's the greatest thing ever to hit the ground running. 'Aw, honey,' he says, 'it's just a business deal, that's all. He just wants to make money, and the more he can get Elvis to make the more he can make.' Huh, I know better than that.

"Oh, he wants the money all right. Old fat-bellied thing with his cigars and his bald head. But he wants more than that. Jesse, his eyes just glitter when he looks at Elvis, and Elvis depending on him like he was his daddy. Not that his real daddy can be depended on for nothing. If it

was left up to him we'd still be back there in Tupelo scuf-
fling around in that dirt. You remember how I had to
force him to load up and move to Memphis, get out of
that mess down yonder."

"Yes, ma'am," I said and changed ears on the telephone.

"And he has him on the road so much now that Elvis
don't get any rest at all. Oh, Jesse, his eyes has got that
look they get when he's having them bad thoughts, and
he's got back to dreaming and sleepwalking at night off
in them strange places where there ain't nobody that
really knows him or cares a real hoot about him. And
that puss-gutted Colonel booking him here and booking
him there and sitting back just a-counting on his fingers
and not caring nothing about Elvis in any true way. You
know what he said to me when I mentioned that I was
worried about Elvis being lonely and by himself in them
hotels and motels on these singing tours?"

"What?"

"He said, and Vernon sitting there in new clothes and
shoes that's not even broke in yet, that he has to chase
people out of Elvis's room every night. I knew what that
meant, and he looked at me and made his eyes jump up
and down and Vernon didn't take no more notice of it
than a bull will of an orphan calf. And laughed like he
does around that cigar, just a lot of air coming out of his
mouth and not hardly any sound. He meant women, Jesse,
that's what he meant, women in there with Elvis in them
rooms."

"The Colonel said that?"

"Right there to me, Elvis's mother, and made a nasty
joke of it, and Vernon just passing it off like it was nothing for that man to talk like that in front of me. He used
to work in carnivals, Jesse, and you know what kind of a
life he got used to, doing that."

"Elvis ain't expressed no worry about nothing, has he?"

"Of course not, he hasn't said anything to worry his mama. But he's sleepwalking, Jesse, and not able to fall off to rest when he needs it and having them dreams again about people trying to get him like back in the Lauderdale Courts."

She took a break for a minute, and I could hear her breathing over the phone, short heavy sounds like she'd just climbed two sets of stairs in an apartment house and had three more to go. I knew what was coming, and I lay back across the mattress and braced myself for it by putting one arm over my eyes and jamming both feet up against the iron bed frame.

"Jesse," Gladys said. "I want you to go with Elvis to be on that next Ed Sullivan show. Live with him in his room and see he gets some rest and protection. Be his family."

"Colonel Parker ain't going to like the way I look."

"You still got your hair bleached out real blond, hadn't you?" she asked.

"Yeah," I said. "But still."

"Keep in the background. Nobody'll notice nothing. You're his blood kin anyway. And the Lord knows he needs you with him now."

That was the first time she'd said anything like that to me, about the way I look and I could feel the bed frame shaking from my feet pushed against it. The telephone next to my ear was hot, and it felt like the sweat between me and the earpiece was scalding water too hot to stand.

"Elvis has got to ask me himself," I said. "And then maybe I won't even do it."

"He's trying to take him away from me, Jesse. His eyes are hungry when he looks at him. There ain't no bottom in them, and Elvis is falling on down into there away from his mama. It's things down in there I can't save him

127

from, and they're waving up at him and he's just a boy and he's letting them call him on."

That's when her voice broke, and she cried into my ear while I laid across that bed with every muscle as stiff and fixed as a dead man.

"Please, Jesse," Gladys said. "For Elvis."

I didn't say anything.

"For me," she said.

"Well," I said.

11

You couldn't really tell it on the TV screen, but Ed Sullivan was a little short bunched-up dude with a head about four sizes too big for him. He was a mean little shit, too, ordering people around in that New York voice like everybody but him was a sixty-year-old fieldhand. I remember when I first saw him he had a woman about twice his size backed up into a corner of the big room we were in just chewing her ass out about something. She was holding one of those clipboards with a bunch of papers stuck in it, and a big wad of them pulled loose when old Ed got so close to her that she had to jump back to keep from letting him touch her. I walked over and reached down to pick them up for her, and Mr. Entertainment spoke to me without looking away from her face to see who it was he was talking to.

"Let her clean up her own mess, you," he said in that dead little voice of his.

That "you" pissed me off. Nobody had ever called me that before, and his saying that to me was one of the reasons why I was willing later on that week to fool his little scrunched-up New York ass. Names people apply to me have always been touchy for Jesse Garon.

Elvis and Scotty and Bill rehearsed all week for that

show coming up on Sunday night. I mainly just laid back and watched the passing scene, now and then helping out on a back up guitar and listening to the TV people bitch at each other about the way they were doing their jobs. Besides Elvis, there was a bunch of goddamn dancing dogs and a set of jugglers and a comedian that talked so fast he looked like he was trying to spit out a mouthful of something that was burning his gums.

All these folks and a bunch of others met every day for three or four hours at a stretch, took their turns standing up in front of a bunch of TV cameras, did their thing over and over again, and dreaded seeing old Ed show up to frown and spin around on one foot while he watched what was going on. Once I got close up to him, and I swear he smelled like he was made out of varnish and new plywood. His skin looked like a high grade quality roof-liner for a Cadillac, and there wasn't a tooth in his head that wasn't the same size and shape as the other ones. He was a piece of work, let me tell you.

We were all staying at the Warwick, and every night at about eleven, eleven thirty, we'd let in some women and pick some out of the bunch for bivouac and war maneuvers. I remember I kept changing to a new one every time, but after the first night we were there Elvis seized on to a little bitty Mexican-looking girl about five foot tall, and he didn't look around for a different one from then on for the rest of the week.

I had my own room, plenty of whiskey and any kind of thing to eat I wanted, and I was pretty much satisfied to let it roll until Elvis had been on the Ed Sullivan show and I could get on back to Memphis and Manassas Street. Bubba was too busy at night to have any problems with bad dreams or sleepwalking that I know of, so I figured I was doing Gladys's bidding at a pretty low price.

All that changed on me on that Saturday night right

before the big day was to happen. I was sprawled out across my hotel bed, about half-asleep and half passed-out, lying beside a big old long-legged blonde girl who had just wore me out. I remember she had kept asking me to talk because she loved the way I said my words. I had finally said enough to satisfy her and was fixing to go down for the count when the phone rang.

"Hey," a black woman's voice said, "is this Jesse?"

"Yeah," I said. "But there ain't none left, so I got to pass on this one. Catch me next time."

"I ain't studying that shit. He done told me to call you, and I want you to see about this crazy fucker."

I knew it was Elvis as soon as I heard her say *he*, so I woke up fast and asked her for some of the details. She was so damn pissed off it was hard to get her to talk at first, but once she got started she about burned my ear off with her story.

Elvis had got it in his head to go up to Harlem and listen to some blues and maybe dip into some coffee-colored poontang, I imagine, and had taken off in a limousine about midnight. I expect he was having a Beale Street flashback and was looking for New York City's version of the Blue Light Cafe. I don't know. But whatever his mission was, he accomplished it at a place called the Bottoms Up Lounge where he had sung with the band, sung by himself, eat some collard greens and neckbones, put on a solo dancing exhibition, testified about his love of Negro music and the saving power of Jesus's blood, gone upstairs to a little room with two women named Marvel and Teen, did the deed with one and the other and then both, passed out, came to, and gone crazy.

"He backed up in the corner like a wildcat," said Teen. "Squalling and crying and hitting out like something trying to get him. Only thing he say is get Jesse Garon at the Warwick."

131

"He naked," said Marvel, coming on to take her turn at the phone, "he ain't got no clothes on. He ain't wearing a thread. Oh, he pretty."

When I got to the room at the top of the back stairs at the Bottoms Up, Elvis was barricaded in the far corner with a single bed pulled up in front of him, and he was still wearing his birthday suit. One of the women kept trying to hand him his pants, and every time she would he'd take them from her and throw them back across the room. She'd walk over, pick them up and try it again while the rest of the people who'd gathered by then looked on and made interested comments.

"He don't want them pants," said one dude dressed in a gray suit and a thin mustache. "No way, mister."

"I wish Elvis Presley would put something on somehow," one of the women said. "I getting to where I just about can't stand it."

Everybody whistled and made noises with their mouths like some kind of a jungle tribe when she said that, and Elvis drew back even further into the corner, looking like he was trying to find some way to slip through the crack where the walls joined.

I got them all out of there except for Teen and Marvel in a couple of minutes, and then I was able to take a good look at Bubba, treed in Harlem.

It wasn't good. His eyes were half-rolled back in his head when they weren't roaming all over the room as if they were trying to pick out something they particularly didn't want to see, and his chest was heaving up and down with his breathing like he'd just finished singing "Mystery Train" for two hours in a row. His hair was plastered back with sweat even though it was cold enough in the room to almost see your breath, and he was whispering something to himself in a low tone, over and over, that obviously wasn't doing him any good to listen to.

"Elvis," I said. "What's happening? You been having a good time?"

He wasn't having none of that, and it wasn't until I had reached out my hand and put it on his shoulder that he took any notice of me and seemed to come to himself some.

"Jesse Garon," he said. "He was in here with me. I believe he must have come in under the door when I had my back turned to it."

"Who? That cat in the gray suit? He didn't come in until you started carrying on and all that, I imagine. Did he?"

I turned to look at Teen and Marvel who seemed to have calmed down a good bit themselves by now and were watching the cornered Elvis Presley with real interest.

"Naw," said Teen. "Not nobody come in here but us until a lot later on when he start up. Ain't that right, Marvel?"

"Lord, girl, I can't think to talk no more, standing here looking at Elvis Presley like this. Hold me up, honey, I'm gon' fall."

Both of them hollered and squealed like colored girls will do and slapped at each other's shoulders while they staggered around that part of the room laughing.

"Woo," said Marvel.

"Mercy," said Teen.

"You ready to get your clothes on now and go on back to the hotel?" I asked Elvis.

"He was in here. He come in low, and then when I heard him and looked back over my shoulder he had reared up as high as a man's head to see what I was doing."

"What the hell you talking about? They said there wasn't nobody else come in here."

"He started talking to me. Leaned over and said it in my ear where I could hear it real plain. He made me hear it and know what it was."

"What?" I said. "Who?"

"Maybe Elvis mean a hound dog," said Teen and bent over almost double with laughing at what she'd said.

"Girl," said Marvel, pushing at her with both hands. "You crazy as a old bug."

"He told me too far ahead, Jesse," Elvis said, talking with his eyes shut as tight as if he was being made to look directly into the sun. "I don't want to know all that right now. You know I can't make it with all that in my mind."

"What, goddamn it? Who?"

"Him. That snake. That big snake with the blood in its side. It showed me its tongue."

"You mean when we was kids?" I said. "Back in Mississippi? That ain't nothing. You must have just had a dream again. That's all it was."

"It was a snake all right," Marvel said, "I believe it done bit me too."

"Woo," said Teen. "Bit me too. Bit me where I itch."

They fell around the room laughing some more, and I tried to get a good long look into the eyes of the Hillbilly Cat while he stood there weaving from one side to the other in front of me, his head thrown back and his fists all balled up. I remember that room was beginning to feel like it was getting smaller and smaller, the walls drawing in and the ceiling sinking down inch by inch toward the top of my head. I was about to have to come out of there.

"A dream," I said. "That's all."

"She can handle that," Elvis said. "She wants to know what things can tell her about what's coming. You know that's why we're here, Jesse. I don't want to understand it."

Elvis sank down to the edge of the bed and reached out to pick up one of his shoes. "It's got knots in it," he said, picking at the shoe strings and beginning to cry. "Jesse, look at all these knots I can't figure out."

"Give that to me," I said, "and get your clothes back on. We'll get on back to the hotel, and everything'll be all right again."

"I can't even tell you what's going to happen," Elvis said. "I don't want to put the words to it and say them to anybody. It told me too much for me to stand it."

"Listen," said Teen. "Why don't y'all both lie down here and let them old snakes stand up and bite us some. I bet they hungry."

"Girl," Marvel said. "My little old mouse itch. It need a snake to charm it and give it a bite."

"I wish I could, y'all," I said. "But it's been too much snake business already in here tonight. Catch you later on in this thing. Do a little mice-catching on down the road apiece."

"Uh huh," said Marvel. "Woo."

"Let that thing strike," Teen said.

I got Elvis dressed, down the hall and the stairs, and out into the street in about a minute and a half, but we had to walk almost two miles before a taxi would stop for us. And even then, inside the car with the doors closed and the cab driver playing his radio loud enough to wake the dead, Elvis kept looking around to be sure the snake hadn't come along with us to ride back to the Warwick and check into his room.

I had never really talked to the Colonel before that next day when he came into my hotel room to get me to play Elvis on the Ed Sullivan Show. He didn't talk to many people at all, in fact, ever. Just rolled that cigar around in his mouth and listened to the numbers fly around in his head. People he did talk to, he had a reason for doing it, always, and that was sure the God's truth that Sunday afternoon in New York City.

"Son," he said, "I don't know what your history is, nor how you came to be sitting where you are right now in that upholstered chair in New York. It might be you're who they say you are, and it might not. Maybe that crazy boy down the hall is telling me the truth when he says you and him are related the closest way there is for two people to be kin. Two selves just as much the same as you will ever see in the world."

He stopped for a minute and rolled his cigar and looked down at first one of his shoes, then the other one. That seemed to satisfy him, and he went on talking.

"I bet you think that all of the litter of a female canine, say, or a hog or a domestic house cat comes from the same egg and sperm, don't you? I'm here to tell you it don't. Why, a litter can have more than one father even, at the same time. It just depends on how many got to her when she was in heat. Did you know that?

"It's not that way with the human species. No sir. It's a kind of a wonder, that origin of two in one, doubled selves out of one, a little miracle in this here old world."

The Colonel looked out of the window toward the building that was standing right next to the Warwick. His eyes were glistening, and he had to swallow twice.

"But that's enough of the genetics lesson, ain't it, son? We got things to do." He stopped and gave me a long look over a perfect little ball of smoke that had just come out of the end of the cigar. I remember it was as white as snow and it just hung there for a lot longer than it seemed like it ought to be able to do.

"Jesse," said the Colonel, "can you do what he says you can?"

"Sing, you mean? Dance?"

"Yeah. Sing. Dance. Hit at a guitar."

"Better than anybody. Better than him."

"Like him?"

"Let me put it this way. On a good day he can almost match me."

"Let's see you," said the Colonel. "Sing that 'Heartbreak Hotel' song."

I was just a kid then, you got to understand, and I didn't have to think a second before I jumped up and hollered that first note and slid up into it and then down, down to that first dark mention of that forsaken hotel. I swear it was the best I ever sung it and there wasn't one instrument backing me up, much less a goddamn echo chamber.

When I finished it, the Colonel summoned up two more perfect balls of smoke out of his cigar, let them hang there between us for me to look at, and then stood up.

"You stay here," he said. "Don't leave this room until I tell you to, and don't use that telephone. I'm going to go to the drugstore and get that hair dye and do it myself. There ain't to be nobody else involved. You get me on that, son?"

"What about Elvis?" I said. "Where's he going to be?"

"Jesse, the boy is a little overexcited now, as you know. I'm going to give him something to help him relax, and that's exactly what he wants to do. He ain't up to much right at the present moment. And he sure can't get up in front of them TV cameras tonight and take a chance on losing everything before all these people that's going to be watching."

"You want me to be him tonight, then. Be Elvis, that's what you're saying."

"Son," said the Colonel. "I just want you to be yourself. Nobody but you. And that'll get the job done just fine. And if that ain't the truth, I'll ride a hog out of here side-saddle."

The Colonel didn't have to ride that hog. Nobody even blinked when I walked up to them there behind the stage wearing one of Elvis's sportcoats and carrying his guitar. My hair was dyed as black as the pupils of Mama's eyes, I had my mouth held just right, and I was ready for action.

Back when Elvis was still in this world in the flesh, eating and driving and forgetting lyrics, people always looked at me and saw him, and that's the way it was. You might think that after he was gone they'd see me and be surprised or shocked or that they'd be at least seeing somebody other than him. That's not the way it works, see. They're surprised all right. Hell, I've seen folks driving cars rear-end people after they caught a glimpse of me on the street. Oh, they're struck by the vision all right. But they're not seeing me. Still not seeing me.

No, what they're seeing is a body and a face that looks just like him. I'm talking about hair, nose, lips, eyes, you name it. Only difference is I never got hog fat like he did.

Nobody but the set of jugglers from Yugoslavia even looked at me that night of the Ed Sullivan Show, in fact, and it wasn't until right before the show was about to start broadcasting that anybody said more than one or two words to me. The one who did was Ed Sullivan himself, striding right up with a woman chasing him with a powder puff and stopping about six inches from my chest.

"Elvis," he said, talking directly into my breastbone without raising his eyes to my face because, of course, he didn't want to admit that he ever had to look up to anybody, "let's make it a really good show tonight."

"Yes sir," I said and bobbed my head just like Big E would have done it.

"I know you've been upset about this whole obscenity thing, and I hope to do you a favor tonight. If all goes well."

"I appreciate that, Mr. Sullivan," I said to the top of his head.

"So if you could just, you know, lay off all that hip-jerking stuff, I'll say something positive to America for you."

"You don't have to worry, sir. I'll just sing my songs and do my job."

"Fine, fine," Ed said to me, and then to the woman with the powder puff, "get that damn thing out of my face."

Ed put me on last, of course, since Elvis was the reason that fifty-four million people were watching Ed's show that Sunday night, and he wanted to make everybody stay tuned to watch every damn commercial they put on during that whole hour.

I watched most of the show on a monitor in a room with Bill and Scotty until right before it was our turn. The jugglers from Yugoslavia, some kind of a dancing bunch wearing ugly white costumes, a comedian who was about as funny as death, and I don't remember what all else. I just looked at the screen and didn't say much, just ate what all was being served, and fiddled with the buttons on Elvis's coat.

That wasn't his way before a show, I knew, but I didn't feel like jabbering and talking and pacing around the room like he'd always do before taking the stage, and after a while I could tell the way I was just sitting there was beginning to worry Scotty.

"Elvis," he said finally, "hey, guy, you all right?"

"Yeah," I said. "Fine. I'm just watching the jugs on this female juggler. How'd you like to balance them babies?"

"You ain't climbing the walls," Scotty said. "Just wanted to know if you was feeling O.K."

"Watch me when I hit that stage," I told him. "I'm

going to hump that damn mike to death."

"It'll piss old Ed off," Bill said.

"Piss *on* old Ed," I said. "Maybe I can get his heart to pumping."

TV lights are real bright, if you don't know it, and every time I've ever looked up into them, it's always acted on me in a strange way. It feels like to me that I'm about to walk off into the sun or something and become part of something big that's happening just a little bit out of my reach. That feeling makes me want to move toward whatever it is out there and reach for it, grab ahold of it and see what it is. It's about like jumping into a big white bed with a clean new woman for the first time, and I'm here to tell you it just turns my natural ass on.

So when Ed Sullivan said Elvis's name and I walked out there and felt that sound from the audience rising up like a wall in front of me and saw that white film of light like a big sheet covering up something I wanted real bad and all I had to do to have it was to rip that cover off, I just bobbed my head, cut loose, went crazy and danced.

If you're reading what I'm writing here, you saw that show, either right when it happened if you were a normal American at the time or later in one of these retrospectives if you were too young or too far back in the sticks to get to a working TV set in 1956. What you saw was Jesse Garon at his peak, and damn I am sorry that they kept that camera aimed above my waist and didn't let all you good people see what I was doing with my Southern half.

I'll tell you what. If that microphone stand would have had a female equivalent of what I was throwing at it, we'd have got hung up like two bluetick hounds in Mississippi. They'd have had to throw two buckets of ice water on us for one to be able to leave the stage unattached. Jesse Garon as Elvis Aron that night on the Ed Sullivan Show did things with his physical being that the reverse of that situation never would have even known to try. The flipside of this twin act couldn't have cut it.

I sang, too, of course. But that wasn't why all that electrical current across America was being made to flow in the same channel in all those TV sets that night. It couldn't have been just that, or nobody would have got that much satisfaction.

After I throwed the first hip out-of-joint move at that helpless mike stand and let loose with the first few words of the first song, the live audience in that place grabbed at its head with both hands, opened up its jaws to full capacity, squalled out every bit of sound it could muster from its guts, liver and lungs, and let its goddamn backbone slip.

That's the best it ever was for me, for Jesse Garon Presley, there in that CBS auditorium in 1956, in front of three cameras carrying my image into all those strange houses, being Elvis Aron in a way I swear he never could have matched.

When I finished the last song and the last guitar lick was hit, old Ed just couldn't stand it. He had to get out there in front of those people and all that electrical power and try to shut down as much as he could of that discharge and energy I had whipped up.

"Ladies and gentlemen," he said, reaching up and grabbing me around the neck as though he had finally been able to will himself to touch something he was sure would ooze a substance on him that would never come off, "let me say one thing about this young boy."

Then he went into that rap that I'm sure you've seen many a time, that little speech about Elvis and decency and cooperation. What he was really saying was that yessir, folks, sometimes a flower will grow out of dirt, even the sorriest kind, if enough fertilizer is mixed up with it and if not too much sun or water gets to it.

That was Ed as official America forgiving Elvis for being a white trash Memphis boy who fucked microphones, drove women crazy and sang like a gin-drunk nigger. Old Ed and CBS and RCA could bear all that, if it lit up enough blue lights in TV sets all tuned to the same station everywhere in the country.

I was hot, I was sweating, I was still jiggling and moving around in my clothes while Ed did his oration. When he finished, the curtain dropped, but not as fast as Ed's arm did from around my shoulder, and he turned toward me as the red lights went off on the TV cameras, his smile still nailed to his face.

"You son of a bitch," he said.

"You don't know the half of it, you little dead fucker," said Jesse Garon, and then I left the stage.

12

Whenever somebody'd talk about "vehicles" for Elvis, it always brought into my mind a picture of Elvis on a tricycle, a little red and black one that Vernon had drug up from somewhere way back yonder when the world for the Presleys was drawed up and concentrated in Tupelo, Mississippi.

A vehicle for Elvis, him riding up and down that dirt road in front of the house trying to find a piece of ground smooth enough to coast over on and free enough from rocks and clods to keep from suddenly tumbling off into the ditch or the roadbed. Me, of course, running behind with a narrow piece of wood long enough to push against the frame of the tricycle and give it enough momentum to keep it moving in spite of the rocks and holes and clods of dried mud it kept meeting in its way.

"I'll give you a turn in a minute, Jesse Garon," Elvis would be saying, "just push me a little bit more. I'm fixing to hit a smooth spot in a little ways further on."

I knew better than that by then, naturally, but I kept on running behind, pushing and getting up speed. Hell, there wasn't nothing else I could do. It never seemed like there was any choice in the matter for me, so I just lowered my head and kept that stick as steady as I could hold it while I pushed Elvis on his vehicle toward that ideal smooth spot somewhere on up the road.

Elvis always did have that problem with his vehicles. And it seemed like the more he got, the more they would throw wheels, develop cracked frames, loosen up in the joints so nothing would fit right or hold together, flake off paint to show big spots of rust and corrosion beneath, lose cotter pins and main bolts, wobble all over the road and hunt for rocks and holes instead of steering around them, rear up and fall back on their rider like they had minds of their own and were bound and determined not to let anybody ride in peace or find that smooth spot where you could take your hands off and stop pushing. Somebody just didn't seem to be making those vehicles right, and quality control wasn't even worth a belch in a high wind.

When Bubba went to the big screen he thought at the first he was going to be James Dean, but by the time he had stopped climbing up on those three-wheeled vehicles and running them off into the ditch, I think he was just glad enough he hadn't knocked out some front teeth or lost an eye in one of those unexpected dismounts. Thank God that Big E went on to the big vehicle upstairs before all these damn karate and kung fu pictures from Hong Kong got so big with the film lovers of America. I fully believe we'd have seen Chuck Norris with his hands full, otherwise, defending his title as kung fu king against the King himself.

I was around during the filming of two of the movies Elvis was in. One of them was the picture that everybody says was probably the best one he ever did, *Jailhouse Rock*, and the other one was so damn putrid it smelled like a north Mississippi outhouse on a hot day in August. That sucker was named *Spinout*, and let me tell you, child, it did. That little vehicle spun off that dirt road into the bar ditch so quick and hard that it's still dust hanging in the air to mark the spot.

I was actually in only one of them, there when I did that dance scene of a convict sliding down that pole and skipping around with the rest of the boys wearing stripes. It put a lump in my throat pretending to be just one of the boys in the prison, thinking back to how my dear old daddy had served his time in Parchman himself after he'd forged the check for that hog in Tupelo in 1937. Like father, like son, as they say.

Of course, Vernon wasn't really no more of a criminal than I was in *Jailhouse Rock* when I put on that tight-fitting suit of striped clothes and saved Elvis's ass and the picture. Daddy was just dumb, dumb, dumb. Like father, like son, as they say.

After I got back from the New York trip where Ed Sullivan wouldn't let the cameras show my natural movements, I just submerged myself in Memphis and tow trucks and long-legged high-assed women. I didn't want to see nor hear nothing about Elvis Presley and what he was or wasn't doing to the moral habits of American youth. I didn't pick up a newspaper, read a magazine or watch the TV or listen to a radio for about a year I swear.

It's hard to do that. Particularly when every time I'd catch a glimpse of a grocery store newsstand there'd be a picture of somebody looking just like me staring right back in my face. Or when a car, say, would be stopped next to me at a light and I could hear a voice on the radio that I could make come out of my own mouth if I wanted to.

That makes for hard living and a narrow view, and it will cause something to get a real twisted feeling in your stomach just below your breastbone. Hell, it will even affect your breathing on long sad nights when you can't get to sleep and there's nowhere to go and nobody to go with you.

Don't get me wrong. I was doing stuff. And I was doing my job, and running the bars and driving fast in short bursts up and down every street in Memphis and every road where Arkansas, Mississippi and Tennessee touch, that sore spot in the middle of the country.

I even finally found me a little old freckle-faced red-headed girl that talked me into letting her move in with me. We rented us a two-room apartment with a refrigerator and stove, she started cooking collard greens and banana pudding, and I stopped changing into my cat clothes as soon as I would get home from work. I talked sweet to her, loved her up enough, I guess, to satisfy, and really tried to make me up a life I could live all on my own like a regular person ought to be able to do in Memphis. Her name was Frankie, and she had the cutest little feet I ever saw on a woman. They were white, white, and God did she like for me to kiss them.

It went along fine for several months there, me avoiding information from the media and her sweeping and cooking and singing to herself in the mornings and afternoons. I remember the whole time we lived together the weather was real cool for Memphis, raining a good bit in the middle of the day but clearing up bright and sunny by the late afternoon, and we hardly ever had to use the window air conditioner I had bought us from an old boy from Stamps, Arkansas.

I kept my hair short, bleached blond, and I had grown me a mustache which had come in a reddish brown.

I think I was about getting ready to make it then, there on Angelus Street, but maybe that's what they mean by hindsight. It felt real good there for a minute.

Everything changed one evening when I got in from working a light day shift. I think it was on a Friday.

Frankie met me at the door at the bottom of the stairs

we had to climb to get to the apartment. She looked like she'd just taken a handful of speed, and I knew she didn't do pills. Her hair was floating up from her head like it had suddenly learned how to beat gravity, her eyes were opened so wide they looked ready to move out and live on their own somewhere, and she was talking so fast it looked like she had just had an electric motor installed to make her jaws chatter.

"Jesse, you mean thing," she said. "Why didn't you tell me? I never in my life would have guessed such a thing."

"What did you find out, Frankie?"

"You never will guess who came by here today looking for you."

"Oh," I said. "That. What did he want?"

"Elvis Presley!" she said. "That's who. I was washing my hair and just starting to cook when I heard him at the door."

She stopped talking, looked down at the doorknob, and reached out a hand to touch it as though it were made of something you had to sneak up on to feel.

"He opened this door," she said, "by turning this doorknob and pulling it to him."

"Yeah, that's the way a door works," I said. "It depends on the way the hinges are set which way you open it. Some you pull to you, and some you just push away. Elvis figured that out a long time ago all on his own."

"When I opened that screen," Frankie said, "I couldn't believe what I was seeing. I thought I was blacking out or something, and it wasn't real. And when he said 'hello, sugar' I just knew I had died on the way down the stairs and was opening the door up to the pearly gates instead of Angelus Street. His eyes are so pretty a blue I don't think no shade can match them."

"How many people was with him?'

"Nobody, Jesse. He was by himself. He drove off all by himself in that deep blue Cadillac. It was so quiet you couldn't hear it start up."

"So it's something that bad, huh?" I said out loud, but of course Frankie couldn't hear it at that point no more than she could have heard a bolt of lightning hit my tow truck sitting out on the street.

"And you his cousin! Lord, Jesse, you never told me that. How could you never have told me that? If it was me I would wear a sign across my chest and tattoo it on my forehead."

"I got a tattoo," I said. "Half of one. Up on my shoulder."

Then I followed her upstairs to where the water had boiled out of all the pans on the stove and the minute steaks and the cornbread were going up in smoke. She led me directly to the bedroom by the hand and tore off her blouse and dropped her shorts and panties like they were on fire and pulled me down on top of her there where she had fallen spraddled across the new flowered spread she had picked out at Goldsmith's the week before.

She was sopping wet and her nipples were drawn up as hard as unripe strawberries and about as big. I'm ashamed to admit it now, but I was ready for her too, by then, and I went on in there and stayed for a long, long time while supper burned in the kitchen and all that smoke drifted into the bedroom.

I never came the whole time, never even got close to it, but Frankie did over and over, and I stayed right with it until she was worn out and the steak was a cinder and the cornbread nothing but burnt charcoal. I figured I owed her that much since I was never going to touch her again after I had her move out the next day for good. And I made her take that Goldsmith's spread with her, too, when she left. I kept the air conditioner.

Elvis caught me at home the next day about dark, driving up by himself again, this time in a different colored Cadillac. He piled out of it wearing big shades and a hat pulled down low enough to hide half his face. I remember he was smoking a thin black cigar to look cool, but he was still as jumpy and nervous as a cat with kittens.

"Jesse Garon," he said. "Long time no see, buddy. You're a hard man to find."

"I been right here in Memphis," I said. "Ain't been doing nothing interstate or transcontinental."

"Where's that little lady of yours? She's a cute'un."

"She don't live here anymore," I said. "Gone."

"That's too bad," Elvis said. "Why did you get shed of her? Too country for you?"

"Not country enough. Not by a long shot."

"Well," Elvis said. "Look, let's go in the house. I got to talk to you, Jesse."

He meant it, too, like he always did. What he wanted was for me to go with him to California while he worked on this new movie they were putting him in, one about a singer who got throwed in jail unfairly and against his better judgment and who had to sing his way out of confinement. It sounded like a life story to me, but when I told that to Elvis, he didn't laugh or show a sign.

It was the old problem working on Elvis, the same old thing that had hung around so long by now it was like a stray dog that had taken up living behind your house. You could kick at it, chunk things at it, call it names and not feed it, but if one day it didn't show up by the back door begging for scraps, you would begin to miss it and wonder where it was. Still, you were afraid it was going to come back, and the thing you dreaded was the surprise you'd get some morning when you heard a whine, looked out the door, and saw it was back for a spell. Reared back on its haunches, looking to you for something it needed that you didn't want to give, and its eyes set just a little to one side of your head as though it was seeing something behind you that you couldn't tell was there.

So I went. Why did I do it? Why did I ever do it? That's what I'm trying to answer here. That's why I'm holding things up to the sun and turning them around and around to let the light rays catch every part of them, things that I've lived my whole life so far being afraid to ever think about, much less to reach down and touch them without gloves.

One thing was sure, I was half of a chemical bond that wouldn't quit, that just kept pulling like that little pair of magnets I got once in a Crackerjack box. They had little plastic dogs glued on top of them, some kind of a terrier, and if they were lined up right they stuck tight together, nose to tail, like one of them was in heat and the other one was randy and ready to serve. But if you turned one of them around and tried to put them together that way, you developed an opposition that would never let up, that wanted to push things apart and keep them there.

That little pair of dogs scared me so damn bad that I had nightmares about them for weeks after I'd buried them there in Tupelo. Separately, of course, with one in the pasture behind Uncle McCoy's house and the other in the backyard of Vernon's and Gladys's house in town, at least eight miles apart.

But I could imagine them, even that far apart, still pulling at each other there in the dark under the ground trying to turn and hook up the way they had to be. Not wanting it, just having to do it because that was the way it was, the way the force field wanted it.

So I went to Hollywood with Elvis to make a picture about a jailhouse and a life sentence. And I expect those two little dogs are still sending out secret force fields down there in Tupelo, trying to get things set in the right direction and joined up tight for good.

13

What Elvis liked most about a movie set was that it was all front and there wasn't anything behind it. I remember when we first walked up to the one there in the studio where they'd be shooting *Jailhouse Rock* he grabbed me by the arm and pulled me around to the side so I could see everything at an angle.

"Look here, Jesse," he said, pointing at a fake wall set up on edge, "it's just like you'd take the face off of something and set it up sideways like a mask. There ain't nothing to it when you see it from the side. But walk around in front," and he did, motioning for me to follow, "and you got your standard reality. Chairs and tables and lamps, just like in a real living room."

I saw it meant something to him, so I nodded and tried to look interested, even when Elvis opened the door leading out of the fake living room and then slammed it hard enough to make the wall shake and the floor hum.

"That reminds me of Tupelo," I said. "That solid construction around the door facing. I bet this one would even keep some of the wind out."

"Mr. Presley," said a man in a purple outfit who'd just come up from behind us, "are you ready to start getting settled in?"

He was talking to Elvis, but he was looking at me. Even his shoes were purple, I noticed, and the only thing he was wearing that wasn't was the white scarf around his neck. His skin was a light shade of the same color and a perfect match for his watch band.

"Who's this, Elvis?" he said. "Family?"

"My cousin," Elvis said. "He's here to observe. He's from Memphis."

"Aren't they all? Well," said the purple man, "we've got a movie to make, and it's going to be marvelous. We're going to let you dance your ass off in this one, sweetness."

I don't know if you remember anything about *Jailhouse Rock* other than my dance to the title song, but don't worry. I'm not going to tell you the plot of it. Let's just say it was several cuts above those dogs Elvis wandered through doped to the gills in the '60s. *Harem Scarum*, for God's sake. *Blue* fucking *Hawaii*. And Jesse Garon's other vehicle, *Spinout*.

But here's how I came to rock the jailhouse in the best dance number the King ever did. That's what I want to tell, not review those sorry movies of Bubba's or try to remember when in the hell he was in which one with what piece of ass. Let some sick silly fucker from New Jersey or somewhere work on that one.

All right. Back at that time Elvis was staying in a place he'd rented in Los Angeles with all that Humes High bunch right there with him. Like always, there were more overweight and under-brained people around the place than ticks on a hound pup in Arkansas.

What Elvis had done, of course, as soon as he started making it even semi-big was to move to the head of the classroom from where he'd been sitting on that back-row seat there in the school house on Manassas Street. And he wanted all the big dogs to be right there with him so he could be the biggest dog of all and show them where he really had belonged all along back when they thought he was just that little poor-assed country hick who couldn't make the football team and who wore off-brand clothes that couldn't stand to be washed more than once without changing their whole nature.

He wasn't still just the little shit who was always on the edge of pictures in the high school annual, the one standing off to the side in the photograph of the library helpers or the one at the back of the workshop with the chair leg in his hand and the goofy smile on his face.

You look at some of those pictures sometimes that they've resurrected of Elvis in Humes High, and you'll see what I'm talking about. The ones they've found with him in them always show his face out of focus, looking like it's about to blur out all the way and slide off the edge of the print and be gone forever, never really there in the first place anyway. If ever a sad-assed pitiful fucker looked like he was doomed to disappear without a trace as soon as he walked out the door of whatever room he was in, it was my twin brother Elvis in those Humes pictures.

But like I said, he made it to the middle of the frame and took the position where the hard tight focus comes to its highest resolution, and he wanted people around to see it. He needed witnesses. And the people he picked out of the mug book were the stars of the Class of 1953 at Humes High School in Memphis, Tennessee.

Why give them names? Let's just use their titles. That's what they were and all they were anyway. And Elvis had a country boy's instinct for knowing what people's right labels were almost all of the time. He didn't miss big but on about two or three folks, and you can guess who the main one was, if you try.

So when I walked into that house in L.A. with him at

about midnight my first day in California, I was greeted
at the door by the Senior Class President. He was sucking at a fruit drink, and the part in his hair was perfect.

"Hey, everybody," he hollered over his shoulder, "El's
here. He's back."

"Looking good too, big guy," he said and clapped Elvis
on the shoulder like John Wayne would have done to
James Stewart. "You want some orange juice or something? How about you?" The last part was said to me
because the Senior Class President wanted to know what
the hell was going on and why was I here anyway.

"Naw," Elvis said. "Naw, I want y'all to clear out of
the room for a little while. I got to talk to my cousin
Jesse."

"Hey," said the Senior Class President. "No sweat.
Everybody, El needs a little room for awhile. So let's take
it out of this part of the house right now."

"El," called the Most Popular Boy from where he was
sitting on a sofa beside a six-foot blonde with a full foot
more of beehive hairdo. "How's it hanging?"

"I'll get everybody out of here, boss," a big red-headed
guy said, from here on to be known as All-District Tackle.
"Come on, you sapsuckers. Move."

"No hurry, y'all," Elvis said and motioned to me to
follow him over to one corner of the room where a big
wrap-around couch took up two walls. "We just got some
business, me and my cousin."

"Jesse," he said in a low voice to me after we'd plopped
down on the big couch, "you ain't going to be able to go
by that name anymore around me."

"What the hell you talking about?"

"I mean the name Jesse. You got to get another name
to call yourself when we're together from now on."

"Who said?"

"I said. Just now. Wasn't you listening?"

"I'm not used to taking orders from you, Elvis," I told him. "Just think back if you will for a minute and see if that ain't right."

"Listen, Jesse. I ain't just saying that to be giving you orders. What it is, see, is just that people's started doing all this research into my background, and we don't want to raise no dead."

"I ain't dead, Bubba, and I can prove it."

"Hell, I know you ain't dead. Shit. But think what it would do to things if people was to start making connections. The Colonel says..."

"What could happen? What's the worst?"

"Like I was trying to tell you. It'd just make things get complicated. Colonel says it would fuck up the image. Blur it. Knock it out of focus. Cost us money and momentum."

"I don't give a shit what you call me when I'm around you, Elvis," I said. "Cause I believe you ain't going to be getting much chance to call me any name face to face anymore."

"Just a minute, Jesse," he said and reached out his hand toward me. "Don't say stuff like that. What do you think I asked you to come out here with me for? I need for you to be with me. I got to have you out here now."

"What you need with me? Looks to me like the whole Humes High senior class has done moved in with you. Can't you get what you need from the Class Firecracker?"

Elvis looked at me for a minute without saying anything, his lip pooched out like it would get when something went against him when we were kids. Like maybe Gladys hadn't moved fast enough to do something he wanted or Vernon had hollered because the radio was on too loud or I had refused to be "it" more than twice in a row in some game he had set up and just had to win.

"Jesse Garon," Elvis said, "yeah, some of my high

school buddies are around all right, but none of them can be what you are to me and you know it."

"What you want from me, Elvis? What in the pure dee hell can a tow truck driver from Memphis have that the Hillbilly Cat could want?"

"They don't call me that name no more, Jesse. I done out-grew that label."

"I'm sure sorry I brought it up, then," I said. "What are you now, cousin? Frank Sinatra, Jr.?"

"I don't want to fight nor argue with you, Jesse," Elvis said, putting up both hands toward me as though I was going to take a swing at him. "You got to help me out here. It's things that has come up. Things in the night that I can't handle by myself."

"You mean the same old stuff? Sleepwalking? Not getting no rest?"

"Yeah, that, but worse. Dreams. Bad dreams that I can't wake up from. They are asking me to do stuff I can't do by myself."

Here's what it came down to. Elvis was having another bout of craziness that would come on him from time to time from ever since I could remember. It was the same thing that made him jump up in the middle of the night in the Lauderdale Courts to fight with people that were trying to take something from him. People that nobody else could see there in the dark in Memphis or later on in hotel rooms in New York and in rented houses in California and finally in Graceland itself right up to the very end.

It was just something inside him, of course, and nowhere really in the world, but it was a thing that only Gladys could believe and only I could feel.

"What can I do about it?" I said. "I ain't no damn doctor."

"You're the only thing I got, Jesse. You're the only one

that can listen to me. You know me the way nobody else does."

"What about all these big men on campus, like I said? Can't they do you no good? Sing you the school song or say the motto?"

"All they're good for is having a good time with, Jesse. They don't really hear a word I say to them. No more than that art statue over yonder does."

I looked at what he was pointing at, a metal object about the size of a Chevrolet engine block made into the figures of a naked man and woman giving each other head.

"Where'd you get that?" I said.

"It came with the house."

"Sure is shiny. Must be stainless steel," I said. "What about Gladys?"

"I can't tell her stuff no more, Jesse. She's always on the edge of going into some sort of a state or a fit or something, I don't know. Besides, I done things by now, you know, that won't let me get that close to her no more."

"Shit. You ain't killed nobody, have you?"

"Nobody I can name," Elvis said. "Or that I ain't scared to."

What it really was, of course, was the story that was in *Jailhouse Rock*. That was what was kicking Bubba into the big tailspin.

He was scared of it then and he always hated it later on. Wouldn't let anybody talk about it in front of him and sure as hell wouldn't ever watch it again after it was finished and turned loose on a waiting world.

As for me, *Jailhouse Rock* is the only movie my brother made that I've ever been able to bear to sit through. One reason, of course, is because of my big dance number in it, the one all these critics and writers say is the best piece of choreography Elvis ever did, the one where I let my backbone slip and my get-along rip.

157

The main thing about it that's made me even finally buy a videotape of the son of a bitch so I can watch it in motel rooms when I can't sleep sometimes after I've done a show is not the jailhouse rock dance, though. It's because the story inside that black and white piece of celluloid is about a singer ripping everybody off. Taking their songs, their arrangements, their movements, taking everything they got, and just hauling ass.

I don't know if anybody remembers anything about *Jailhouse Rock* anymore except my big number, but if they do, it's one little scene where Elvis finds out he's been fucked by a record company executive who's stolen his tape and given it to his own boy. Elvis looks surprised and says something like, "He stole my style, he stole my everything."

I like to watch *Jailhouse Rock* every now and then for the same reason Elvis never could stand even to hear about it. The story that picture show tells is the reason Elvis begged me to come out to L.A. during the making of it, too. It gave him dreams at night and made him feel sick in the middle of his sleeping. Got him up and walked him around and tried to throw his ass out of windows and out in front of cars.

I got to give him credit for that. Elvis would fuck you blind, take away from you what you just had to have to live, treat you like he didn't even know your name. Do all that and do it as well as anybody I ever seen. But he'd feel bad about it. God, he'd feel bad about it. Get even plumb sick, sick enough to lose sleep, want tablets and eat capsules.

He would wear your ass out, but it gave him the colic to do it. And then he would have to come around to get you to hold his head while he threw up in the commode and tell him it was all right and would he like a little sip of water, maybe, or half a glass of Coca-Cola or a handful of uppers.

That's the way it was with *Jailhouse Rock*. When he was acting out that story of the old boy who killed a man with his bare hands, went to the pen for it and learned to sing, came out and screwed everybody but a good woman, Elvis was having more gastric distress and late-night walk-arounds and stumbles than he'd ever enjoyed before.

Gladys wasn't there to help him, and for damn good reason too. He sure as hell didn't want Mama to realize all the pussy he was getting and the pills he was already into by then. So that left pretty much only one old boy to turn to. You got it. Jesse Garon. Little old me. All those Humes High senior class standouts couldn't do a single thing for the way Elvis would feel in the middle of the night, and I'm including the Class President and the Most Likely Boy in the count.

No, ladies and gentlemen, the only one that could help him feel the way he used to those times in Tupelo and in the Lauderdale Courts late nights listening to the radio blues was the other one, the Dead Twin that wouldn't go away, wouldn't finally lie down and be covered up and done with it. I had something he wanted and couldn't quite get, and Lord knows I thought Elvis had something I wanted, a thing I had been cheated out of before I even knew it existed.

So the Live Twin took from the Dead One once and that made him have to go do it twice. Because once you rob somebody of something, you have always got to go back and be damn sure you got it all. Or it never will give you any peace.

But I hope you have seen my dance in *Jailhouse Rock*, the one I have been talking about. Before now there's only been an audience of two to watch it and know what they were really seeing. And one of them checked out in 1977 in the air-cooled comfort of South Memphis on a hot August day.

I expect you have seen my performance of the jailhouse number, though, if you have been alive long enough in the twentieth century and watch any TV at all. It starts with the drums setting a beat and me and about twelve other guys packed up on this false front of a cell block, each of us behind his own door hanging on the bars like monkeys. All of the doors swing open on the same count, and I strut across the top platform moving from your right to your left as you watch it, and then I slide down a pole and hit the floor dancing.

By the time I'm on the ground level I'm about two lines deep into mouthing the words to the song, and I am slipping, jerking, and popping every spinal disc I own, sometimes a little behind, sometimes a little ahead of the beat, holding steady to one side and the other and then just when you think I ain't going to make it, pouncing on that rhythm and riding it, riding it, riding it until you can see the smoke start to rise and hear the oil start to popping with the heat.

I throw that baby's feet up until they're pointing at the sky, I find the center of where that dance is living, I give it a probe to be sure I found the right spot, I play with its privates until its eyes roll back, and then I just gallop that mount up and down the countryside until it comes on home to the barn on its own, teeth showing and hair flying.

I did it in one take, of course. Hell, there ain't enough room in the world for more than one round of that baby. They were just lucky they had a camera there to catch it while I was burning it down, because once a fire gets set you can't light the same match twice.

When I finished it, gave it the last pump and the final frog-gigging, the director said "cut" and everybody on the set just stood there and looked at me until finally the old boy playing the cop, the one you see skipping around during the number with the billy club in his hand, started clapping real slow and real hard. It sounded like two pieces of meat thudding together the way he did it, not like the little dry sound that applause usually makes. By the time he'd brought his hands together three or four times, everybody had joined in so I was able to leave the studio without saying anything, just walked off through a side door and out into that California sun listening to those hard licks people were making with their hands as I left. I took that with me. I still got it.

14

I left that afternoon on a Trans World flight for Memphis, and I didn't see Elvis again after *Jailhouse Rock* until he had already gone in the army and had to come back from that training base in Texas to Memphis because Gladys was dying in the Baptist Hospital.

Yeah, I had watched him be inducted on television all right and get his hair cut and I'd read the Memphis newspapers about all that shit, and I'd listened to the disk jockeys play all his songs one after the other on the day he went in to be drafted. You'd have thought it was his funeral day, listening to those records coming in a steady series from every station in Memphis, and to tell the truth about it I thought about that induction day those nineteen years later when the same programming started pouring out of the radio speakers on that day in August of 1977. "Hound Dog," "Rip it Up," "Blue Suede Shoes," "Don't Be Cruel." You name it. All of them came to the party.

Vernon and Gladys and the whole damn household moved down to Texas with him when Elvis got sent there by the army to some post down around Killeen, and it wasn't until late in August that I heard anything from any of them. I had moved up out of town by then to a little suburb north of Memphis and was thinking about buying the house I was living in.

Late one afternoon I was out on the backside of it looking up under the crawlspace and thinking about ways to shore up the foundation when I hear a car drive up in front and start honking. I kept on poking with a screwdriver at a cement pilar that looked like it was crumbling away, figuring that the fool in front would either get tired of leaning on his horn or leave, but he kept it up and then started hollering my name.

After about the second time he called me, I recognized it was Vernon and gave the screwdriver one last shove and then walked around to the front.

"What's he want, Vernon," I said, "this time?"

"Son," he said, "it ain't Elvis. It's Gladys."

He was sitting sideways in the seat with the door open and his shoes stuck right in the middle of a big pool of oil where I usually kept the tow truck parked. His shoes had been white when he shoved them out of the car, but now they looked like a zebra's hide.

"You going to ruin them shoes," I told him. "You keep sitting like that."

"She's going, Jesse Garon," Vernon said and started to cry, "she ain't going to make it in this world no more."

"What's wrong with her? Where is she right now?"

"In the Baptist Hospital. They don't know. None of them doctors can tell."

"Well," I said. "Maybe it ain't as bad as all that. She's been sick before."

"No, son. She told me she ain't going home alive. Said it just the one time and hushed like she does when she knows something's going to happen."

I didn't know what to say to him. I knew what he meant. I just kept looking at that oil creeping higher and higher up the white buck shoes he was wearing, ruining them forever.

"Son, she's asking for you. I wish you'd go to the hospital and see her."

"She wants to see Elvis, Uncle Vernon," I said. "Call him up in the army. They'll let him off."

"I done called him, and he's coming right now. But it's you she's asking for. 'Jesse Garon' is all she's saying. 'Get Jesse Garon to come here now' is all she'll say to anybody."

"Just look at your shoes," I said. "Just look at them. They ain't never going to be the same after this."

They had her on a high-up floor and way down a hall toward the back of the hospital, so it took me a while to find her room. When I walked in, Gladys had her face turned toward the door, and her skin looked the color of a squash late in the season, past yellow and almost into orange. They had some kind of a clear tube stuck in her nose and taped to her face, and I remember during the time I was there little bits of some kind of a liquid would come out of a bottle fastened to a stand by her bed and trickle down the tube into her head at regular spaces. After the first time it happened I would look off whenever I would see a bubble start to slide down the plastic tube toward my mother's nose and into her head.

"Jesse Garon," she said and held out her hand toward me but then drew it back when it hit up against the metal stand, "you've bleached your hair back to blond again, haven't you, honey?"

"Yes, ma'am. That's the way I like to keep it most of the time."

"Y'all both got natural blond hair," Gladys said, "from Vernon's side of the family. Before his hair turned white it was real blond."

"I remember," I said. "Back in Tupelo when I'd come to visit."

"You don't know what it was like, son, living back there in Mississippi at the beginning. You don't know why things were like they were."

"I got some idea," I said and watched the first bubble begin its slide down the tube into her nose.

"Him off in the penitentiary at Parchman them three years. Can you believe that happened, Jesse? My husband in jail for breaking the law by forgery? I still can't think it's true. I come of good people. Never lie nor cheat nor ask anybody else for help."

I didn't say anything, and she got quiet for a minute, looking over toward me with her eyes fixed right on my face until I had to stare a little bit above her head to be able to stand it. I never was able to look her in the eyes for more than a few seconds in a row during all the time I knew her. And that's right up to now.

"You think I never gave you nothing, don't you, Jesse," Gladys said, "your whole life."

"I'm doing all right," I said, "now."

"On the day of the night it happened," she said, "I slept late in the morning. I couldn't seem to wake up and that never was like me when I was young back then."

"You're not old, Aunt Gladys," I said, "right now. You're coming out of this all right. Be home tomorrow. You wait."

"Let me talk, honey. I want to tell you what you got to know."

She took a deep breath and put her hand up to her nose and touched the plastic tube gently like it was a boil sore to the touch. I could see she had one of those plastic bracelets on her wrist with some writing on a piece of paper stuck in it. That was the worse thing in the room to me, her name on her wrist like that.

"It was a bird that finally woke me up enough to get out of bed. It was just singing outside the window, sitting on a limb of that magnolia tree right up next to the screen, and it got so loud and sang so many different kinds of notes and calls that I finally roused up and hit on the screen to make it fly off, but it wouldn't even though it was only a foot or two from where I was hitting with my hand.

"I could see it real clear after I'd opened my eyes from the dream I was having about a whole bunch of people in one place more than could fit into the room, so they was all mad and scared and yelling at each other. It was a mockingbird, and it sang every bird's song I think I ever heard before that morning, sitting there on that limb and opening its wings up real slow until they were all the way out and then snapping them shut and then hopping to a limb right next to that first one. I laid there and listened for a long time before I finally got up and looked for Vernon, but he was gone, maybe to work. I don't remember if he had a job then or not."

I'm telling this a lot faster than it really happened. Gladys kept stopping between sentences and looking deep, deep into my face and she seemed so tired it was hard for her to get words out fast enough to satisfy her. I remember she kept clenching and unclenching her hands and picking at the edge of the sheet lying over her as she talked.

"She was sitting in the kitchen at the table when I walked back in there looking for him. But I wasn't scared to see her then, and I remember at the time being surprised at myself because it didn't bother me none or even startle me much to see her."

"Who you talking about?" I said. "Did I miss something?"

"The old woman. The one I'd been seeing walking the roads around that part of town where we lived for two or three weeks before she showed up in my kitchen. Just a sitting there at the table, not saying anything. She was wearing that same headcloth I'd always seen her in. Had some kind of designs on it in white thread that looked like star patterns against that black material.

"I remember I spoke to her. Asked her if she wanted some coffee. I didn't even say a word about how she got in the house or why didn't she knock or let me know she was there. She didn't say nothing back to me at first. Just sat there looking up into my face with them real dark eyes, almost black, until I finally said to her what do you want to tell me, what did you come here for."

Gladys stopped talking for a minute and closed her eyes and lifted both hands up slowly to the side of her face and touched them to her temples the way you'd try to set a coin on edge to make it balance. She had rings on both hands that Elvis had bought her, diamonds and some kind of green stone. Seeing them made me think about the earrings I had bought her once at Woolworth's in Tupelo. She had never worn them because her ears weren't pierced, she said, and the ones I'd wasted my money on were made to stick through your ears. I tried to fix that scene real clear in my mind so I could keep on standing to listen to what she was telling me there in Baptist Hospital.

"She never told me her name or spoke mine, neither," Gladys said. "She just lifted a little sack up to the table and put her hand down in it and pulled out two rocks, real smooth rocks, one of them a white color and the other one dark. She held them out to me, one in each of her hands, and when I tried to take them with my right hand she wouldn't let me, wouldn't let go of them until I took one in each hand. And then that's when she talked.

"'Girl,' she said. 'It's your choosing to make. Nobody can do it for you. It's two of them coming to you. One is to live, the other one is to die. One is to have nothing of this world, the other is to have all. What one gives up, the other takes. What one takes, the other one loses.'

"Then she didn't say nothing, just looked at me with them black eyes and me with one of them rocks in each hand, and that bird outside the window still singing every song it knew, making bird calls I'd never heard in Mississippi before and never heard no bird make since anywhere.

"And then, Jesse Garon, one of them little smooth rocks made a little jump, it felt like, and moved in my hand, and it scared me so bad I turned around and ran to the door to the bedroom and threw both of them at the same time at the bed. They landed real far apart on top of the bedclothes, more than three feet, I'd say, and then they just started rolling toward each other and come together in the exact middle of that bed and touched and stayed there, still, and when I went over to look at them it wasn't two rocks anymore at all but just one. And it wasn't the size of both of them together, it was just the size that one of them had been by itself, and its color wasn't dark or light but in-between, a gray color with no specks or streaks in it at all.

"And Jesse," she said and turned to look directly at me, "when I picked it up it was heavier than both of them had been apart and when I went back into the kitchen that old woman was gone and the chair where she'd been sitting was pulled up to the table like she'd never been there and that back screen door was latched on the inside and the front door was locked."

I just sat there for a while and listened to my pulse beat in my ears and kept my eyes fixed on Gladys's hairline right where the little widow's peak comes down in a point on her forehead. If you look close in pictures, Elvis had the same pattern in his hair. So do I.

"Well," I said, finally, "that's kind of a mystery or a ghost story, isn't it?"

"The rock's there in that little coin purse inside that big one," Gladys said. "I want you to get it out and take it with you. I've carried it as long as I've been able."

It was there, all right, and I've still got it, set into a bracelet I wear on my left wrist during shows. It doesn't look like much, but it is real heavy, sometimes so much I have to take it off between sets to rest my arm.

"That was the night your daddy and me got you and Elvis, right there on that bed where them two rocks had settled into the middle of the mattress and become one."

That was the first and only time I ever heard her mention anything about what goes on between a man and a woman in a bedroom, and let me tell you hearing Gladys on that subject I didn't know how to handle it. I just sat there looking at that gray rock, tumbling it back and forth from one hand to the other and trying to avoid looking into her eyes.

"And Jesse," she said, "when y'all came them nine months later in January on that freezing night, you was the first one out of me and into the world and when the air hit you you just shivered once and never made one cry. Doctor Hunt said he'd never seen a baby pink up so fast right after birth as you did. The first breath you drew was a full one.

"I said to myself right then, it just busted out, loud enough you could have heard it under all the yelling I was doing with Elvis, 'Lord, let this first one live and the other one die. Let him be the heavy one, Lord, and live in this world and know it for what it is, and let the other one be light and rise up and never know life like my first son has to know it. Let the first one be in it, and the second above it and the first have the earth and the dirt and the ground and the second the air and the light and the empty places.'"

Gladys stopped talking then and closed her eyes and seemed to sink back from where she had been raised up in the bed propped against the pillows, and for fully five minutes she never said anything, and the only sound in the room was the soft sliding noise of the machine running those bubbles through the tube and the click of the gray stone against the ring I was wearing on the little finger of my left hand.

In a little while I eased to my feet and started to move toward the door to leave, but as I reached out my hand for the knob, Gladys's eyes opened and she looked at me and made that same gesture toward her temples she'd made before, lifting her hand up real slow to just barely touch the sides of her head.

"You have always thought I denied you and didn't love you, Jesse Garon," she said.

"I've had some reasons, a few I can come up with. But it's all right. It's fine."

"You are the first baby born to me, and I picked you to live and Elvis to do the only other thing that could come to my children."

I didn't say anything, but just stood there in the Baptist Hospital weighing that extra heavy stone in my hand, waiting for her to finish whatever she had to say.

"Jesse Garon," she said, her voice dropping into that rhythm like a Pentecostal preacher will get, "all your time you have been living, and all Elvis's time he has been dying. You have been moving in a solid path and he has been floating, floating with just a little thin line connecting him to the ground. And that line is weakening, and it's hard to see, and it's not made long for this world."

"I gave you to suffer," she said and turned her entire body toward me there in the bed far enough to tilt the metal stand holding up the bottle of liquid hooked to the tube. "Son, you owe me for that, for me choosing you to be the one to live."

"I don't understand," I said. "None of this. But I thank you for what you thought you were doing."

"You'll thank me by helping him. Let his going be as easy as you can make it. Watch that line as long as you can see it, as long as it will float and stay in the air and hold to him."

"I will," I said, not knowing what I was promising or how to see what she was talking about. But I needed to say yes to her again like I always had done, and I thought it would be the last time I would ever have to do that again. I was young.

"You go on now, son," Gladys said. "My Jesse. I got all the dying to do now before Elvis gets here to see it."

I opened my mouth to say something to her, but no words came into my head to let come out, and I walked out of the room still looking at her until I closed the door between us.

The last thing I saw of my mother were her eyes opened wider than I'd ever seen them before, like naughts, letting everything she could see of me come in with that fading light late in that day in Memphis.

Elvis went crazy, of course. I wasn't around for most of it, but I heard all about it from some of the Humes High standouts later on, and I did see what took place at the funeral and in the house after the burying was over with.

"Your cousin sure loved his mama," the Senior Class President told me. "He was just heartbroken when he heard the news. And Billy (that was the name Elvis had folks calling me by then when I was around), I have never seen a grown man cry as much as he did or seem to mean it more."

"Oh, he meant it all right," I said. "He meant it a lot more than you'll ever know. That boy can feel."

A couple of the things Elvis did in those first few days before and during the funeral have made a lasting impression on Eastern rock critics and biographers, as the magazines call them. But hell, those expressions of grief just came with the territory at a pentecostal dying and burying in north Mississippi.

What son doesn't keep leading mourners and friends and fans over to the casket to lift up the lid and show them his dead mama's feet, how little they are and how pretty? What boy worth shooting doesn't point to her hands and kiss them over and over and talk on about how much they did for him? Emptied bedpans at St. Thomas Hospital. Cut up okra that stuck her fingers and made them bleed just to fry it because he liked it so much. Held his forehead while he puked.

And how else is a boy to show how much of a lasting change his mama's death is going to work on him if he doesn't keep pointing out things she ain't going to be doing no more? Like chickens pecking around the back yard she never will feed again and brand new mixmasters she never will turn on to whip up cake batter with another time.

And isn't a boy deep in grief, even if he is the king of rock and roll, going to grab his old gray-haired daddy around the neck and demand to know what they're going to do without our little mama now?

"My poor old daddy," he's going to say in front of whoever's there to hear it, "he ain't never going to have him another wife. They ain't never going to be another woman for him to love."

See, that kind of carrying on just gives the kind of Yankees that work in the media real uneasy feelings. They don't think it's natural. It's what they call *morbid*, a word I never heard before I was a grown man living on my own and poking around where I had always been told not to. That's just a word in a book to a Southerner.

Right before the funeral itself, Elvis naturally made the folks in charge unscrew the lid to the casket so he could see Sat'nin one more time. And he talked to her and made promises and praised her for her makeup and the size of her feet and told her he'd be with her in Glory just as fast as he could arrange it. Three of them finally had to pull him away from her so they could get on with it with him yelling to her as long as the lid was up about what all he was going to do and how fast he was going to do it.

And after the thing was down in the hole and the black guys dressed in overalls had wandered up from their truck and begun casting long looks at the green covering laying over the stack of shovels, Elvis finally spun around in a full turn where he was standing at the edge of the grave and fell full length on the ground, eyes rolled back in his head and his mouth open so wide you could see to his tonsils. It looked almost like an album cover.

They hauled my brother back to Graceland in the back seat of the biggest one of those black limousines with two of the Humes High standouts holding him down. When they got there, they carried him into a dark room and a doctor shot enough dope into the cheek of his ass to stun a bull elephant. It worked, too, for about an hour.

I was still watching the two black guys throw shovels of dirt on top of my mother's copper vault when the Class President pulled up in one of the Cadillacs and called me to come get in with him.

"We scared about Elvis, Billy," he said. "He thinks you're somebody named Jesse and he's got to see you. He keeps calling that name, and the doctor's afraid to give him no more shots.'

"I'll be on directly," I said. "I'm almost through here. Go on ahead and tell him I'm coming."

The Class President gigged the Cadillac, and it left with a roar, kicking up about two cubic yards of flying gravel, and I turned to watch the last few shovels of dirt put up on Gladys's grave. You'd be surprised how long it takes two men to fill up a grave and how much dirt is left over. Those boys were big, they worked steady, and they knew what they were doing. And it was still over an hour before they got the last bit smoothed down and mounded up right enough to suit them.

I gave each of them a twenty-dollar bill and tried to look full-on at the head of the grave and the shape of it. But I couldn't do it for longer than a second or two, so I got in the car and turned toward Graceland. As I steered through the cemetery gates I could see in my mirror the two black guys throwing their shovels up in the bed of their pickup and rolling up a big green mat that had covered the dirt during the praying.

There were cars lined all the way around the big circle drive at Graceland, and when I walked in the door I could see enough people wandering around the two front rooms to make up an army unit. Most of them were eating and drinking, and those that weren't were busy picking up things off coffee tables and what-not shelves to shake and look at. There was a constant rumble you could hear through the whole house of people talking, and now and then a high-pitched laugh from one of the women friends of one of the guys would percolate to the top.

"Elvis is in yonder," the Class President said as soon as he saw me, pointing at the door of a room down a hall and toward the back, "I sure am glad you finally made it. He's just calling and calling."

"I'll go see him," I said. "See can you get this bunch cleared out or quieted down one."

"Right," he said. "Will do. Is Jesse your middle name?"

"No," I said. "It ain't."

"I know you're a Presley," said a little old woman that looked like a bird hopping around with a plateful of ham slices and fruit salad in her hand. "But which one are you? Whose boy are you?"

"That ain't been fully decided yet, ma'am," I said and walked down the hall to where Elvis was denned up.

He was lying on a bed with both hands up to his head like he was trying to keep two sides of something together that were trying to fly apart. Two of the class officers were in close attendance, and one of them was about two-thirds drunk.

"Whoa up there, hoss," the drunk one said when I walked in and put out a hand toward me to stop. "Who do you think you are, coming in here?"

"Ask your boss," I said. "Maybe he'll be able to tell you."

"Aw, Jesse," Elvis said and sat up, "Mama's gone and I got to go back to the army. You know I did it all for her, every bit of it."

He started crying again then, his face looking like it would when we were back in Tupelo and somebody had been picking on him or maybe some kid had made fun of his clothes. His overalls or those damn high-topped workshoes Vernon had found somewhere for him to wear to school that time.

"Because," he said, barely able to get the word out past all the sobbing, "she did everything for me."

At that, he fell back across the bed and buried his face between two pillows, and I told the Humes High crew to go on out, and I would take care of it. They were glad to, particularly the old boy who wanted to fill in that miss-

175

ing one-third.

I didn't say anything for a while. Just sat down in a chair and let Elvis carry on until he got tired of that round and sat up again to face me.

"What are we going to do now, Jesse, with Mama gone?"

"You're going to go back to Texas to the army," I said. "And I'm going to move out to the west."

"Why are you leaving here?"

"Because I don't live in Memphis no more, Bubba, and I hear that western call. I'm fixing to pull a Hank Snow and just move on."

"You ain't going to be able to stay away from here, Jesse," Elvis said. "You can't live away from me."

"You just wait and see. You just count the days I'm gone."

"Not for long," Elvis said, and his eyes cleared all of a sudden like they'd turned to glazed ice, and I was looking into Gladys's face. "We come into this thing together. We're one by ourselves, and we always are going to be. You'll be back. You're right here."

"Don't float off," I told him, trying to make my voice as hard as I could and hoping both him and Gladys would believe it. "Don't let that line break in two."

And then I left Graceland for what I meant to be the last time.

But, shit, it wasn't.

15

I signed on for the westward movement. Had a garage sale and sold all I could, and what I couldn't I gave away. Only thing I saved back was a box full of tools, some clothes and the whiskey that was left, and the record I had made for Marion Keisker back there in 1953 on Union Avenue at the sign of the Sun.

I threw all that in a '59 red and white Ford station wagon and headed for Texas early one morning just when the light was hitting the top section of the Mississippi bridge into Arkansas. I watched the Memphis skyline shrink up in my rearview mirror. I tuned the radio to a country station out of Little Rock, and I decided to grow a full beard and let my hair turn whatever color it was able to.

"Elvis," I said, leaning out to look myself in the eye in the side mirror, "put it where the sun don't shine and the wind don't blow. She left, you're right. I'm gone."

I wanted to put some running water between us, and some mountain ranges and some dry, dry deserts and wide wasted places. It took me eight days of steady driving, steering that Ford west with my right foot stuck in a go position and my eyes on the white line of the road, before I found a place where I could stand to stop.

It was a little town up in the Sierra Madre Mountains in California with not even real sidewalks, just boards like long porch floors in front of the grocery store and the filling station and post office. Downieville was its name, and it set right beside where two little mountain rivers come together to make one bigger one.

That's where I used to sit in the afternoons, at the fork where they joined, and watch the ripples and waves they made as they kept coming together, over and over, one a little wider than the other but slower as it moved. And one of them had warmer water in it than the other by at least fifteen degrees. But if you went down a little ways and stuck your hand in the river they make together, it was all one temperature, just an average kind of thing.

I went back there last year to check it all out. Downieville was just like it ever was. Rivers coming together at that same fork at the same temperature, board sidewalks still in place, Ed Clifton running the same garage by the one-lane bridge in the middle of town where I signed on to work the second day I spent in the mountains.

The big difference was up the road about a mile, past the graveyard stuck on the slant of a hill so steep you can't stand up straight on it, and next to that line of houses built on the bank of the river. What I'm talking about is something not there any more, just a little grassy place now with a driveway up to it from the road.

I guess she had sold the trailer to somebody or dragged it off herself somewhere and nobody had ever put another one in that same spot. Because when I walked up to look at where I had lived with Wanda those years I couldn't even tell exactly where the thing had set. You would think pipe connections or the electrical set up or the same view you would get out of the bedroom window every morning would be a tip-off, something that would last to let you know where you had been.

But it wasn't there anymore. All I could get was a general idea, like looking at something with my glasses off or after having been spun around enough times to make me dizzy. You know the way the horizon would lift and fall when you did that when you were a kid and then tried to focus things. Nothing came together, and you liked it.

So I walked up there from the road and stood about where I figured our bedroom had to have been and tried to remember how it felt back then. And for a minute or so I got damn close to it, too, but it faded out like a radio station from Mexico bleeding into Memphis late on a cool night when the air is clear, and then just slipping on back across the border to home.

I worked on cars and logging trucks five and six days a week. Sometimes seven. I moved in with Wanda, a good old girl I met one Bingo night in the Downieville city hall. I heard about Elvis finally marrying Priscilla who I hadn't even met yet, though he'd been raising her for years. I saw on a back page of a newspaper that Vernon had married a woman named Dee Stanley, and I wasn't surprised. I started listening to the Beatles and the Rolling Stones and Janis Joplin, and getting a lot of gray in my beard and hair. I drove all the way into San Francisco lots of weekends to let Wanda eat Chinese food, she liked it so much. I learned how to cook.

I tried it all as hard as I could. I sucked it up and kept my head down. I started reading all kinds of books and learned the names of mountain ferns and flowers. I got as close to being a regular citizen as I ever made it. For almost ten years right there in Downieville.

I remember I woke up one morning early, an hour or so before I had to get up to get ready to go down to fight with those transmissions and timing links, and I could tell from the way Wanda was breathing she was still asleep. When I opened my eyes she was lying facing me, so close to the end of my nose I couldn't focus on her, but I knew what she looked like, anyway. I laid there for thirty minutes, watching the light get brighter through the window of that trailer house and listening to that woman breathe in and out as regular as the water running in those mountain rivers outside, and I felt like for that whole time then that I didn't want anything.

I wasn't hungry, or thirsty, I didn't feel like I wanted to crawl on Wanda and wake her up for a quick tussle before I left for work, I didn't feel any dread about going down to Ed's place to work, I didn't feel like there was a thing I needed. It just got lighter and lighter in that bedroom and a little breeze came up and moved some leaves around just outside the window, and I just laid there and watched.

I think back to that morning more and more these days, especially when I'm lying in a motel bed after a show trying to get off to sleep. Oh, I keep books by the bed, but I mainly just lay one across my chest, open to my last place, and remember that time I didn't want a thing. Nothing. There in the mountains.

What happened? The clock radio went off, Wanda coughed deep in her throat and turned over, and Elvis came on singing a piece of shit called "Stay Away Joe." I flipped it off as fast as I could reach the radio dial, but by then I felt the lack again, and within two minutes I had Wanda's legs up over her head and I was trying to find what I needed between them one more time.

"I don't want her seeing you," I told him that afternoon when he showed up outside the trailer. He was wearing some kind of shiny white coveralls and had a cap pulled down low over his forehead. He looked round before he opened the door to the black Cadillac and put his feet out onto the ground and swung around to sit facing me.

"Whatever you say, Jesse," he said. "Who is she?"

"None of your goddamn business," I told him. "She's at work and I want you gone before she gets back home."

"Why you so mad at me?" he said and took off his sunglasses. He had picked up weight in his face, and his cheeks looked different from the way they always did. Lower somehow. He put his glasses back on.

"How'd you find me out here? I ain't put up no road signs."

"It took a lot of work and time to do it, Jesse. I've had people looking off and on for years."

He was talking in that voice he would always use back when we were kids and he was trying to get me to break down and listen to him again after he'd done something to make me realize who I really was still. Maybe he'd seen me talking to Gladys, laughing with her at some story or foolishness while she worked in the kitchen, more than likely, while I sat there shelling peas or hulling pecans or something. And he'd come in and wanted all of everything again and had said something to get it. And I had sat there with the hulls and shells, watching the sweet parts inside go sliding off somewhere else.

"You know what it took, Jesse? You'll be interested in this. I had an old boy buy up a bunch of magazine mailing list names and then look through all of the *Popular Mechanics* and *Sports Afield* and a bunch more of them for Jesse Garon. And he finally found it listed here in California. Wasn't that something?"

Wanda had given me a magazine package for Christmas a couple of years back. She had bought it from a kid that lived right there in Downieville and went door to door selling them for awhile. He was part Indian.

"I knew you wouldn't give up using your own name," Elvis said. "It wouldn't be right for you to do that. You couldn't."

"I'm going to surprise you some day," I said. "She's going to be back here in about thirty minutes, like I told you, and I want you gone. Long gone."

"Why do you hate me?" he said and started crying right in the middle of the word *hate* so it strung out for a long time. "You're supposed to love me and do for me."

Elvis leaned forward and dropped his head into his hands and knocked his glasses loose from one ear so that they dangled for a minute and then fell into my driveway among all that California gravel and grass.

I believe I must have watched them the whole time he was there sitting in that black Cadillac like I was afraid they were going to move off on their own or something. I know I couldn't keep my eyes off of them. They were dark at the top of the lenses, shading off lighter at the bottom, and the frames were silver-colored.

In a minute or two, Elvis looked up at me through the fingers he was still holding across his eyes, opened his mouth like he was about to say something and then dropped his head back down again before he did.

"Mama told me I could depend on you always, Jesse."

"Well," I said. "She was a believing and an optimistic woman when she told you that."

"Said we had a bond holding us together stronger than anything time could do to it. It comes out of blood and the night and the moon, she told me."

"I figured the moon would get in there someplace," I said and tried to look away from the sunglasses and Elvis's shadow falling on them, but I couldn't seem to. "Wouldn't been a moon in the sky, I don't know what Gladys would've had to blame stuff on."

I was talking as hard-edged as I could make it, you got to understand, and I was doing my dead level best to keep any give out of my voice, but something had started up by that time right at a certain point in my head.

It wasn't exactly a pressure but more like a gap, and I was just beginning to realize it. A little space or hole that I could feel a wind starting to blow through from way back somewhere away from me. How did it get there, I was thinking.

"You never have made it easy for me to say anything to you, Jesse," Elvis said. "Not when we was kids together and not since all this here." With that, he pointed to the sunglasses in the gravel and moved his finger in a little circle that took in the last fourteen years.

That little movement had in it all the movies and singing and women and cars and hotel rooms and airplane trips and clothes and shoes and hair dye and the big men from Humes High and Vernon and all the rest of it. And right in the middle of it was an overweight country woman high up in a hospital room in Memphis turning the color yellow as she died.

"All you ever said to me is something you wanted, something you thought I had," I said and listened to the little shifting sounds the vacant spot in the middle of my forehead made as that wind started to move it down and away from the dead center where it began.

"You got part of it, and I got part of it," Elvis said, "and ever once in a while we got to swap back and forth to keep it one thing. It's always been like that. Sometimes one of us is the shadow of the thing, and the other one is the thing itself. And then it switches because it won't stay still and be the same forever and all the time."

"It's got light in it," I heard myself say as I listened to keep track of that empty space moving down through my head toward my throat.

"And the dark's in it," he said.

"She said sounds would be mixed together," I said as the wind moved the empty space past my vocal cords and down into the top of my chest.

"Two voices," said Elvis. "Wrapped around each other, but you can't take one away and have the other one still be. Won't last on its own."

The space was sliding down through my lungs, taking its time at its own rate, making a catch in my breath, and I couldn't speak until it had moved further down past my diaphragm into my belly where it seemed to lodge and stop for a while.

"You can't hear but one voice sometimes," I said when I could get my breath. "I wonder sometimes if the other one's not gone for good."

"It's always there," Elvis said, looking up at me now from where he had been leaning over sideways in the car seat. His eyes were just what they had been back there in Tupelo when he was afraid to go to school that time because of the boys bullying him and later in Memphis when he'd wanted me to see him in the Humes talent show. And I had. I did that for him.

"You just *think* it might be gone," he said, "but it never is. That voice is there, right behind the one you can hear, making it stand up so it won't die out."

It's not right what growing up with a person can make you do to yourself. You know what I mean. Seeing them scared, losing something they wanted to win, not having what they need, times when they felt like they weren't anything and never going to be noticed by another soul, all that kind of thing makes you weak later on when you try to get away from all that weight that has been dragging around your neck all your life.

And when that person is the main part of the weight, it makes it so hard a little, empty spot will form up in your head and move wherever it wants to all through your body and all through your life. And it will stop when and if it wants to, and not before.

So when I felt that space that had moved from my head all the way down into my belly begin to settle in and make a home for itself in my very gut, I knew it was happening again. The old sickness. That damn condition that has dogged me from the time I could first wonder who I was and where I had come from and who were all these people just outside and around me that I never could quite reach out and touch.

I could see them, I could smell them, I could hear them talk and use my name, but I could never put out a hand and touch what wasn't me and not just be killed by that fact when I did it.

"I feel like I'm dying," he said. "I feel like I been sinking deeper and deeper into something like a big room full of cotton or thick fog or something. I feel like it's been going on for the last I don't know how many years. Just sinking further and further, and it's real gradual, just a little bit at a time so I don't notice much, but I can tell it's happening more and more every day I live."

I remember he stopped for a minute at about that point to fumble in a regulation-looking doctor's bag he had beside him in the floorboard of the Cadillac. He took three or maybe four of the capsules he got out of a good-sized bottle in it and looked up at me again.

"What is that?" I asked him. "Some of this new stuff they're all doing in San Francisco?"

"It's medicine," Elvis said. "It's a doctor prescribes it for me for my nerves. Anxiety. You know. Thinking about bad shit. Not being able to sleep and all. Worrying."

"Uh huh," I said. "She's going to be back here any minute. And like I said, I want you out of here."

"All right. It's like this. I been wasting myself all these

years making these damn movies. They ain't worth a shit, and I know it, and it's killing me."

"Make some good ones then."

"It ain't that easy," he said. "It's too late. I ain't never going to get a script worth a damn after all the stuff I been in. He's done seen to that."

"Puss gut?"

"All right, yeah. I know you never liked him none."

"Neither did Gladys. She didn't trust him as far as she could have picked him up and throwed him."

"I know it, Jesse," said Elvis. "You don't have to tell me that. Mama made her feelings damned clear to me long before she passed on."

"Died," I said.

"Died," he said. "Died. All right."

"Well, what's the big deal?" I asked him. "What did you want with me after all this time we spent apart from each other? You want me to go back to Graceland to talk to you, or play touch football or ride motorcycles?"

"No, Jesse. I want you to help me come back alive. I got a chance to do it, if you'll be with me again like you used to be, like it was in the beginning, like it ought to have always been."

The wind had come up off the river and was moving the tops of the evergreens around across the road at the edge of the bluff down to the water, and I lifted my eyes to watch that for a while before I said anything else to him. Behind me the metal sides of the trailer were making ticking noises in the sun, and the screen door shuddered as the breeze hit it and rattled the catch holding it shut.

"What's going to bring you back alive, E?" I asked him. "What can help you breathe now."

"Singing," he said, as the mountain wind moved the pine needles and pushed against my door. "Standing up in front of live people and singing to them like I used to."

He stopped for a minute and looked at me until I couldn't keep from looking back at him. Right into his eyes. Blue like mine.

"Like *we* used to," Elvis said. "Back there when it all started up."

"I never got a bit of credit," I said. "Not a speck of credit from you or from her. Not word one."

"I know it. But you made it all able to happen. You propped it up and kept it running."

"Look," I said, "you got a wife and a family now. It's in all the newspapers and music magazines. Don't you get any satisfaction from having them behind you? She's an awful pretty little old thing."

"That's it, Jesse. Little. You said it right."

"What you mean?" I asked him.

"She's just real little. That's all. Priscilla's just a real little girl."

I didn't know what to say to that, but Elvis seemed to think he was on to some truth judging from the way he was nodding his head and moving around in the car seat like he was gathering himself together to make some movement with a purpose to it. So I pushed it on a little further.

"What's *little* got to do with anything? Don't she do you no good?"

"I don't know," he said. "Naw, she can't, I don't believe. She's just real little and ain't never going to get to be any real size."

"She looks just like you," I said. "That hair dyed real black. Eye makeup and all. Clothes she wears."

"She wants to look like me. I wanted her to do it, too, starting out. Dressed her in the same kind of outfit I would have on. Got this special perfume for her, you know. All that kind of stuff. Necklaces and rings like I had on.

Shoes."

Elvis stuck out his foot toward me and looked at it for a minute. He had on some kind of black snake skin boots, as I remember. Maybe it was lizard.

"It ain't there, Jesse," he said. "I don't get what I need from that little bitty woman."

"Why?" I said. "She don't like to do it?"

"Naw," Elvis said. "It's not that. That's part of the thing, see. She wants it all the time. Wants us to be together and looking into each other's eyes and holding hands and kissing every chance we get."

"Sounds like a lot of fun."

"You wouldn't like it all the time, Jesse, and you know it. Priscilla wants every damn bit of me. Every day, every minute, all the goddamn time."

"Well," I said. "Wives, you know, expect that kind of thing, I imagine."

"Ain't going to be nothing of me left. She's working on one side of me. That bald-headed fucker working on the other."

"Hey, Hillbilly Cat," I said, "I thought you liked pussy and rock and roll."

"I do, Jesse," Elvis said and gave me the look of a man that had just seen something that he expected was on his trail and now knew sure as God it was gaining on him in great leaps and bounds. "I love pussy, but I don't like to have to get it from just that one woman all the time. And I got to sing my songs, but I need to sing where I can see them hit and take hold of the people that's listening. You know what I'm talking about. I ain't never heard nothing about you fucking up and getting married to one thing."

"No," I said. "You haven't. And you ain't never heard of me singing a song of my own to a bunch of people that came to hear just me sing it, neither."

"Are you going to do it for me, Jesse?" he said. "Are

you going to be my brother for me again?"

The wind was blowing a lot harder by then, bending treetops back and forth, lifting up pieces of trash out of the road in the front of the trailer, and making a whistling noise through the screen at my back. I could smell supper overcooking on the stove, and I knew I couldn't eat any of it.

"Tell me where you're staying in San Francisco," I said, "and I'll get back to you."

He did and started up the car to leave.

"But don't hold your breath," I told him as he backed out of the driveway.

He didn't need to.

16

And that's how the Singer Sewing Machine Company and Jesse Garon Presley gave Elvis mouth-to-mouth resuscitation back in 1968 and brought him back from the dead. For a while at least, that is until the last big slide that took him out long before they called him officially gone.

What got him up on that little bitty stage surrounded by the old boys from Memphis and looking out at a live audience in front of a TV camera was two things. Me and fear. Not the kind of fear that comes with a jump at you and gets you all revved up and white-eyed and makes you move out and do it quick, now, don't think about it.

No, the other kind is what Bubba was feeling for the first time. You know the type I'm talking about if you've lived long enough in this world. I mean the feeling that comes on you gradual, a drop at a time, the way you feel when you've looked in the mirror for the eighteen thousandth time and seen that same face looking back at you. Notice those little lines in your teeth? Are they really there, or are you just imagining it? Are they getting easier to see? Damn, that beard is heavy, seems like I need to shave twice a day and it's whiter coming in around the chin and lip. Shirt's tighter at the sides than it ought to be, no matter how much I try to hold back from the table. But it seems like I'd rather eat something than do just about anything else these days, more and more. Tired at night, earlier than I ever used to be, but still I don't sleep as sound as I feel like I need. Roll and tumble around and watch whoever I'm with sleep quiet beside me. Just lying there in one position, mouth open a little and drawing breath regular and deep and never making a peep. While all's I can do is watch.

I imagine something like that came on Elvis one night in particular. Maybe he was sleeping beside Priscilla, maybe some other woman he'd hooked up with. It was past midnight, and he was there in the dark by himself, awake in spite of the pills he'd taken to put him out.

When he went to bed she'd wanted it, maybe him or at least the attention. Maybe he'd turned away from her and not said anything and she'd pouted or else asked him what was wrong. Then he might have picked a fight to keep from having to climb on and try to ride it one more time.

Say he did try it, maybe, and it wouldn't work right, and she could tell he was not interested. And she cried, or worse than that, just got real quiet and rolled away to go to sleep as quick as she could.

Whatever hadn't happened, he was there in the dark, in the quiet, and it was a long way to when he could get up and find something to take his mind off where it had crawled to. And that place where it had reached was a bad place to be. It had lights in it and lots of people and they were moving and scurrying around like they knew where they wanted to go and had a reason to get there. But it was all quiet, not a sound, not a voice, not a note of music and none of the instruments would work, and he was the only one who noticed it or cared. And no tune to carry.

I imagine he tried to make his mind get ahold of something he could stand to think about for longer than a minute or two, and he had come up snake-eyes. Crapped out and folded and nowhere to go, but still here right where he was to begin with and knowing every minute more and more that that was where he was always going to be. And two eyes looking back without a blink.

He could think back to Tupelo, and think back to the Lauderdale Courts, and back to the early road trips, and the crowds, and back to Gladys and Vernon and the Colonel and Priscilla and me, but there wasn't a place he could visit that would hold him still and quiet and let him rest.

He had kicked himself loose from all of that, and he was floating as high and wobbly and unfastened as a kite that had broke its string.

He was going places, but he wasn't going to be anywhere.

Why did I go? Why did I leave Downieville on that river bank and the trailer house and Wanda to follow him to a place he was never going to be?

It was love, of course. Love, that sickness and infection that has kept me in a fever flat on my back all my life from Tupelo to Memphis and out and back and all those places in between.

That's what's always betrayed me and been my downfall. It's always been full of promises every time it popped up and crooked a finger at me and told me it would make things right this time. Here, Jesse, it's always said, this round belongs to you. You and the world have finally found a fit, and you're going to join up so tight with it that the seam will look like it was sealed by a magic carpenter. I know it didn't work out those times before, but now you got a lock on it. Trust me, Jesse. This is Love talking, your old friend. Pucker up.

That's what happened that time in Downieville, California. It's what made me walk out on a woman I had got used to and could stand to be around most of the time. It's what made me throw all my tools in the bed of the pickup and leave my last paycheck down at Ed Clifton's without asking for it. It's what made me sit there on the cement block step up to the trailer house and listen to Elvis explain why he had a need for me to be with him one more time, Lord, never again after just this once, I promise, I swear, you got to believe me, please.

Or maybe I just wanted some blues.

All I know is I eased out of bed beside Wanda the next morning just when the windows started getting light, being careful not to make a sound and leaving everything I owned behind me. Except for the pickup and the box of tools.

Something kicked up in the middle of my chest right below the breastbone when I looked at her lying there on her side of the bed. She had short curly hair, and she had been all right to me, and she never asked me to buy her a thing the whole time we were together, although I did, of course.

I almost leaned down to wake her up, then, but I remembered the dream too strong I had just come out of a few minutes before, and that saved me from reaching out and doing it.

Wanda, if you are reading this I want you to know I thought you were a good woman and it was a hard thing for me to do to leave that place in the mountains with you. But you didn't really need me, and I thought Elvis did, so I went. You are a fine person and we had some good times, and I wish you the best. I hope you got a good deal on the trailer.

What it was really that morning that took me out of

that trailer and put me behind the wheel again was something in that dream I just mentioned. Things that talk to you in the night when you're asleep and can't nobody else hear were always like a big secret radio from God to Gladys and Elvis, and that night six thousand feet above sea level in California I received my own personal broadcast from that station.

I had drunk most of a bottle of red wine, cheap but good, after Wanda got home and we ate supper. I remember she had only one glass of it, holding her little finger cocked up as she drank, like she always would do. She didn't have to learn to do that. It just came with being really female the way she was. She never put on. So I hit the bed hard like I hoped I'd be able to do, and I remember being glad to feel myself drifting almost as soon as I laid down.

I was on a lifeboat with a bunch of other people, four or five men and two women. The enemy had sunk our ship, and we were the only ones to live and find something floating to crawl onto. Everybody had a part to play, like in one of these old movies you see on TV late at night when there's only two or three of you watching in the whole range of the transmission signal.

I was the American, the tough guy that everybody was afraid of and the one that was going to make it all the way through to the end and get one of the women to go back home with.

One of the women was soft and sweet and wore her hair tied back and she cried when the wounded guy went crazy and drank sea water and died.

The other woman wore a suit and smoked cigarettes in a holder and didn't take nothing from nobody, and she was the one that knew that one of the other men in the boat was an enemy spy with a secret bottle of water to keep him strong and talking back to me.

I watched myself in that dream like it was a movie for what seemed like two hours. But I felt all the time like I was in it, too, while I was seeing myself do things. You know, catching fish, trying to rig up a sail, thinking about ways to send signals and get help, telling the enemy guy off, flirting with the women, throwing the dead man overboard to the sharks that kept circling and following the boat we were all in together.

Finally, in the scene at the end when everybody learns the truth about everybody else, I had to comfort the sweet girl and then hug the tough woman I was going to end up with. And when I did both those things—I had already whipped the enemy guy's ass by then and knocked him overboard to the sharks—when I looked at each of those women up close in the face as I reached out to hold them, both of them turned out to be Gladys, and I was looking right into her eyes from about two inches away, as deep as that sea water.

I pulled myself out of the dream as fast as I could, like you'll do when what you're dreaming scares you so bad you've just got to get back into the real world, your muscles twitching and not moving right and nothing in your body doing what you're telling it to. And just before I broke out of it and came to in bed beside Wanda in the trailer house, I looked out over the edge of the boat and watched the sharks pulling the enemy guy down as he reached his arms up out of the water to me, and of course it was Elvis. And I was inside and outside of myself at the same time again.

I couldn't afford to dream anything like that anymore, so I slipped away from the mountains and came on down to sea level one more time, looking for the other half, trying to see where I was, hoping I'd left myself somewhere I could find.

I had seen plenty of pictures of her before, when I'd pass by newsstands on those Chinese food trips in San Francisco and she'd be beside him on the cover of some magazines, but it wasn't until about a month after I'd left Downieville that I saw Priscilla in real life for the first time.

It was real life all right. So damn real it left me with an eardrum I thought was busted and with a hole in the middle of my heart that ain't never filled up since. It's not going to, neither. I learned that a long time ago.

Here's the scene. Elvis was rehearsing the stuff he was going to do on that Singer special. Going over songs and lights and backup musicians and camera angles and directors and costumes and goddamn choices of shoes and I don't know what all else. It was the worst I'd ever seen him up to that time, and I'd seen him bad.

I remember one afternoon listening to him argue for an hour with somebody about how far a chair he was going to sit in would move back when he stood up. Elvis was scared the thing would go too far back so when he sat down in it again after having made a dramatic jump up out of it to sing part of a song that he might sit back down in it wrong. You know, have to fumble around with his ass trying to hit it right or flop back too far and have the thing scoot underneath him. Something that'd look bad.

So they practiced him sitting down in it and jumping up and sitting back down again and measuring how far it had moved in between times until I had to walk off or punch somebody's lights out.

I was just hanging around during that whole time being a cousin on the set and whenever there was anybody else around, listening to records by the Doors and Joplin and the Beatles, talking to Elvis about Tupelo times for hours on end every night in rooms with the shades all drawn, and drinking what Vernon would have called *boo-coo* whiskey. And old Daddy never knew he spoke a word of French.

The Colonel was always there on the set, prowling around sucking on long cigars and being fat, and the high school All-Stars from Humes were underfoot everywhere you'd turn.

The afternoon I met Priscilla, I was back in one of the dressing rooms sitting on a sofa with my feet up on a little table and having a quiet little talk with myself about why I was there and why not get the hell out now and worry about it later. I don't know where Bubba was. Maybe off getting a rubdown or eating cottage cheese to help starve some more weight off or looking at Tarot cards.

Anyway, there I was all by myself when the door flew open and Priscilla ran in and stopped in front of the table where my feet were and pulled a gun out of her purse.

She pointed the thing in my direction, I remember it was a little bitty blue colored piece but the muzzle looked as big as a Chevrolet exhaust pipe, and pulled the trigger. It sounded like World War Three.

"Goddamn," I said, "shit," and tried to crawl back in between the cushion I was sitting on and the back of the sofa. It wasn't but about three inches of space I was able to open up behind me, but I believe I was about to get about halfway into it by the time she hollered.

"Crawl, Elvis, you son of a bitch," she said. "See if you can hide."

"Don't shoot," I said, "please, shit, don't shoot."

I remember I was feeling around all over my chest with one hand to see if I was hit and holding the other one out toward Priscilla like I was a traffic cop trying to flag down a Mack truck.

"You can stop checking for blood," she said and

snorted at me. "This gun ain't nothing but a starter pistol."

She had the bluest eyes outside of mine and Elvis's I had ever seen up to that time, and she had these cheekbones that left shadows where the light hit them. I believe her mouth was perfect, and I didn't care what Elvis had told me, she wasn't too little at all no matter how I looked at her or what part I picked out to study. And let me tell you, I kept on watching close the whole time she was talking, so I know what I am talking about. That scene was burned in so hard to my optic nerve that I swear I can still see the outlines of it sometimes at night when I close my eyes just right.

"I'm not going to shoot you," she said. "I never planned to give you that satisfaction. I just wanted to see you squirm and beg and back up for a change."

"Well," I said, "I appreciate the compliment." And then I tried to tell her she had the wrong man treed, but she broke in and wouldn't let me talk and shot off her starter pistol again. Twice.

"Who is the Girl with the Vise-Grip Lips?" she said, her eyes as narrow as the muzzle of the gun she was waving.

"Wait a minute. Give me a chance to explain something to you."

"I'll give you a chance to explain, you sorry mean bastard," she said. "That's the way she signed the letter I found under my pillow this morning. Who is she, I asked you."

"I ain't Elvis," I yelled at her to stop her finger from tightening on that trigger again. Those pops in that small tight room were about to bust my eardrums. I kept expecting to feel blood dripping onto my collar any minute from the way my ears were feeling, and I was ready to do anything to get some relief.

At the same time, though, I was purely enjoying just looking at Priscilla with her being so mad and worked up. I swear her hair was standing up from it all. It had broken loose from that beehive she used to wear back then, and it was working and moving and it was alive all over. Just like she was.

Right then was when I felt my heart open up for the first time all the way to a woman and I understood what it meant to say that word and really feel it. I know it doesn't sound possible, and it looks like I'm just doing some selective remembering when I say that, but I haven't been lying before and there's no reason to start now this deep into it.

All right, I'll say it. It was love. Right there at the beginning with Priscilla waving a fake pistol around the room and firing it off every minute or two to express her feelings, that's when I knew I was bad wounded and not ever going to get over it all the way again. She had winged me with one of her shots, and that explosion from the starter pistol had announced a race where I was a contestant who was never going to cross the finish line and get any rest. She had got me going, and I knew right then I was never going to be able to drop out or stop in that race.

God, it was depressing to sit there realizing what I was in for on down the road. It couldn't come to any good, and I knew it, none of it, but like Marlon Brando says in *One-Eyed Jacks*, she didn't give me no selection. It was a long race and one I was never going to have a chance in, one I was bound to lose, but I was going to have to run it just as hard as I could toward a finish line that moved off just ahead of me forever.

When I need to think about loving Elvis or Mama, love was a sickness, something like a fever and a set of chills that kept you either burning up or freezing to death, and you either couldn't take enough covering off of you to stay cool or put enough on to keep from feeling yourself turn to a block of ice. It was a condition is what I'm trying to say. Love was something outside of you that took over and did whatever it wanted to do to you and then just left whenever it felt like it.

After that scene with Priscilla and the starter pistol, though, I came to a new way of thinking about that thing that Elvis always had so much of and I had so little. After Priscilla, love was not a condition for me ever again. It was a lack.

It was like being born with a part missing, and that part was a small one and a secret one, but one I just had to have. The feeling was kind of like this.

You're lost in a field full of snow, and it's winter and nobody around and no place to get to and you're dying of thirst. So you eat snow for water, and it melts inside so you get the moisture you need, but it never feels like you ever get the drink of water you are dying to taste. There's enough that gets through to keep you living, but you never can feel any satisfaction at all. So you keep on eating and feeling emptier every bite you choke down, every freezing mouthful you can gag.

"Please put your gun down, please," I said. "I ain't Elvis, but I do know a young lady that goes by that name you just called. I mean Vise Grip Lip."

"What?" Priscilla said. "You're not? You do? How can that be?"

"No, I'm not," I said. "Yeah, I do know her. I'm his cousin is how you made the mistake."

"Wait just a minute," she said. "I'm trying to think. I don't believe it."

But she did stick the starter pistol back in her purse and sat down on one of the sofas in the room. I was glad to see her off her feet, to tell you the damn truth, and to get a chance to get a better look at her sitting still. I kept looking at her as much as I could stand it the whole rest of the time.

But that was just for a few seconds at a stretch. I knew if I let myself get beyond some kind of a limit that was out there somewhere I would completely lose my fucking mind and start babbling stuff I ought not to.

"Your hair's lighter," she said, "and your eyes are different. The same color but you look out of them different. Other than that, you look just alike."

"Well," I said. "Like an old boy said to me back in school one time, hillbillies breed true."

"Was she writing that to you and thought you were Elvis?"

"Who? What?"

"That woman with the name," Priscilla said. "You know, something something Lips."

"Oh, yeah," I said and saved my brother's ass one more time for a little while. "I reckon so."

"Charming," she said like the word was a bug that had flown into her mouth and she had to spit it out.

"Do you do that a lot?" she asked. "Get women to think you're Elvis so you can go to bed with them?"

"Oh, hell yeah," I said. "That's the only way I can ever get any action."

"I believe you're lying to me," Priscilla said and got up from the sofa to leave the room. She stopped at the door to look back at me, and I allowed myself one quick look at her eyes before I shifted to another interesting spot on the wallpaper.

"I'm sorry about scaring you with the gun," she said. "What's your name, cousin?"

"Jesse," I said. "Jesse Garon."

"Uh huh," Priscilla said and left, and I sat there feeling that hole in the middle of me getting bigger and deeper and more empty by the second.

17

You probably saw that Singer Special when it came on the air, if you've come this far and are still with me. Elvis wearing that shiny leather outfit, every hair as black as a Mississippi delta midnight, all the good old boys from the good old days sitting around on that little stage, sucking up to the kid hard enough to lower the air pressure in the room, women sitting close up all around in the audience with that little glint in their eyes. That light, the thing you see in the face of somebody just before they bite into something they're dying to eat.

Go back and watch that show one more time. Rent you a tape and slap it on that VCR you're probably still paying for. Take you a long hard look at who's singing to you. See the cheekbones. And the deep tan and the tight body.

A television camera won't pick up the skin texture on the palms of the hands, though. If it could, you'd be able to see where the blisters broke years before and made deep callouses. You'd see how heavy-duty grease will get down inside of the layers of the skin and won't come clean all the way no matter what kind of chemicals you use and how hard you scrub it with wire brushes. About all you can do finally is bleach it out and hope for the best and trust folks to look at some other part of the machine.

How far do I have to take it? How many hints do I have to drop?

Let's just put it this way. Jesse Garon got his first satellite exposure that night they did the live taping, and he got it because of buttermilk, bellyache and chemical interaction.

Here's what Elvis told me right before everything got strange and strung-out and crucial during that whole mess. Right before I got the call to put on that black leather Jim Morrison costume and go out and save the world one more time for Bubba and the Colonel and Vernon and a woman that had been dead for almost ten years. Jesse Garon to the rescue.

"Jesse," he said, sitting in a dressing room and just drenching wet with sweat, "I can't seem to get enough to eat."

I didn't say anything. Just sucked at my can of Tab and let him ramble.

"Back when all this first got cranked up, I ate stuff like shrimp and veal cutlets and all them high-dollar cuts of steak. Fancy green salads with all different kind of fruit in them and little pieces of toasted bread over the top of it. Mushrooms. All that fancy stuff that cost a lot of money. I liked it pretty much. It was different, you know. Never had it before. I learned how to do it. I wanted to learn it.

"But now. Now all I seem to want is what Mama used to cook whenever Daddy would bring in enough money to buy something or we'd get some of it give to us. You know, turnip greens cooked down good with some salt pork, mashed potatoes and milk gravy. Cornbread and buttermilk.

"Buttermilk, Jesse. Lord, buttermilk. You remember

that good stuff. How we used to do with cornbread mashed down in it? You know, let the cornbread get a day or two old, covered up with waxed paper or a cheese-cloth or something. Maybe put a little sugar in with it, mush it on down in there and mix it up until it's good and smoothed out with the buttermilk. And then eat that! You didn't even have to chew a bite. That stuff would just slide on down your neck."

Listening to him talk, I could almost believe it was 1955 and Elvis was describing what he had discovered under-neath the clothes of an eighteen-year-old blonde in a motel room in Tyler, Texas or Columbus, Georgia or Tuscaloosa, Alabama. I wouldn't have been totally surprised if he'd have had to reach down and adjust the front of his pants so he could sit more comfortable, just thinking about what he was painting the picture of. It was the same way of talking.

"Remember that, Jesse?" he said, looking in my direc-tion with his eyes fixed on some point five miles off and a sweet little smile on his face. "Living back then?"

"Can't help but," I said, thinking about the nightmares I would have now and then about still living in one of those shitty little apartments somewhere in the guts of Memphis. And to tell you the truth that's something I still haven't outgrown over the age of fifty. That stuff's still lurking in the night.

"I tell you what I found back in Memphis, Jesse," said Elvis. "It's this brand of buttermilk that's got little specks of butter stuck all through it. You know, suspended like, so it don't fall all down to the bottom together or rise to the top in a layer or nothing like that. You ought to write this name down so you won't forget it. Southland Field of Clover. That's what it's called.

"I got me this colored woman, see, to bake me up a pan of cornbread whenever I want it. I get me a quart of that Southland Field of Clover, mix it up and just go to town on that son of a bitch."

Elvis stopped for a minute to play back over in his mind what he'd just described to me, the dream still on his face and his mouth half-opened like he'd just finished off a glass of what he was drooling for, and then he let this big belch come rumbling up from his guts so long and hard I could smell it from across the room. I swear people out in the hall could have heard it through the closed door, I don't care how deep a conversation they were in or how bad stoned they might have been at the time.

"I can't seem to get filled up, Jesse, no matter how much I eat or what time of the day or night I do it. And I just got to keep that weight off to be able to let people see me and still get what they need. It's hard, it's hard to do it. It's a motherfucker.

"I want to eat my fill of all that good stuff I never got enough of when we were little living back there in Mississippi. You know what I'm talking about. Butterbeans and sweet potatoes and that bacon fried real hard and dry so you can put it with lots of mayonnaise and eat it on white bread. Not toasted. I'm not talking about toasted. You understand, Jesse?"

"I know the feeling," I said. "Not ever getting filled up." Of course, Elvis didn't know what I was talking about. And he couldn't have given a damn if he did. His mind was in his belly, and it wasn't finding the way out.

"The thing is I can't get it all down not near enough to satisfy me. It's like there's a big old empty room somewhere down inside of me, and there's a hole in the floor of that room and everything that goes in at the door is going to leak out of that hole and not never going to stay. I thought about that little rhyme Mama used to always say to us, Jesse. You remember? 'What's round as a biscuit?'"

"Deep as a cup," I said.

"And the whole Mississippi can't fill it up?"

"A sieve," I said.

"That's it. A damn sieve. That's what it's been like for me. That's why I got to take this medicine all the time. Keeps me from wanting to eat stuff when I shouldn't be hungry. Supposed to, anyway."

He stopped talking again and leaned down to open up a little leather case setting beside his chair on the floor. He took two of the white ones and two red ones and offered me the bottle they came from, but I said I wasn't that hungry yet.

"Sometimes," Elvis said, "I'll take three or four of these or some other kind that the doctor's prescribed, it'll be the middle of the night, and I'll have to go get me something to eat before them little fuckers even hit bottom. And then about the time I'm in the middle of eating whatever it is I found I want, them damn pills will kick in and make me so sleepy and tired I can't even make my jaws work to chew the fucking stuff. Sometimes I'll pass out with my mouth still full and wake up in the middle of the floor with somebody trying to take me off to the bedroom."

"Priscilla?"

"Who? Her? Naw, she says she don't like to be around me when I'm eating."

"Does she ever cook much?" I said. "Mess around the kitchen? Do recipes and all that stuff?"

Wanting to know things about her, anything I could know about her, started for me right then. And it ain't let up or quit since. I'd like to know what she's doing right now.

"Priscilla can't cook shit," Elvis said. "Can't even fry an egg right. Can't make coffee. And that kitchen is got every kind of appliance a woman could ever want. You know what else, Jesse? You know the worse thing?"

"What?"

"The trouble with shitting."

"The what?" I said.

"I can't shit worth a damn no more," he said. "Eat all that stuff and can't get full and then I take all them pills to get some kind of a balance on my system, and it sets up some kind of a goddamn blockage. I tell you the truth, Jesse. I'd give a Cadillac, hell, I'd give a parking lot full of Cadillacs to be able to sit down on the commode and do my business in five minutes and get up and go on my way. I'll sit there sometimes for half the morning trying to get something busted loose. And it'll promise and promise and then back out and seize up and not amount to no more than a mockingbird can shit."

I just sat there and listened to Bubba, the twin with the bowel complaint, as long as he wanted to talk about it. Don't get me wrong. It wasn't that I wanted to hear all the details of E's potty problems, but that was on his mind, and any time in his whole life whatever was on the boy's mind came out right then. And whoever was around was privileged to listen because whatever it was he was talking about involved him, see, and not wanting to hear him tell it was like going against the Bible or slapping your own mama.

So that's a large part of what all those outstanding graduates of Humes High did for a living. Listened to Elvis, the Man, Big E. Said *uh huh* and *boy howdy* and *you ain't just a shitting* and *tell it like it is* and learned to laugh at awful jokes when drugged, comatose, asleep or maybe even dead. And if they laughed loud enough and often enough and looked interested enough when they were listening to whatever was coming down from the Big E, then maybe they'd get some leavings to have all to themselves. Maybe a cripple or two left over or maybe one that the boss had just took one bite out of and then put back in the package for lack of an appetite.

"Trash pussy," I heard one of the Class Officers call it one time. You know, the kind that's got too many bones in it to be fit for the big table, but sweet enough to keep for the help to eat. You don't throw it back, but you don't count how many you caught either. Put it on a stringer, take it home and rough fry it in deep lard. Forget the lemons, the white wine and the fancy sauce. Just get drunk on beer and eat the pure hell out of it, fins, tail and all.

I listened to Elvis for a while myself, of course. Almost fifty years' worth, as I count it. I know I'm not that much better off myself.

"You know what I'd really like at times like that?" Elvis said and threw down a couple of more pills. "What I think would be the cure for me when everything just gets all blocked up, and I'm in that kind of a fix?"

"What?" I said after waiting a minute or two because I was afraid of what he was going to say.

"One of them warm soapy enemas Mama used to give me when I was a kid and couldn't do do right. I hated it back then. I used to run and crawl under the bed and hold on to the springs so she couldn't pull me out. She'd have to get Daddy to help her pull me out and hold me down."

"Goddamn, Elvis," I said. "I don't believe I would've told that."

"I'll say one thing, Jesse," he said. "I wouldn't run and hide now. It wouldn't be no struggle for her this time."

"I was scared you'd say that. You better watch who you reveal that secret dream to. People will look at you funny for that kind of thing."

"You ain't been in L.A. much, have you, Jesse?" Elvis said. "That ain't nothing, what I just said. It's people all over this part of California making a living by giving folks enemas. And they ain't working in hospitals, neither. Why, there's a real good-looking young girl lives close to here that Jake Stovall goes to real regular for just that kind of business."

"I'm just a country boy from Memphis," I said. "I'll keep regular in a less exciting way myself."

"Yeah," said Elvis. "I guess I'm like you. Except for wanting what Mama could do for me."

By that time I felt like I had to come out of that room or else suffer a permanent case of constipation, so I got up from where I was sitting and began to ease toward the door.

"I got to get something to eat, Jesse," Elvis said just as I touched the doorknob. "I feel like I'm starving to death. Let's get them to bring something in here for us, and we'll eat us a meal together."

"You got to go it alone this time, E," I said. "My stomach's been kind of acting up, and I feel a spell coming on. Going to be a bad one too, I believe."

"Well," he said, "take you something for it. Ask Doc for something special. He's got specifics for everything that can happen to you from eyeball to asshole."

"He sounds like the man to know."

"Except for when you're hungry. I hope it's something worth eating around here."

Elvis got up and came to the door and started yelling down the hall for somebody named Ronnie, and within fifteen minutes he was into the eating binge that put Jesse Garon up on stage in front of a live audience of four hundred people and a satellite TV hook-up bringing him to millions more around the world. White and black, red and yellow, big and little, old and young.

That high point of exposure for the dark twin started off at about four o'clock that afternoon with two cheese sandwiches and a quart of buttermilk, it went on through the rest of that night with eggs fried hard and ham, with a double order of pancakes and syrup, with a visit to a soul food restaurant in East L.A. and some of everything Minnie had to offer in the house, with a quart of cherry ice cream and Pepsi over it, with as many almond Hershey bars as a man could grab in two hands out of the box, with another quart of buttermilk, and all this accompanied of course with pills to make the man burp, not throw up, be able to void, calm down, sleep, wake up, secrete more saliva, feel lively, and get rested.

And the thing ended up at noon of the last possible day for the taping with the Comeback King lying in a dark room way up in a hotel sucking on an oxygen mask, his heart beating off and on whenever it felt like it, and his mind as gone as the 1937 Plymouth we had moved from Tupelo to Memphis in.

"He's going to be just fine," said the Colonel, sucking to get his cigar well lit, as he looked down at the oxygen mask. "Elvis'll be able to start the show just when he's supposed to. Yessir, he'll be there when the sign is made and the roll is called."

Nobody said anything. Not the nurses, not the doctor, not the studio executive, nor the director. They just stared at the man in the sickbed. As Little Richard would have said, all their lips were tight.

"Won't he, Cousin?" said the Colonel and flicked his eyes up at me. "Don't you think so, knowing him like you do?"

"Well," I said and looked over the edge I was standing on to watch some more clods break off and tumble down, down into the dark spot at the middle of everything before me. "I guess so. I imagine."

"Sir," said the boss nurse to the Colonel, "You're not supposed to smoke around an oxygen tank. Please remove that lit cigar from this room."

"Certainly, ma'am," said the Colonel. "But don't you worry none. There ain't nothing going to blow up around here."

18

Part of it was him, and part of it was me, of course. I was the "live" taped part, and Elvis was the "taped" taped part of that Singer Special. When you first saw it come on then or later on in the discount movie house or on your own VCR, you probably wondered why folks that put that much money and time into a thing would forget to give the King a strap for his guitar. Or why every one of the good old boys on that stage looked so damned surprised and scared when I got up to move around a little bit when I sang "That's All Right, Mama."

That's the one that's come to mean the most to me. It's the one song that brings it all together, somehow, and even now I end my show with it because it rounds things off for me. The first shall be last, and the last shall be first, it says in the Bible. And that first song is the last one for me, because it takes it all on back to where it started up for me. And for him and for all of us, there in that little house in Tupelo, Mississippi, with the wash-tubs turned upside down in the backyard and with two of us alive and only one soul to share between us, as Mama always said it was forevermore going to be.

The thing of it that night was I hadn't done but one little run-through, and that was by myself in an empty room with a guitar. And I hadn't set foot on that stage in the middle of those old soft-bellied boys from Memphis until it was time to do it for real. Another thing was that there wasn't a damn toot of dope in me. Not a pill, not a snort, not a lungful, unless you count a finger and a half of vodka as amounting to anything. I never have and still don't.

But I did it. I put on that Jim Morrison look-alike suit, I showed my teeth, I stood up and whipped on that guitar, I threw back my head and howled out the lyrics, I forgot a few lines and I made some up. Hell, I even swapped a few jokes with all those old boys whose names I couldn't keep straight and made it all look like I enjoyed it.

I brought back my twin brother from extinction, from that ten years of those damn movies that had taken almost every drop of blood out of him. I propped him up on stage like a wind-up toy and set him to running, and I made everybody jump back and look again. I made rock stars sober up and call up their agents late at night for some pillow talk to calm them down and give them sweet assurance. I made the money men check their wallets.

It had been a long time between drinks of water for Jesse Garon, and I was one thirsty son of a bitch. I drunk deep, and I drunk long.

Like always, it wasn't my song, but I fucking sung it. And then some.

Now, here's the best part. Here's what I think about at night when I'm lying awake in some motel with an air conditioner turned way too cold, and I'm Lance Lee between shows in Jackson, Tennessee or Columbus, Georgia, and I can't turn off and go to sleep and the vodka won't kick in like it's supposed to and let me.

You might think it's all the applause I got after every number I did as Elvis on that Singer show or the way the director looked at me after he'd seen the move I put on that guitar or the big wad of cash I found stuck down in my suitcase in the dressing room later.

It was none of that, and it wasn't Vernon Presley's handshake or the way later on Elvis couldn't make his eyes look at me when he said thanks, Jesse, and Mama would have been proud for you. No, you got to guess again, but you never will, so I'll tell you.

Here's the best part, the thing that lets me get off to sleep on those bad nights on the road when there ain't nobody there but me and I can't feel too sure even about that. It happened right after the whole thing was over, and I had told everybody flocking up to me that I felt like I wanted to be by myself for a while and thank you and all that but I'm tired.

She came toward me down the hall that ran between the dressing rooms, and she had on a short skirt and a blouse with four or five colors in it, and I could see her walking toward me all the length of the hall and she was swaying like the pendulum on one of these big old-fashioned clocks, a perfect rhythm from one side to the other and not missing a single beat. I still remember the sound of her shoes, the clicks they made on the floor.

I stood there holding the doorknob and watched her all the way up to me. She stopped about five feet away and looked up at me like I was a stranger to her, or like she had just seen me for the first time but was recognizing something she always wanted to find and had given up looking for a long time ago.

"Elvis," Priscilla said and hugged her arms up to her like she was cold, "you didn't seem like yourself out there. You were just so full of life when you were singing and moving around. It was just like you were really doing it."

She stopped and moved a step closer, holding her mouth

like she was fixing to say something else that she wasn't too sure the person listening was going to like.

"Not like you were just acting," she said. "Do you know what I mean, honey? Don't get mad now."

"I ain't mad," I said and reached out and pulled her to me. I never will forget that first kiss from Priscilla. It tasted like I don't know what. The way some kind of flower smells, maybe, but not too sweet and nothing bitter at the middle of it. And there wasn't any teeth in it, and it was warm and dark, and it let me on through to her, finally, after a second or two when she was surprised at first and still had some of her mind in the way. But that left quick, and everything was gone but the warm part and the way you feel when you happen on a waterfall way up one of those rushing little streams in the Smoky Mountains and there's nothing there but the sound of the current and a little mist rising and the light is real green and dim through the leaves.

Then we were in the dressing room, and she asked me to lock the door, and I did that and kissed her again and it took a little while but we got back to the place where the smoke was hanging on the water and I took her to the head of the falls and we stayed there on the edge for a long time and listened to the current move and we finally let it take us with it over the lip of the stone drop and we were in the water and the air for a long time turning and moving together and when we finally hit the bottom we floated together to the bank and stayed there together in the shallow part for a long, long time before we finally had to come out and lie on the hard ground.

"God," she said, "you wanted me. I could feel it. I could tell."

"Of course I did," I said and started trying to curl little parts of her hair around every one of the fingers on my right hand. The hair was soft, but it was stubborn and had a mind of its own.

"I want it to be like this all the time," Priscilla said. "I want us to feel this way when we're together, close and in love, and I want you to be this way with me every-day."

"I am," I said. "I love you. I love you all the time."

I surprised myself saying that to her, because I hadn't planned to say anything like that at all. I didn't even know it was in my head until it had popped out of my mouth and I heard myself telling my brother's wife I loved her. It felt real strange to me for a minute, and everything in the room seemed to take on a kind of a hard edge, like a little light all of a sudden appeared along the surface of every-thing there and made each thing stand out from the things around it, all by itself alone, not connected to anything around it. Just separate like it was all there was in that place. The single bed we were lying on, the lamp beside us, the coffee table in the middle of the room, the combs and brushes and jars of makeup on the shelf in front of the big mirror. Us. All of it just there, but none of it con-nected.

"Do you really mean that, Elvis?" said Priscilla. "Do you love me all the time?"

"Can't you tell?"

"It felt like you did when you kissed me so hard awhile ago and held me like you were, I don't know, desperate or hungry for me or something. If somebody had asked me right then if you loved me, I would have said yes."

"You mean like this?" I said and moved so I could kiss her and did that for a long time, keeping my eyes closed so I couldn't see how everything in the room was sitting all by itself with nothing to hold it down but gravity. And I dove on down deep and held my breath and de-cided I wouldn't come up until I had drowned and just floated to the top with my eyes closed and water coming out of my mouth and my heart gone and not pumping and every muscle dead.

Later on after we had come to, Priscilla cried and asked Elvis to promise her to keep things between them just the way they were there in that room after he had come back alive singing in that special, and I said he would.

I said that for the other twin, but I meant it for me, and every kiss I gave Priscilla and every feeling that came from touching her I stored up and kept just for me, for Jesse Garon, the brother the earth wouldn't give up, the one always held down.

But I wanted her to keep thinking it was Elvis she was with, Elvis who was crazy in love with her, and she did. She believed it was him, her husband, and I let her think that. And I knew I was giving up myself to make her keep believing, but I was glad, glad, glad to do it. Because that was the only way I was ever going to have her, and it was worth it to me then, and it always has been and always will be.

When I made some excuse and left her there in the dressing room to go off and change into the cousin again, I looked back once to see her eyes on me, and she was right there for the twin that had just loved her. She gave me that smile. But I could tell that everything else there still had those hard clear lines along every edge of it, bed, chairs, bottles, ashtrays, all of it. And nothing was touching anything else, but was separated from whatever was next to it or on it or under it, and there where I had been with Priscilla might as well had been a model room like you can see in a big furniture store. Nobody lived there or was ever going to, and the lamps couldn't be plugged in or the chairs sat in or the bed laid down on for sleep.

19

I hung around Elvis and Vernon and Priscilla from that point on for several years, right up to the time in fact that she left Big E for that karate instructor. Oh, I took off now and then, sometimes for three or four months at a time, traveling here and yonder and taking jobs wherever they needed a man that knew what was going on in the guts of a car engine and how to fix trouble and make it right. I tried Eugene, Oregon and Beaumont, Texas and Kansas City, Missouri and one time even as far north as Bar Harbor, Maine. Too cold up yonder for my Mississippi blood.

But I never could achieve escape velocity, like Mr. Spock says on TV, and I always ended up coming back to Memphis to circle around that planet that had put the pull of gravity on me and wouldn't let up. It was just like that, too, being around her. Priscilla didn't no more know she was the thing that kept pulling me back to Graceland where all that bunch lived than the earth knows it's pulling a wadded-up cigarette package to it when somebody's smoked the last one and lets it go.

I couldn't stay away from her for long. I couldn't give up watching for her around that house, waiting to leave it myself until she had done it first so I could see her going out the door and getting into a car. Or maybe I'd invent some game to play with Lisa Marie that would make her not want to go to her mama when she called her for something, and Priscilla would have to come in the room where I was to get her, and I'd get a chance to make a joke and see her laugh. You know, stuff like that. Silly shit.

I'd do things to be able to be around her for a minute or two that makes me laugh now to think about them. I'd offer to hold a damn umbrella over her when it wasn't even raining yet, I'd try to carry stuff for her that a three-year old could have managed, I'd try to figure out what she was going to pick up next so I could get there first and hand it to her. The things a fool in love will do to make himself useful and maybe noticed.

I used to be worried at first that Elvis would notice me bird-dogging his wife and would catch on to what had happened to Jesse Garon. How could he miss it, I'd ask myself. Couldn't he tell that I couldn't keep my eyes off of her whenever she was in the room and that I ran around like some kind of a goddamn English butler opening doors for her and handing her stuff? Couldn't he see I was in love with his wife?

I felt guilty enough right after that hour I spent with Priscilla in the dressing room in L.A. to be scared he'd come after me with one of his .357 magnums when he'd figured out what had took place. Hell, I just knew as soon as Priscilla would have come up to him and said something about that sweet time together they'd spent after the Singer Special he'd have realized it. He'd have put two and two together and come up with Jesse performing as the King one damn time he shouldn't. One special appearance by the dark side unrequested, one stand-in he hadn't asked for.

But one he damn sure needed.

He never did, though. He never said a word about it or made a sign that anything strange had happened after the big special where Jesse Garon had staged a comeback for him. And in more ways than one. In front of millions of people and of one in particular.

To tell the truth about it, by that time in his life Elvis probably thought it *had* been him who'd done such a turn-key job with his wife when she mentioned to him that magic hour in the dressing room. I bet he just patted himself on the back if he noticed what she was saying to him at all, reached down and arranged the hang of his equipment in his jumpsuit, lit up a little cigar and smiled at one and all.

You got to understand that Bubba never was a man to question the reason for or the truth of a compliment, particularly in the later years of the reign.

So, like I said, I hung around off and on for a long time, dreading seeing Priscilla and needing to in the worst way all at the same time. It was like having a bad tooth in your mouth, one that was so far gone it hurt to touch with your tongue, much less get something hot or cold on it. But no matter how sensitive it got, how careful you had to be not to aggravate it so it wouldn't start throbbing, you just couldn't keep from reaching over there with the tip of the tongue to punch at it and feel that pain, that little steel icepick going straight to the root. Finally you want to give it a good hard suck to see how much it can hurt, how red it can turn the inside of your head as you lie there at night not able to go to sleep because it won't shut off.

I even found myself asking Elvis questions about her, how they got along, what they talked about when they were by themselves, what kind of things did they fight about, all the kind of questions you can find in a damn fan magazine. I made myself sick with it, and I sucked at that sore tooth until it roared.

"You're a lucky man, Jesse," Elvis said to me once during one of my little self-punishment sessions. "You ain't never been married and had to deal with all that shit that comes with it. You just fuck one of them for a while and move on to the next."

"I thought you wanted to get married to Priscilla," I said. "Bad enough to import her from Germany to raise in Memphis."

"I always want to *get* married," he said. "Every time I fall in love. I just don't want to *be* married."

He gave me a long look over the lip of the cup he was drinking from and then set it down slow on a table there in front of him in the Jungle Room in Graceland where we were sitting.

"It's a big difference," he said. "I done figured that out, but it's come a little late. Now you, you got it doped out right. Keep looking for that strange pussy. Before you finish the one you're on, be looking around for the next one to nail."

He talked a tough game, my brother did, a hell of a tough goddamn game.

Well, I hung around to feel that pain and lie awake nights, I talked to Priscilla about Lisa Marie and what kind of clothes everybody was wearing and how weird hippies were and what it would be like to go to college and learn stuff. I read some of the books she told me she had and thought I would like. We talked about the people in some of them and how we would like to meet them or not and what kind of lives they led. One of them was a book called *Wuthering Heights* and it was about two old houses in England and these two people that loved each other. The man was dark-complected and nobody knew where he had come from as a kid. He tried to dig up the woman he loved out of the cemetery after she had died. I knew the feeling.

So I sucked that tooth and fed the pain to make things be real, and I went on the road with Elvis time and again when he was making all those tours and doing all that Vegas shit. Times came when he couldn't meet the bell and had to stay in the dressing room, listening to the pills sing him to sleep, and it was dye bottle time for Jesse Garon and another chance to sing Elvis's song and dance Jesse's dance.

And so I sucked it up and blew it out and hit the ground running, and I made them twitch between their big toes. When the big light hit me, I moved around in it. I have always done that.

I did that stuff for years, and nobody knew about the doubling that was taking place, the old bait and switch the Colonel and me and Elvis were running to keep everybody happy and buying in. I do know one drummer we used in the road band caught on to us once in Seattle when he happened to walk in on me and Elvis together. I was dressed to go on because Bubba had developed the shakes so bad he couldn't hold a mike in his hand, and I was there in the hotel room to ask him something before the show. I forget what.

That old boy's eyes bugged out when he saw the two of us looking up at him so much I was afraid they was going to pop like little balloons. He never said a word about it later, but he knew something heavy-duty strange was going on, and I would catch him studying me when I would be in my cousin phase. You would have thought he had seen Heathcliff walking along in the woods with Cathy's ghost. Priscilla, if you are reading this, you know what I'm talking about.

His name was Henry, and he was like all drummers, never real sure of himself, that's why they got to make all that noise, and I don't believe he ever really trusted himself to think he had actually seen what he had. He was good, too, with the sticks. I liked him. He would get up on his toes and lean into them hides. I'm sorry he's not around to hear me testify and set his mind at ease after all this time. But he was killed in a wreck with a truck on I-40 close to Jackson years ago.

Maybe Elvis up yonder with Old Shep in that happy home can run into him and set him straight about those years when Henry and the whole damn Presley-watching public was seeing double. I'm doing my damn best to, and I could use some supernatural help now and then, so Bubba, pitch in whenever you can.

I helped Elvis in more ways than one, and I would appreciate some payback. I figure I was responsible for at least two of those five years of wedded bliss that the King enjoyed with Priscilla. By the time I fell in love with her at the Singer Special thing, she was already seeing that karate guy, and that was less than two years after she and Elvis had tied the happy knot in Vegas in the first place.

So what I'm saying is that the split was already there by the first time I ever touched her there in that dressing room in L.A. And if I hadn't showed up they wouldn't have been married three years, much less five.

My loving her the way I did the times when I stepped in for Elvis kept that dying arrangement alive long after the doctors had done give up hope and called it terminal. I know it must have been a strain on Priscilla, that kind of going back and forth from one thing to its opposite all in a day's time.

Think about it. Suppose you're a young healthy woman with nothing but time to kill and your husband, the famous rock and roll king that every female wants, has just made mad love to you until you can't even get your breath. And he's told you he loves you more than anything, more even than getting up on stage to sing, and he's cried pure tears of joy just to see you naked in bed with him. Maybe he's even just pushed you into a handy closet he's so crazy to touch you and bent you over a shoe rack he's in such a hurry to get inside. The love he makes to you is so desperate and wild and needful you can't even keep your mind about you and you've had to scream your loudest into a double handful of dress material you've stuck your face in so nobody in that part of the house will think somebody's killing you.

Your famous husband lies beside you on the floor after it's over with, crying and kissing you all over your face and throat and hair and telling you he can't live without you and that he's crazy to touch you when he's away from you and that he can't ever get you out of his mind and never wants to even if he could. When he leaves, he's trembling and looking so deep into your eyes you're afraid he might tip over and fall inside your head and never come out again, and you hold him to you so tight you can feel your muscles and his moving against the bone.

He's gone, and you see him again in a couple of hours when you walk into a room where you didn't expect him. This time he's lying back on a long white fur-covered sofa wearing different clothes and holding a remote control for the TV in front of him, and he looks up at you once when you walk in the door, and his eyes touch you the same way they would a glass that had just been full of buttermilk but now was empty and had set out long enough for the heat to begin to get to it. He says something like "there ain't a goddamn thing to watch on this television here" or "your makeup needs fixing" or maybe he says nothing and hits the button on the remote control and watches the channels roll: static, football, game show, static, desert movie, static, static.

You can see why you'd want to leave the room and the

house and him and your mind.

Priscilla got finally to where she didn't know what to say to him or how to act or what to do. She lived for the other Elvis to show up, the one who could match the way she could feel, the one who cried whenever he left her, but he didn't show up that often. Because when he did, it killed him. What she wanted was a man that would be mostly the same for most of the time, but what she got was one that was both dead and alive at the same time.

She was a damn strong girl. I say that because the whole thing didn't kill her. She was dealing with a love life that would have blown out all the fuses on most women, left them living in the dark with not a speck of light to keep them company and nothing warm coming in at the vents. But she stood that for a long time, being married to two halves that never could join up right to make one and she never did go completely crazy but the one time, and that didn't last long. Just long enough to get her out of Memphis and the house in L.A. and my life and our marriage that Elvis fucked up and ruined.

Don't take my word for it about her being tough and staying with a thing way past the time most women would have called it quits and gone to the bottle or pills or shrinks or to spending all the money they could lay their hands on. Just look at her in some of the old *Dallas* reruns. Nobody in that show can ever stay with her one on one and look as alive as she is. She's always looked stronger than anything around her, no matter how little she is, no matter how much name the other people's got.

I've taped all the parts of that show that she's been in, and I carry around the cassettes in a black leather suitcase when I'm on the road, cloning the King. I even got every episode of *Those Amazing Animals*, and nobody else in the world can say that, I bet.

I told you I am in a fix. I know that, hoss. You don't

have to say it. I know how it feels inside my chest. I'm living here.

That one time Priscilla went crazy, actually lost the balance in her mind and checked out of her mental hotel and didn't leave a forwarding address, was when she went off with that karate guy, of course. I knew at the time she had to do it. I could see it coming and even Elvis knew she wasn't acting right, but that still didn't help the way I felt any. It still won't, no matter how many times I go over it in my mind. I can't make it right, no matter how I try to figure it, no matter which way I turn it in my hands and hold it up to the light.

Here's how I found out about it. I heard a gun shot, a heavy caliber from the sound of it, then two more, then several other ones too close together and overlapping to keep count of. When I opened the door and put my head around the casing real slow, I could see that Elvis was in the middle of the TV room with both hands full of Smith and Wesson. They were chrome-plated, there was smoke curling from the muzzles, and there was so much smell from burnt powder in the room that it made my nose itch and my eyes burn. Fine pieces of glass, chunks of wood and plastic and a cloud of plaster dust were covering tables, chairs, floors and every available surface. It looked like a troop of boy scouts had been turned loose with hammers to work on merit badges in destruction.

Elvis was staring at one particular spot on a wall of the room like it was the face of somebody that had just called Gladys a redneck whore, and as I stepped on into the room, he raised the .357 in his left hand and pulled the trigger again. It clicked on an empty chamber, but the one in his right hand didn't, and a basketball-sized hunk of wall just vanished in front of us.

"Little target practice?" I said, my nose itching and my ears ringing like a busted guitar string.

226

The Humes High School Heroes were all bunched up
against the wall behind Elvis, their eyes big as the bottoms of beer bottles and their hands over their ears, and
one of them, the Class President, I believe, or maybe it
was the Most Likely Boy to Succeed, was crying in a little
soft girlish whine.

"Boss," one of them said, "look who's here. Your
cousin Billy." And then to me. "Say something to him.
Talk to him. Try to talk to him. Please."

Elvis didn't look around. Just stood there with his
mouth working like he was carrying on a conversation
with somebody that didn't need ears to hear and who
wasn't about to talk back to him. He lifted the revolver
in his right hand again, took good aim and pulled the
trigger. This time it clicked too and didn't fire so I took
the chance to walk up closer to my brother, the gunfighter.

"Big E," I said. "What's happening? Run out of
ammo?"

"I'll kill the son of a bitch," Elvis said to the hole he'd
just opened through the wall into the next room. "I don't
take that kind of shit from nobody. That goddamn nigger
bastard."

"Who you talking about?" I said. "Jimi Hendrix?"

"Wouldn't have been for him, she wouldn't have done
it on her own."

"Who?" I said, but I didn't want to hear the answer
because I already felt it down in my guts, low and dead
center, right where I lived, in the middle of me. That little
blank spot that had followed me around for years all the
way from Tupelo to Memphis and away from there and
back again was seeking its final and true home, and I
could feel it zeroing in. Here's the place, it was saying,
I'm home, what's for supper?

Over Elvis's shoulder, one of the Humes High standouts
was mouthing something at me and when I focused on

him, I could read his lips.

"Priscilla," he said with no voice, just the lip movements, "she's gone. Left him."

"Y'all go on out of here," I told the gang backed up against the wall. "Me and Elvis have got to talk."

I didn't have to repeat myself. They all tumbled out of the room, scattered down the hall and ran out the front door of Graceland like they'd been told there was a four-foot mound of cocaine piled up in the driveway and each of them had a shovel.

When I looked back at Elvis he was patting all of the pockets in his pants and coat trying to locate some more .357 cartridges, and he kept doing that over and over for a lot longer than it would take a man to realize that everything was gone and his secret hiding places were empty.

"What you looking for?" I said. "I can tell from where I'm standing that it's gone."

"I got a whole stick of them upstairs," Elvis said. "They just not where I want them. Go get them for me, Jesse."

"Naw," I said. "I ain't. I don't believe that wall and them TV sets can't take any more punishment and live. You don't want to kill them, do you?"

"Why did she do it? Why would a woman want to leave me? Don't she know who I am? Look at all I give her."

Elvis swept his hand around in a little circle the way he had done all his life, a little motion that took everything in around him and everything that had been in the past. It included the white sofas and the big lamps and the glass tables and the curtains and the remote control units for the TV sets and everything in the other rooms and the cars outside in the driveways and garages. It had stages and white lights and sound units and movie screens and jet plane trips and people standing with their mouths open in a yell and tears pouring down their cheeks.

There was Memphis in it and Mississippi and Las Vegas and California and the Colonel and Vernon and a dead woman buried in a coffin that cost more than her husband had ever earned on his own in his whole life. There was a stand of pines and a big snake in a hole under a flat sheet of metal in the middle of it and two voices wrapped around each other so tight they almost made up one. But not quite.

And the one thing that wasn't taken in by that little motion of Elvis's hand that became a circle getting bigger and bigger and going further and further back in time and out in space was standing in the same room with him, smelling the burnt cordite and the plaster dust and the exploded picture tubes, close enough to touch but never quite doing it.

Jesse Garon. The twin dead at birth. The one that walked and breathed and spoke and sang in his brother's dreams and that disappeared everytime he woke up. Jesse Garon, the other half of what came of that night under a blue moon in Mississippi in the middle of the Great Depression. The man that made sweet love to a woman who never even saw him as she whispered her need in his ear and called him in a soft voice by his brother's name.

"How could she look at all this and leave?" said Elvis. "The goddamn little bitch."

"Little brother," I said and stopped to take a deep breath and wait to hear what I would say. "Maybe she took a good look and really saw it. And then maybe she had to leave before her eyes burned out."

"Oh, Mama," Elvis said, starting to cry and letting the revolvers slip out of his hands to the floor so he could rub the heels of his hands into his eyes. "I'm glad for the first time that you're dead. Dead and gone and don't have to see this happening to your little boy."

With that he collapsed onto the floor beside the .357

magnums hard enough to jar the busted TV sets and set some more fine shards of glass to falling.

"I wish," I said, sitting down on the sofa closest to Elvis's head so he could hear loud and clear what I was saying, "I wish Gladys *was* dead. I wish she'd go on and die and stay dead like any decent woman ought to. It's about time."

"You sorry bastard," Elvis said, his eyes popping open so quick and wide it looked like they were set on tight little metal springs, well-oiled and on a hair trigger. "Saying a thing like that. You never loved my mama. Never in her whole life did you give a damn about her. And she could tell it. She knew it. She knew things. She knew you didn't care nothing about her."

I leaned forward toward where Elvis had surged up from lying on the floor when he had heard the name of Gladys taken in vain, and I took him by the head, my hands on each side of his face and made him look directly at me. His eyes were drawn up like BB's, the blue of them like patch ice on a pond in January, and there was no more depth to them than there is to a dinner plate.

"Listen here, Mr. Rock and Roll," I said. "You want to know why Priscilla left you here? Here in this big house with all your asshole buddies? I'll tell you. She left you because of Gladys. Not because of no karate teacher. Not to run off with Mike. Because of Gladys. Gladys. Our sweet mama."

I let go of Elvis and sank back into the chair behind me. It seemed like it took me two minutes to reach it and like I'd gained a hundred pounds along the way.

"You're crazy, Jesse," said Elvis. "Priscilla never even met Mama. She was gone before Priscilla even got here."

"There's dead, and there's dead. And there's alive, and there's alive, and you and me both are some of each."

"You talk like somebody fell out of a tree," Elvis said

and lay back down beside his firearms. "My little girl is out there running with a home-wrecking nigger, and you're saying things that don't make no sense at all."

"Priscilla ain't no little girl no more," I said. "She's a grown woman."

"Oh, yeah," said Elvis. "She thinks she is. She believes she knows all kinds of shit. To hear her tell about it, you'd think she went to school at Southwestern. I believe this and I believe that. Don't you think this and don't you think that. Let's discuss this and let's discuss that. Shit."

"You sound like you're glad she's gone, then," I said. "Like that's what you wanted. To get shut of her for good."

"Jesse," he said and rolled over on his side to look directly up at me, "you know there's a lot more better looking women than Priscilla is out there. Bigger ones, too. Sweeter ones that'll appreciate me and treat me right. That ain't what's bothering me. You know that."

I didn't answer him. I just let him ramble. For one thing, I didn't care to carry on a conversation with a man lying in the floor with two just-emptied .357 magnums that he kept caressing like a woman's thigh, and for another, I was having a hard time making the connection between my mind and my tongue work. I'd think of something to say, maybe about the part Gladys was still playing in our lives or the reasons why a man's wife will pack up a small suitcase and leave the house, and the cars, and the pool and him for good, and I'd try to put the thing into words for Bubba's benefit, but everytime I opened my mouth to speak, Priscilla's face would rise up before me like a wall I couldn't get through. And I'd sit there feeling her move further away just like I was watching her in a car driving off in a straight line down a highway that went from where I was to a horizon so far away I couldn't see the limit of it. The car got smaller and smaller, and I had to keep straining harder and harder to keep it in sight, and there weren't any glasses anywhere in the world strong enough to help me.

"Look at me, Jesse," Elvis said all of a sudden in a different tone from what he'd been using. "Look at me and listen to the sound of my voice."

I looked over at him, and he was sitting straight up in a lotus position and staring right at me. I had once seen fifty Californians lined up in rows doing the same thing, so I wasn't surprised at the idea of it, I was just puzzled to see a Presley from Tupelo, Mississippi going Eastern in a house in South Memphis.

"Naw," said Elvis, "don't look all around. Just concentrate on my eyes. Look just at them, and listen to what I say."

So I did. It had used to be like looking into a mirror, but now something about Elvis's eyes wouldn't let it be a perfect fit. Something was a little off, and I looked close, trying to figure out exactly what it was, what the thing was that wouldn't let me see exactly my own eyes when I looked at his.

"That's right," Elvis said in a voice deeper than his ordinary one, "just relax and listen to the sounds of the words I'm saying. Don't try to worry about what it all means."

It was something about the way they were fixed, I remember thinking, like they were focused on some point about two feet back of me and a little to one side. If I turned around real quick, I might see it too. But I knew it wouldn't be worth looking at, whatever it was he was seeing where nobody else could look.

"Do not be nervous or tense," Elvis said in that same voice, "do not be nervous or tense."

"I will not be nervous or tense," I said back in his voice and waited to hear what the great hypnotist was fixing to put on me.

"Look into my eyes," said Elvis. "I want you to kill him for me, Jesse. Kill him dead."

"I've been trying to kill him, Elvis," I said," and I hope I can finally do it. But he's a tough motherfucker to off."

"You know him already?" Elvis said in his normal voice and then, shifting to the hypnotist tone again, "when did you run into him? Where did you meet him?"

"Before I even knew it," I said. "He's been with me as long as I can remember. And I just can't seem to shake him. Not in Memphis, not in California, not even in my sleep. He is always around, looking right back at me out of every mirror, out of every dream, out of every dark room I walk into."

"You ain't talking about Mike," Elvis said. "You hadn't been listening to my words at all, Jesse, not a goddamn one of them."

"Oh, I been listening to them," I told him. "I've been hearing every word you've said since before I can remember, and I've been marking them down and counting them up. I've heard you when you didn't hear yourself, and I've listened to you when you didn't even know you were talking.

"And you're not the only one who's been talking," I said. "You're not the only one who's said words that I've listened to and got by heart and studied over and tried to understand until I thought my head would bust wide open and all the world would come pouring inside my skull and back me out of it until I was gone, gone, gone."

"If you're talking about Mama, she's dead," said Elvis in his usual voice, the one with a tear in it, "dead and gone off and left me here all by myself. You were supposed to take care of me and do for me, like she told you to."

"I did that, little brother," I said and tried to look into his eyes, but they were glazed over and the surface of them was like blue stones. "I did all that as long as I could stand to do it. I did it until I died right here in Memphis. Died sitting up and breathing, wide awake, and the worst part is that I can't lay down and just go blank and get to that place where it's nothing there at all, not even me."

"If you won't kill him for me, Jesse, then what am I going to do?" Elvis said and began to cry, still sitting in the lotus position with his hands turned palms up on the bend of his knees. "Somebody's got to do the killing for me around here."

"Give yourself some credit, Bubba, " I said. "You're doing a damn good job of that yourself. You turned out to be a real craftsman at that chore, a master mechanic. If you don't believe me, ask Priscilla."

"You got to help me, Jesse," Elvis said in that voice from our childhood, the one that always showed how afraid he was. "Mama said you would."

"Not this time, brother," I said. "I'm gone now, and it's for good."

I left him there in the TV room, sitting in a floor full of busted picture tubes and coffee tables and chunks of wood and plastic. He was still in that eastern stance the last look I gave him, and I fully expected that that would be the final first-hand image I would ever have of Elvis, him paralyzed in a lotus position and a long, long way from the two-room house Vernon had built for the Presleys in Tupelo, Mississippi before the war broke out.

Thinking back to it, one of the damnedest things about that night I fled Graceland—and our broken marriage and my twin brother—was running into Jerry Lee Lewis down at the gate.

I could tell it was him way before I got to the fence by

all that bunch of yellow hair shining in the street lights, but even if I had been a blind man I would have known it was Jerry Lee because he was informing the world of that fact over and over in the loudest voice he could muster. He was drunk, of course. But saying that about the Killer is like admitting if you get in a boat on the Mississippi in Memphis and let it drift you're going to end up passing by New Orleans. Nobody's going to argue the point.

"Yonder he comes," Jerry Lee announced to the empty street and swivelled his head about to look for the crowd he always believes is around him, "the so-called King of Rock and Roll, Elvis the Pelvis Presley."

Jerry Lee was by himself. The car behind him with its front wheels run up on the curb was empty, and I couldn't see another soul at the Graceland gate. The night was clear, and the moon was yellow, and the leaves, as the man said, came tumbling down.

"Killer," I said. "How's it hanging?"

"You ugly thing," said Jerry Lee. "I have always been better looking than you ever was."

Jerry Lee reached under his coat down into his left armpit and pulled out a little shiny pistol that sparkled in the streetlights like a Vegas silver dollar. He held it up in front of his face and looked at it like it was a clock he was having a hard time reading the time from.

"That matches that silver coat you got on," I said through the bars of the gate. "Shiny like it is. Pretty."

"Yeah, Elvis," he said like a man looking at a grandchild, "It's pretty, ain't it? Got a double action, too."

We both stood and admired Jerry Lee's sidearm for a minute until he thought about something and shook his head back and forth like a man either trying to clear the cobwebs or whip some water out of his hair one.

"You think you're the King, Elvis," he said. "But I'm a man here to tell you you ain't."

"No, I don't," I said. "I don't think that. I know better than that, Piano Man."

"I always did get more women than you ever did, Elvis," said Jerry Lee. "Fucked more of them. Married more of them, too. Hell, you ain't married but the one that I know of."

"You're right, Killer," I said. "Just the one. Now she's done left us. I ain't got a one left."

"It's more of them out there," he said. "It's thousands of them."

"Well, yeah," I said. "If you want to start counting them up. But I ain't never been no damn good at figures."

"Reason I come here tonight," Jerry Lee said, putting out one hand to hold onto the gate between us, "is to tell your ass that I was always bigger than you, and you know it's a fact."

"You didn't get no breaks," I said. "Not a one."

"No," he said. "Shit. They was worried about Myra being fourteen, being my cousin. They shut me down just for that. I was married before then when I was fifteen myself. There ain't nothing to that. They didn't even know that part."

"You can't figure it out, Jerry Lee," I said. "What makes some things happen and some things not. Might as well blame that moon for it."

We both turned our heads up to the sky to look at the moon hanging over South Memphis, big as a wash-tub and yellow-orange and with one side that looked like a wolf had taken a bite out of it. I couldn't look at it long.

"Well," said Jerry Lee. "Just as long as you know the truth."

"I do, Killer," I said. "I do."

"I might ought to shoot this piece off a time or two," said Jerry Lee in a quiet voice. "But I sure do dread it."

"Don't do her, then," I said. "Memphis police will come and then the *Commercial Appeal* and all them live minicams from the TV stations."

"Yeah," he said. "Shit. I guess I'll go home. See if anybody's up."

"I'm leaving, too," I said. "Give me a ride down the road a ways, Jerry Lee."

"All right," he said. "Pile in. But you know something? You never could play no guitar, much less a piano."

"Naw," I said, "I know it. Couldn't write songs neither. Just sing somebody else's."

"I ain't through yet," said the Killer. "I'm still whipping that sucker. Got a lot more whiskey to drink, women to marry. Look up yonder at that damn moon. It's just like the yellow of a big old egg."

"Yeah," I said, opening the car door. "It's something else, ain't it?"

But I couldn't look up at the sky again, no matter how I tried to twist my head to do it.

20

I saw Priscilla one more time after that night I left Graceland. The idea to do it as Elvis had come to me first thing, of course, and I had to fight it off for almost a month before I was able to trust myself to go to California and hunt her down in her love nest. What I kept saying to myself is maybe if I go in as Elvis I can bring things back together again, get the little family re-established, talk her into coming back to Memphis to live in peace and love and Graceland.

I knew I was lying to myself, of course. The first thing Elvis himself would have done if Priscilla had come back was to fuck it up again, and she would have the whole thing to do all over. Besides that, I was having myself a little trouble at that point in my life keeping things separated and apart and in the right places.

Things was going down like this about then. Nights, I would go to sleep after a long dose of whatever I was taking as medicine to help me make it. Gin, sometimes, or vodka, or white rum. Less hangover in the white liquors than in the dark ones, you understand. Or maybe it'd be a woman I'd picked up in one of the bars I was running through by the dozen then. And we'd have rolled around and wallowed and hollered and done our thing and drifted on off to the land of dreams.

That was the hard part. That's when your heartaches begin, as Bubba said in one of the early ones. Because what would happen then was I would dream, and what I would dream was that I was Elvis.

It was like living his life for him in story after story, and it was hot and tight being inside his head and it was hard to see out of his eyes through all the fog and rolling clouds and rising mists. And I couldn't get comfortable no matter how I turned or twisted or tried to run and hide. It seemed like I was always hungry and wanting some particular thing to eat, but whatever I tried to get down my throat wasn't it. It had the wrong taste and the wrong feel and the smell was enough to make me gag, but I couldn't stop biting it off, chewing it up and swallowing mouthful after mouthful of it until I felt like my belly was about to explode.

When I'd wake up from those nightmares it would take me sometimes almost an hour to begin feeling like I was myself, Jesse Garon, again, and the longer they went on and the more of them I had the less sure I felt every morning that I was going to be able to get all the way back inside my own body and my head again.

Finally one Sunday morning after a Saturday night that had begun on Friday afternoon and run on into a full forty-eight-hour day, I woke up to realize that I had been dreaming all night not that I was Elvis but that I was Jesse Garon. Lying there awake in the bed beside a woman I couldn't remember seeing before, I lifted my hands up in front of my face and curled my fingers and watched them flex and asked out loud whose they were and listened to a voice in my head tell me Elvis's.

I closed my eyes as tight as I could force them and everything before me became a country road I was driving down too fast, the car bottoming out in ruts and chug-

holes and the shocks not working and the engine screaming like all the oil was gone from every cylinder. And
nobody was coming toward me, and nobody behind, and
there'd never been anybody drive that dirt road at that
speed that way before.

When I came to myself I was standing in the shower of
the motel room, the water coming ice cold into my face,
and I knew it had been running a long, long time because
the drain couldn't handle it fast enough and it was wet
from the bathroom all the way out into the middle of the
floor of the room itself.

"What's wrong with you?" the woman standing on the
bed was saying. "Why won't you answer me? Please quit
scaring me like this."

"Honey," I said, and I couldn't tell whose voice I was
talking with, "call you a taxi. I'm trying to get this drain
to work, and it don't want to let nothing out. It's all just
overflowing all over everything."

That's when I started trying not to ever go to sleep
again. It's bad enough to pass out and start dreaming
you're not yourself at all but somebody else you don't
want to be, but at least when you wake up you can usually persuade yourself it wasn't anything but indigestion
and a bad night and the sun's shining and the coffee's hot
and that hand you're reaching with belongs to you and
nobody else.

But when you get a little taste of what Willie Nelson
means when he's singing "be careful what you're dreaming, soon your dreams'll be dreaming you," that, hoss, is
a whole 'nother smoke.

But you know something? You can't stay awake all the
time, no matter how you plan your shopping at the drugstore and the liquor market. What you finally end up
doing is going to sleep and dreaming you're awake, and
that is the worst world there is. No rest in it at all, at all,

and that thing you're trying to escape lives in that world like it's in its natural habitat. It's at home.

So I went to California to see Priscilla one last time, and I went as Jesse, as near as I could remember what he was like. At least I was wearing his clothes and hair color and had about a two-weeks' growth of his beard on my face. Jesse Garon about then had lost a good bit of weight and was in general traveling real light, and he wasn't singing any songs or doing any dancing. He was walking flat-footed.

We had breakfast together, Jesse and I did, at a McDonald's right around the corner from where Priscilla was living with her karate instructor, and after I had drunk my coffee and eaten my Egg McMuffin and had to finish Jesse's orange juice for him and the rest of his coffee too, we got in our Avis rental car and drove up in front of the love bungalow.

Lisa Marie opened the door, took one look and hollered for her mama, and I walked in and set down on a sofa covered with an animal hide of some kind. It was sitting next to a chair that was hanging from the ceiling on some wires, and I could see all kinds of other interesting furnishings in the room. Big candles, rugs hanging on the wall, trailing plants in bottles, flowers stuck in vases, lots of stripped wood. You know what I'm talking about. California dreaming.

"Jesse," Priscilla said, "I'm so glad to see you. Have you been sick?"

"Hi, Pris," I said. "A little bit. Do I look that bad?"

She was wearing some kind of a Mexican thing, lots of color and rough-looking weave in the cloth, and her hair was halfway down her back and it was its own color, a little to the light side of off-blonde.

I couldn't stand to look at her in more than little short blinks, but I was having a hard time keeping my eyes from settling on her longer than was good for them. They kept wanting to focus on the part in her hair and the point of her chin and her fingers as she picked up things. It was like being deep under water with my breath held. I knew I couldn't stay long down there and live.

"You've lost a lot of weight," she said. "Have you been to see the doctor?"

"No," I said. "I don't need to. It's a special diet I'm on. You just deny yourself everything you want."

"Well, don't go too far with it. You'll just waste away to nothing."

About then Lisa Marie came into the room, over her scare, and asked her mother for something, so I had a chance to draw a couple of deep breaths while Priscilla tended to her, and by the time she turned back to me I was smiling like the old days.

"You been reading any more good books?" I said. "Got some hot tips for me?"

"I don't have to read like that any more, Jesse," said Priscilla, her eyes glowing like a spark had just been struck behind them. "I'm living that kind of life now for real. Not just reading about love. I am in it for good."

"That's good," I said and made my eyes drift to the wall of glass on the back side of the room. "I'm glad you feel that way." Far off across the valley beyond the glass I could see a little highway with toy trucks moving down it from left to right. One of them passed two others while I watched. It was real slow, and I saw the whole transaction.

"I'm happy," she said. "I'm alive. Wide awake for the first time in my life. And I love it."

I nodded and tried to think of something to say, but every word I ran across in my mind with the notion of saying it out loud just lay there like a rock I was afraid to turn over. I didn't know what kind of soft, wet squirmy thing might be living under it, hiding under the shiny side.

"Mike is wonderful to me," said Priscilla. "He's not afraid to talk to me about the way he feels about things. He's got real depth, and Lisa Marie is just crazy about him."

"I don't know him," I said, "but he sounds real nice."

"He is, Jesse," said Priscilla. "He really really is."

"I don't guess you been thinking about coming back to Elvis, then. Not missing him or anything like that."

"Missing which one?" Priscilla said. "The one that says he loves me and needs me and can't live without me, or the one that would rather play with his buddies and have other women and ride horses and shoot guns and stay on the road and do anything not to have to be around his wife?"

"I didn't know it was that much difference in him," I said, picking up each rock real slow and shaking it to make those squirming, blind soft things fall off before I had to see them.

"It's night and day, Jesse. Black and white. It's like he's two different people and you can't tell which one's going to speak whenever he opens his mouth. And the Elvis that cares about me and wants me and needs me shows up less and less. I think he's gone."

She had been picking at a loose thread on the sleeve of her Mexican dress, and it was finally coming loose so she gave it a quick jerk and broke it off, but not before it made a little puckered looking ravel in the cloth.

"I got tired of waiting for him, Jesse. I finally just stopped looking for him. That Elvis was fading away from me anyway, and I believe he's probably gone now for good. Just faded away like an old letter written in pencil. Nothing left but a few little marks you can't even read any more."

I looked away from her face because I had to, and I

could see the little highway through the window with the toy cars and trucks running up and down it. I couldn't see where it was heading or where it had come from, but I knew I had to get on it and go in the direction it would point me, wherever that was. I didn't expect it would put me any place in particular that I wanted to be, but I knew I didn't have any choice about whether to follow it or not. Like I said before, in the whole time that I knew Priscilla, in Memphis and in California and in Las Vegas and in my lonely goddamn fucked-up dreams, she never did give me no selection.

21

I left. I drifted, I parked cars, I sold insurance, I changed oil and lubricated transmissions, I drank white liquor and dark, I ate, snorted and smoked dope, I fucked teenagers and grandmothers. I lost myself and Elvis couldn't find me. But, of course, he really didn't have to. He was always right there, every morning, every noon and for goddamn sure every night.

You might know what it says in the Bible about that, but probably not. "Wherever two or more are gathered together in my name, there will I be also." That's what the preacher used to say in that little country church out from Tupelo when there would be only one or two families at prayer meeting. Sitting there beside Aunt Edith and Uncle McCoy in that splintery pew, I never took that thought to be a comfort even back then.

And it sure wasn't any consolation in my own life knowing that I could never be truly by myself, alone, ever. It wasn't that having my twin in the world was any company to me. Don't get me wrong. What it was was the feeling that somebody else was always there, no matter where I was or how far I had run, and that somebody else was a copy of me or maybe I was a copy of him.

I got by the best I could those years. I lived on the edge

and listened to it crumble and break off and fall into the dark emptiness, and I didn't go back to Memphis again until that night when I was living in Oregon, and Gladys came into my room and woke me up.

She wasn't wearing any heavenly robes, and her face wasn't bathed in any kind of a golden light, neither. In fact, after I'd opened my eyes and sat up in bed because of hearing her call my name just the one time—Jesse— short like that and real definite, I could see that she had on a housedress just like the ones she always used to wear. I don't mean one of those high-priced fancy ones from Goldsmith's that she bought so many of after Elvis had ascended the throne. What I'm talking about is one of those flowered kind, the ones that look like they were cut out and sewed up from a big bolt of that cheap material from the back of a department store in Tupelo or maybe from a sack that flour or cattle feed had come in.

On her feet she had a pair of old flat black shoes that were run over at the heels and about to bust out at the sides where her weight walking would have put pressure on them, and she was wearing a patent-leather belt that the buckle had worn about half through where it was fastened.

I'll tell you what she looked like. She looked like she had just walked Elvis down to his fifth grade class early in the morning and was on her way back to the house, already tired and trying to figure out what she could find to cook for supper.

She was a lot younger than she had been when she died there in the Baptist Hospital, and her hair was mostly still all dark and her hands didn't have that puffy look they showed in her last years. Seeing her sitting there in the chair across the room from my bed, I could have believed it was 1948 and we were all still roosting there in Tupelo, waiting for that appointed time to leave the nest and begin that flight up US 78 to Memphis.

I remember thinking to myself that I wasn't scared because Gladys was in that room there with me in Oregon in a state she'd never been in when she was alive, but instead I was uneasy in the same way I'd always been around her. I didn't know what she was going to do next, and I'd never figured out a way to calm myself down while I waited to see.

I looked down at her ruined shoes again and that worn-out belt, and it hurt me to do it. I felt something turn in the middle of my chest, and when it did that, it took me back to when I was a kid looking through a Montgomery Ward catalogue at the pictures of women in new unfaded dresses and unbroken shoes and I was wanting money to buy clothes like that for her and Aunt Edith.

I must have groaned out loud at that thought because she lifted her head and looked at me. That's when I could see the shadow falling over her face and not letting me see her eyes, and that's when I could tell Gladys was truly dead and that the view I had had of her eyes those years ago in that hospital room was the last one I would ever have.

"Are you hurting, son?" she said. "My Jesse?"

"Yes, ma'am," I said. "I am. I have been hurting a long time."

"You always will. That's the way you are alive. Heavy in this world with the hurt. You hurt to live."

"You're young," I told her. "Your hair is so pretty, Mama. Let me see your eyes."

"I can't, Jesse Garon," Gladys said. "Only Elvis can see my eyes now."

"Why always just Elvis? Why always just him and not Jesse Garon?"

"I told you before, Jesse," she said. "Back there with the sun and the moon and the voices mixing. Elvis is light, and you're the heavy one. Elvis rises up and you live in the world."

"What can I do?" I asked and reached out my hands toward her. "What can I find to help me?"

"Go to Elvis one more time," said Gladys, "and this is the last."

"Can't you do it for me?" I said. "This one time, Mama?"

"No," she said, "It's always been for you to do, Jesse Garon, and this is the last."

It was like thunder in the room, but there was no sound, just a silence so strong and deep I opened my mouth to scream with the pain of it and twisted away toward the window and the night outside it, and when I looked back for her she was gone.

And she has never come back to me again since that time, no matter how I have strained to listen or how quiet I sit and wait. And I have wanted her to. That is the hard, fast truth.

22

It was after midnight when the cab driver let me out in front of the wrought-iron gates at Graceland. It was dark, no moon in the sky and some of the streetlights right in front of the place were out, so the cabdriver had to shine a flashlight to see what bills I'd given him.

"It's a ten and a five," I told him. "Go ahead and keep all of it."

"Thank you, sir," he said, and then snapping off the flashlight and looking up at me, "you don't live here, do you?"

"Naw," I said. "Just visiting."

"I didn't really think so," he said. "It was just something about you looked familiar. Maybe I gave you a ride before sometime."

"Maybe," I said and stepped back and watched the cab drive off up Elvis Presley Boulevard, picking up speed as it slipped in between two trucks.

Vester was in the gatehouse and was glad to see me. He thought it was going to give him somebody to talk to in the middle of that hot August night in Memphis, and I could see him rearing back as he cranked up to speak.

"Long time no see," he said. "Where you been? Does he know you're coming?"

"Nowhere," I said. "Everywhere. No, he ain't expecting me. Where is he?"

"Up yonder in the bedroom with Ginger, I imagine. He drove in about midnight, said he was ready for bed. I wouldn't just barge in on him up yonder if I's you."

"I ain't," I said. "You can get on back to guarding. I'll wait to see him tomorrow."

As I walked up the driveway, I could hear Uncle Vester grumbling behind me in his little booth, disappointed and lonely at the edge of Graceland, but I didn't pay him much mind. That was what you bought in for if you elected to hang around the King. It was steady work.

The bottom floor of the house was dark except for a dim lemon-colored light just inside the hall, and I didn't even bother to look up at the top story where Elvis would be because I knew that would be so blacked out and sealed off by special curtains that an Air Force spotlight couldn't have got through to the outside.

I used the key Elvis had given me years before, and like I was afraid of, it still worked. As I stepped through the front door and into the hall, I looked around the rooms to each side, hoping that one of the Humes High Heroes would stop me and not let me go any closer to the man upstairs, but everywhere was deserted and nobody helped me out, so I started up the stairs, one slow step at a time.

Lisa Marie had left some kind of a toy at the top of the landing, maybe part of a dollhouse or something, I can't remember, and I had to step over that to be able to get to the door to the big bedroom where the King took his rest. The knob turned real easy and quiet, and I pushed the door open about six inches and looked inside toward where a light was coming from.

It was a lamp on the low setting, and it was sitting on a little table next to a bed big enough for three or four people who liked their privacy and didn't want to be touched even accidentally when they were sleeping in the night. There was only one person in it, though, and she was a pretty good-looking redheaded girl with bad adenoids. She had her mouth open to breathe and was setting up a healthy but ladylike little snore as she did it. I remember I was thinking that Ginger was a good name for her and that her eyes were set a little too close together for my taste when he spoke.

"I'm glad you got here," said Elvis. "Did she tell you to come?"

"What do you think?" I said and stepped into the room so I could see him.

He was sitting off to the side in a big chair close to the door to the bathroom, and he had these little half-glasses perched on the end of his nose. He had been reading, judging from the pile of books by his chair, but he didn't have anything in front of him when I walked in and faced him there in the half-dark room.

"I'm glad you came right on and didn't wait, Jesse," Elvis said. "You got to help me."

"I don't do no more substitutions," I said. "I done give up show business."

I said that, but I knew nothing like that was the problem. Something else was in the air of that super-cooled room in Memphis that night, and it had the moon in it, though it wasn't to be seen in the sky, and it had the mother of Elvis Aron and Jesse Garon in it, though she had been dead for nineteen years and buried in the side yard of the house.

"What I need," said Elvis, "what I need, Jesse Garon, is for you to tell me something. Tell me something I can't tell myself."

"All right," I said. "What? That you're the King? All right, you're the King."

"Don't play with me, brother," he said and then, noticing that I was looking toward the sleeping girl with the adenoids in the big bed, "Don't worry none about her. Thunder wouldn't wake her up."

Elvis had leaned forward in the big blue chair, and as he did, his pajama top pulled apart and I could see his chest hair, black with a lot of white in it, thick down across two big rolls of his belly. That made something close to my heart twist inside me.

"Damn, Bubba," I said. "You sure got fat and hairy, didn't you?"

"I know it," said Elvis, tears welling up in his eyes, "I tried to fight it. I did for years, over and over, right up to when I come to see there's a meaning in it. It's a meaning in all of it, and I got to accept it."

"A meaning," I said.

"A meaning," said Elvis, "all through history. It's in books and volumes, what these real wise men have said about it. It's for us to try to understand it."

I didn't know just what he was talking about, but I knew it wasn't only his problem with weight control.

"It's about being heavy and not being heavy," he said. "About being able to stick to the ground and not being able to do it."

"You not talking about some kind of diet?" I asked. "Not some damn weight loss program?"

"Everything a man eats speaks to him and for him," said my fat twin. "It's a riddle in every bite you put into your mouth, and the solving of it is the nourishment it offers your body."

Elvis stopped for a minute and looked over at the sleeping beauty in the big bed. She hadn't moved an inch since I had come into the room, I noticed, and she was still making those cute little snoring sounds.

"Poor little Ginger," said Elvis. "She thinks she understands about food, the way that it works."

"Maybe she ain't had all that much experience," I said. "Don't look to have eat much yet."

"All that about what you eat is just a little part of it," Elvis said, waving his hand to get rid of it. "That's not really why Mama got you here, Jesse, to talk about that. I already know most of it. You're the one with the missing part. You know what it is and where it is, and you got to tell me the truth, that last bit of it I don't know."

"Look, Bubba," I said. "It hurts me to be here. It's like I was trying to set a broke bone in my arm all by myself for me to sit in this chair and listen to you. Ask me what Gladys wants you to ask me, and let me leave."

"Why, Jesse," he said, and I swear he said it in deep surprise, "how can it be hurting you to be with me? I'm your twin brother. I'm the same as you. I always have been."

"Yes and no," I said. "Yes and no. Get to it."

"Part of it's this book they got out about me, then," said Elvis. "I thought they was friends of mine ever since high school, and then they do this to me. Telling all them lies about me. Claiming I'm a drug addict. Saying I ain't been fair to them. Making stuff up. Twisting things around to make me look bad. Let me tell you something. Hell hath no fury like a serpent scorned."

"I didn't think that's exactly the way the saying goes," I said. "Not right on the money."

"He's here," said Elvis. "I'll show you. You never did know about it. Only just the beginning was what you saw and all you ever knew about. Just you wait and see."

With that, he got up from the blue chair so fast he kicked over the pile of books sitting by it, and he walked over to a big painting hanging on the far wall. It's probably one you've seen pictures of, if you know your Presley lore. It's him, the King, dressed all in white, his head turned a little to one side so you can see the jawline and his eyes fixed on some point far off in space, like he is looking at planets circling around a sun.

Elvis reached up and pulled at one side of the frame, and the whole thing swung away from the wall on hinges to show the safe behind it, the round combination knob shining like mercury in the light. He spun it once to the left, twice to the right, made some adjustment and then opened the door after the click came, and reached inside. Whatever he was after gave him a little trouble at first because he fumbled with it for a few seconds and then started pulling a long black thing out of the wall safe.

It came out with one long motion as Elvis spun around to his right and whipped the thing at me through the air. I stuck up my arms in front of my face like you will when something you don't know is flying at you, and it wrapped around my hands where it hit, one end of it flopping around and hitting me in the face.

It felt light but strong, and it made a rasping noise as it scraped against my lips and chin. It was as cold as midnight.

"Goddamn," I said. "What is this thing?" and pushed it away from my face to look at it. It felt like it took my breath along as it went.

"I told you he was alive," Elvis said. "Not never going to die."

"That fucking snake," I said. "At the bottom of that hole in Tupelo. It's his hide."

"It come with all this," said Elvis. "Look at the hole in the skin where you stuck that stick and tried to kill him. But you couldn't do it back then, and nobody since has neither."

"How did it get here?"

"I brought it with me from Mississippi when we moved, and I kept it all this time."

Elvis came away from where he was standing by the

wall safe livelier than I'd seen him step in a long time, and he started walking around the room, talking and pointing and using his hands to demonstrate as he moved up and down that deep blue shag carpet.

"I called him Old Tarzan Snake, and I had dreamed him before I ever saw him in that hole where he lived. He spoke to me in my dreams and told me things nobody else could hear. And then you tried to kill him just because he was there, but I came back outside to him that night after Mama and Daddy had gone to sleep.

"Where you'd hurt him, his guts had come through and he was dying slow. And I knew that if he died slow he would be dead for good and never talk to me again and tell me things and let me know what was going to be. So I took Mama's butcher knife and shoved it through his head right between his eyes, and Jesse, he didn't even flop once when I did it. Just laid there and looked up into my face and never blinked and he died just like you'd cut a light off.

"I took that knife and cut into him and skinned him out, and he didn't even bleed when I did it. Rolled that hide up and hid it and kept it with me ever since. And when I come out of the house to look at what was left of him the next morning, the hole was empty and all his meat and bones was gone, and not a sign of blood anywhere."

"Dogs got him," I said, looking down at the patterns in the snake hide in my hands. There seemed to be something in it I could almost read, like when a word is on the tip of your tongue so close you can taste it but can't say what it is, not even if somebody was to put a knife to your throat. "Drug him off into the woods to eat. That's all."

"There ain't nothing nor nobody could eat that," said Elvis. "He just went back to where he come from, where he can't be seen nor heard. But you see his hide right there in your hands, Jesse. And if you listen just right, you can hear him singing to you, too. I could always hear that song, all my life, all my time here."

"Here," I said and tried to give the snake skin back to him with both hands. "Take this damn thing. It's freezing me to death to hold it."

"You never could stand to hold it, could you, Jesse?" said Elvis. "You never could take it in your hands for long. Never long enough."

"What does this piece of dead hide mean to you, then, little brother?" I said, opening my finger to let it fall to the floor in front of me in that space between us. It seemed not to want to come loose and let go, and it fell in what looked like slow motion to me, hanging there in the air of that bedroom in Graceland as though it was as light as a breath and couldn't decide whether to let gravity take it or not. I remember the whole time it took that snake skin to drift to the floor I was shaking all through my chest and shoulders like I had a fever chill. And it wasn't until the thing was flat out still on the floor that I stopped feeling like I was about to pass out from the cold.

"What it means," said Elvis, "is that something put me here in this world for a purpose and I got to serve it on out until it's done."

"Jesus," I said. "You mean Jesus, then."

"Uh-uh," said Elvis. "I don't. Not exactly. Me and Jesus was *both* put here for a purpose, and both of us is had to work on figuring out what that purpose is supposed to be."

"Jesus," I said again, but this time I wasn't trying to call up his name like the answer to a riddle. I said it in the same way you would if you'd just seen a big wreck on the highway or watched the windows in your house bust out from a bomb going off in the neighborhood.

You know what I mean. Slow, and every part of the name long and drawn out.

"It's pyramids in South America," said Elvis. "In Peru and all down in there. They got these drawings on the wall of a man singing to a bunch of people, to a whole society and a whole civilization. These little markings are called hieroglyphics, Jesse, cut into them rocks by these priests. It's signs to people that know how to read them."

Elvis reached down and picked up Tarzan Snake and hung him around his neck like a four foot bandanna and went over to look at himself in a full-length wall mirror. I sat there and watched him like a child listening to his granddaddy, and across the room Ginger kept on drawing air in and out of that pretty half-open mouth, sleeping the sleep of a justified beauty.

"Space ships landed all over remote parts of the world thousands of years ago, Jesse," said Elvis. "They set up colonies and rearranged people's genes. Built all kinds of big runways that you can see from the air even right today. Now it's just jungle and headhunters all out in there."

"You learn that in them books?" I said, pointing to the knocked-over pile by the big blue chair.

"And other ones, too," Elvis said, "that, and private revelations. Yes."

"Revelations?"

"Meditations and visions," said Elvis. "Meditations and visions, vouchsaved. You know what that word means? Vouchsaved? Look it up and learn something.

"We've been here before, Jesse. And we're coming back when it's time. All in the fullness of time."

"Vouchsaved?" I said.

"Vouchsaved," declared Elvis.

I remember we both looked off and didn't say anything for a little space, and I sat there trying to find enough strength to get up out of the chair, but my muscles didn't seem to want to work and my mind wouldn't take charge and make them. I tried to close my eyes to rest them, but they acted like they were on springs and kept popping open, no matter how much they didn't want to focus on my twin with the snake skin wrapped around him.

Elvis looked like he was beginning to wilt. He had stopped striding around the room like one of these TV preachers on cablevision, and after a minute or two he sat back down in his blue chair and began looking all around at the walls like he was trying to find out the source of a sound he'd picked up that nobody else could hear. He had broken into a sweat, and as I watched him it was like I was charmed and couldn't turn away, his face got wetter and wetter until finally drops were forming at the tip of his nose and dripping off onto the front of his pajama top.

"Tell me what you want from me, and let me get on out of here, Elvis," I said. "Put it in words and say it. I feel like I'm freezing to death and I'm never going to get warm again."

"I can't never get it cool enough in here no more," said Elvis and wiped each side of his face with his sleeves like a man who'd just come out of a delta cottonfield in August. "Everybody claims they're cold, but I can't see how."

"Mama said it was the last time," I said, hoping to get that word from him which would let my muscles do what my mind was telling them and pull my body up out of that chair and through that door and out of Graceland forever and for good.

"You got that last little piece I need to have to make it all fall together, Jesse," said Elvis, twisting in his chair as though he couldn't find any way to sit that would satisfy him. As he moved, it seemed to me that Tarzan Snake was settling closer to his throat and taking a tighter grip, but that had to be just the way the light was shining and the shadows fell.

"When I sang that first time at the fair," said Elvis, "it was me that opened my mouth and started the song, but it was you that took it over and finished it up. I could feel your voice starting up in the back part of my head and then coming out of my mouth and carrying the tune out to the end and laying out there in the air for the people to hear it. I never told you that because I couldn't even believe it myself.

"Mama knew it was the truth when I talked to her about it, and she told me not to question it. Just to take your voice whenever it would come to me and use it whichever way I could. That would be the double power of it, she said, and it would be the two of them mixing up together and making one that was more than just the two of them could ever be standing separate and alone. It was the white and the black, the light and the dark. And it was one that floated up in the air and one that stayed in the ground. Not *on* the ground. *In* the ground.

"And you sang through my throat with the air from my lungs again and again, Jesse, you did it there in Humes High at the talent contest, and that's when I knew the power was in me and things had worked together to get me here. The next time was on Union Avenue when our voices come together out of me, there in the Sun Studio with Scotty and Bill and Sam Phillips."

I started to say something, but Elvis lifted up both hands to stop me.

"Why do you think Mama told *me* the call had come when you was asleep there that afternoon in 1954? She knew you had made that four-dollar record, but she knew who it was the voices would gather in and where they'd come out of, too. I was the instrument, Elvis Aron, that the song was supposed to come through, and you, Jesse, you Jesse Garon was the rhythm and the bass."

"It was like the way the lead guitar floats on top of all that the band's doing, and that's what you hear first, and that's all that you know you hear if the music ain't in you. But if it's there, if it's in your bones and your blood, you know where the real stuff is happening, the stuff that holds it all together. It's in the bass and the drums and the beat that's behind all of it.

"That was you and me, Jesse Garon, them different sounds wrapped around each other, one floating on top, light and fast and jumping around and the other one behind so low you can't hear it with your ears. You hear it in your belly and your balls, and it's a feeling you don't have to think about. It's just there, and you can't talk to it or practice it or call it up when you want to. But you can do one thing with it. You can lose it.

"Sometimes I'd be singing, maybe in front of a hall or auditorium full of people or maybe just warming up with just me and the band, and there wouldn't be nothing really happening. There'd be a lot of noise all right, people hollering, women yelling out my name, the girl singers'd be getting it, horns hot. And then it'd just happen. Your voice would just cut in, come out of somewhere, come out of nothing, and just slip in with my voice and wrap around it and join up and slide like a silk scarf falling through your hand.

"'Jesse,' I'd say to myself. 'Come on in here, brother. Give me a hand.'"

Elvis stopped talking to lean forward and wipe the sweat off again, rubbing each side of his face with a sleeve and then lifting up the front of his pajama shirt to swab at his nose and chin. His belly was white as the hospital sheets on Gladys's bed, and sweat was standing in the creases between the rolls of fat. I jerked my eyes away as fast as I could, and he caught me doing it.

"Ain't pretty is it, Jesse?" said Elvis. "But like I said, it's a meaning in all of it, in everything about me. And about you.

"When that voice of yours would cut into my song," he said, back on to the stage business again, "it wasn't anything else like it in the world. I didn't sound like nobody else but me. Couldn't nobody touch it, couldn't nobody come close. Then was when the magic was there, when everything lined up in that long row nose to tail, and it was a fit all the way back through time on up to now and all the way to whatever was coming next. You know the songs it was in. You could tell it. It was there.

"And then," he said, "then, it would just cut off like somebody had closed down a big valve somewhere, and you'd go leave me there all by myself, and it'd be a long stretch before you'd give me your voice back again. And the times between, when it wasn't there, would get longer and longer, and then finally you just left for good and took your voice with you and kept it all to yourself somewhere. And you ain't never gave it back, and Mama said you never was going to, again, ever.

"You let me die up there," said Elvis, and the room dropped ten degrees in temperature as I sat there facing him, "and I want to know why did you stop singing through me. Why did you take your voice away? Why did you do that to me?"

"I'm cold," I said through my teeth. "I'm freezing to death. I feel like I'm turning to ice here in this room."

"Here," said Elvis, holding his hand toward me, "take some of this. It's got the truth in it."

I took whatever he gave me. Maybe it was a way out of there. And I swallowed it all without even feeling it go down my throat, and by the time it hit bottom I could feel myself sliding away from him over that crumbling edge I'd been walking on for so long, down the sloping side which got steeper and steeper and finally dropped off to nothing. I watched Elvis's face looking over the edge of that hole at me all the way as I fell, and his eyes were as blue as mine and every bit of gray was gone from his hair.

I dreamed about Gladys and Vernon and Priscilla and me being in a wagon that rolled along a high track like a railroad from the top of one tall building to another one, but nobody said anything and nothing came together and there wasn't any sense to be made of any of it. The wagon just rolled faster and faster, and nothing steered it, and building after building flashed underneath the rails, and we went on like we were going somewhere definite, but I could tell the whole time that was wrong and a lie. All the light faded and the moon dropped down behind the tallest building, and everything was black and the darkness gathered into a ball I was holding in my own hand, and I didn't wake up after then until I heard Ginger screaming.

"Something's wrong with Elvis," she was saying over and over, "help him, somebody, please."

He was in the bathroom, but you know that, of course. Everybody does.

He was face down on the floor, his pajama bottoms were pulled down to his knees, and some little thin book was lying by his right hand. The snakeskin was wrapped tight enough around his neck until it looked like that might have been why his face was blue, but I knew better than that.

"Go use the telephone, hon," I told Ginger, and after she'd left the room to do that, her face so twisted up it looked like one of these Halloween masks, I kneeled down beside him and turned him on his side, real careful not to let him just fall over. When I did that it made some air come up out of his lungs through his throat, and Elvis made a long groaning sound like a man will do when he lies down after a long day. Your mind will do funny things when a person has just died. I remember when that groan came out of my twin brother, I thought to myself that was the last bit of music he'd ever make and that it wasn't too bad a note he'd just hit. It was pretty close to that long grunt he gives in "All Shook Up" right after "I'm in love."

It was easy enough to get the snake hide unwound from around his throat. I just gave one little pull, and that broke it loose, and it was almost like it crawled into my hand and wrapped around my arm. It was ice cold, but it was as supple as a length of cotton rope.

"Brother," I said and looked at Elvis's eyes, "I did all I could, as much as I could. I showed up every time that the moon made me, and I tried to help Gladys make everything stay right."

He didn't make a sign, though, after that one groan, no matter what I said to him or how close I looked into his face. He just laid there with his tongue between his teeth and that rim of blood around the pupils of his eyes, and he was focused on something far off, studying that and trying to understand it, and I knew that both of them, my mother and my twin, were never going to give me any notice another time in this world.

23

Peple got there and shoved things down Elvis's throat
and breathed into his mouth and gave him shots and took
him off in an ambulance and made long-distance telephone calls and issued statements to the media. And more
people gathered in front of Graceland by the thousands
and drove up and down Highway 51 in cars and pickups
and leaned out of their windows to look. Lots of them
got drunk and drove fast, and one carload ran into the
crowd and killed several people, their shoes bouncing off
the stone wall built around the place.

The airport was full, and the highways into town stayed
full, and people came from everywhere to Memphis. Flo-
rists made big money, and so did the *Commercial Appeal*
and the *Press-Scimitar*. The Humes High Heroes went
crazy, and the Colonel arrived in a New York minute,
and I finally found Vernon by himself in a little back room
downstairs just off the kitchen.

He was sitting in a wooden chair right in the middle of
the room, and he was surrounded by shelves from floor
to ceiling stacked full of canned goods and sacks of flour
and sugar and bottles of cooking oil and spices and I don't
know what all. He looked up at me from a little wooden
box he was holding on his knees and didn't say anything

at first. His face looked redder than usual, and his hair was as white as cotton.

"Is it you, son?" said Vernon finally, holding on to the box like he was afraid somebody was about to try to snatch it out of his hands. "Is it you?"

"It's Jesse Garon," I said. "The other one."

"Well, of course, I know that," he said and looked down at the box and then around at some of the shelves. "Elvis has got so much fatter than you ever been. Yes sir, just put a lot of weight on, lot of weight these last few years."

"You all right?" I said. "Sitting here by yourself."

"I just wanted to take a look at all these canned goods, Jesse," said Vernon. "Got peaches here, chili, every kind of bean and pea, creamed corn, whole corn, them little peeled potatoes with snap beans in with them, turnip greens. You name the vegetable or the canned meat. It's all right here. Anything you want to eat. I wish she could see it."

"You mean Gladys," I said, looking again at the little box Vernon had in his hands.

"She was always afraid there wouldn't be enough," said Vernon. "Many's the night I'd wake up with her out of the bed and know she was in the kitchen counting things and adding them up. Picking things up and moving them around and arranging where they set. Seems like she never could get everything all straight and fixed just like she wanted it."

"She had it all where she wanted it by the time she died," I said. "Didn't you think?"

"I swear I don't believe she did. Gladys never did act like there was enough to count on and be sure of. Not back in Mississippi, and not in all them apartments in Memphis and not even here in this big old place."

Vernon leaned over from where he was sitting and

picked up a can of English peas from a shelf.

"Look at that," he said. "Eighty-nine cents for a can of these. That's your top-quality produce. Yes sir, that's off the high shelf at the top."

"I'm glad I found you before I had to leave," I said. "I wanted to tell you good-bye before I slipped on out."

"Wait a minute," said Vernon, putting the can of peas back on the shelf, careful to find the exact spot it had come from. "Jesse, I got something she told me to give you whenever the time would come."

"What time is that?" I said.

"You know, son. Whenever Elvis would go on to glory and be with his mama in heaven," said Vernon. "Be at peace up there with Jesus."

With that, my poor old white-headed daddy started in to cry, but I was able to stop him in a minute or two by asking about the price of two different kinds of canned meat stacked up on one of the shelves beside us. Both were top dollar.

"Here," said Vernon, reaching into the wooden box and pulling out something wrapped in paper that had turned yellow with age and begun to come apart along all the folded places. "She looked at it a many a time and always said you was to have it when they was both gone."

It was a photograph, of course, a snapshot made with a Brownie camera sometime back before the war started, and the paper it was printed on looked like it would turn to dust if you breathed on it. Gladys was in the middle, all dressed up in something with big flowers on it, and her hair looked like she had just had it cooked and rolled in a beauty parlor. It swept down over her forehead and about touched her eyebrows, and she was looking straight on into that closing camera lens like there was something behind it she had just had a glimpse of and she just had to see closer and clear.

There was a child standing on each side of her, holding tight to each of her hands and staring just as directly into the eyes of whoever was going to look at that picture in the future. I should say there had been a child on each side of her, because somebody had taken a pair of scissors or a sharp blade and cut off the side of the picture showing the boy on the left, so what you saw was the child's hand and part of his arm, but the rest was gone a long time before.

"Well," I said to Vernon, "one more snapshot of the King at an early age for me to put in my billfold and fool people in bars with. Mighty nice."

"Nuh uh, Jesse," said my old daddy, fumbling in the wooden box on his knee, "the one she left showing is you. Elvis is the one she cut off with them scissors when she was laying there in the Baptist Hospital. Said for you to read the back of it."

I turned it over and looked at the four words Gladys had put on the back in ink. You could tell she hadn't pressed down hard, but they were plain enough to read, all right, stacked up in two little columns, two in each one.

heavy	light
stay	rise

No matter which way I turned the picture, over and over again, as I looked at it from first one angle, then another, the four eyes of the woman and child looked right into mine like they knew they were going to when that little ray of Mississippi light shot into that camera and touched that film all those years ago. There was nothing behind the two figures to pin anything down, and there was nothing between my eyes and theirs but the dead air that nobody could breathe.

The four eyes were trying to balance everything in the

light the camera had captured, but the five hands in the picture wouldn't let them make things come out even. No matter how I counted and subtracted and summed things up, the numbers wouldn't come out right. It was the stated problem I knew I could never solve, the answer I would never get.

So I left Vernon there in that room full of canned goods, and I went out the backdoor of the house, and I wouldn't let the Colonel stop me to talk no matter how many times he hollered after me that we could work everything out and make it smooth for everybody.

I went back to see Aunt Edith one day. Drove that road past the new subdivisions and the fast food and the fields covered with kudzu and pulled up into the yard just at dark.

I knew Uncle McCoy was dead, but I expected to find her there, working at the cookstove, ready to feed me and maybe tell me a thing, maybe point out to the back-yard where I played all those singlehanded baseball games.

I might have saved myself the trip. The nurse there with Aunt Edith was glad to talk, to tell me about how sweet the old lady was, how she wasn't mean or cross as most of these old folks get with that new disease that takes their minds and leaves them begging for coloring books and ice cream. Aunt Edith just sat there and hummed.

It's no balance in life, it's only in the songs that you make, and that's why folks still have got to have the King.

And the way I live now is to give the people what they need. And to keep both of us standing and both of us alive.

What I do is work all these clubs in the South right back where it all started. Home again in Dixie. You know the kind of place I'm talking about if you ever been down here much at all.

Generally, the place is at the edge of town, out where the used car lots begin and the fast food places have all popped up. It's a low flat-roofed building without any windows, built of cement block usually, and it's got maybe a canopy out in front going up to the main door. If the canopy is made of cloth, it's all tore to hell and drooping, and if it's made of metal it's rusty and the stains have leaked all down the paint.

What's the name of it? Bad Bob's in Memphis. The Green Frog in Lake Charles. Cowboy in Tuscaloosa. Other places wherever the clientele wants to see a "Living Tribute to the King." Or maybe they call the show something like "Loving You" or "Elvis Live!" That last one always gets me to thinking double. It seems to help me get my lip sneer right.

O.K. Here we are in Tallahassee. The club is called Vereen and Jane's, and it's the 10:30 show. I've been there about a week, and the word has had time to spread. "Hey, you seen that Elvis show out there at V and J's? That old boy has got him down, let me tell you. Sounds just like him and looks almost just like him too. Drives them women crazy."

That kind of thing, you know. Word has got out to the waitresses and the housewives and to these women who sell real estate. So they are coming in strong on a Friday night, and they are bringing their husbands and boyfriends with them. Or if they don't have that kind of connection anymore they are showing up in teams of two and three.

By the time the first show is ready to start, most of them have been in the place for over an hour, drinking sweet cocktails or maybe straight shots of scotch or bourbon. The salesmen have all got a good buzz going, and they are working the tables of the two- and three-women teams like a school of sharks. Everybody's up and dancing to the music of a band called Beauty and the Beats, and between numbers the women are walking back to their tables with a salesman behind each of them cutting his eyes back and forth as he tries to see something better.

The alcohol is working, and the sweat is flowing, and the noise level is moving up notch by notch. Just at 10:30 I look up from whatever I'm reading, and I take off my reading glasses and drop them into the little black bag inside the trunk.

"On my way," I say to the old boy knocking on the door to the dressing room, and I stand up and fasten the belt around my jumpsuit. I'm wearing the white one with the big Aztec suns on the front and back of it and the white boots trimmed with red and gold. I've got a big bracelet on my left wrist, and I pull a couple of rings the size of belt buckles out of their box and stick them on my fingers.

I take out a hairbrush and hit the hair one more lick before walking out the door. It's as full as ever and as black as coal. It'd be as white as Vernon's was at this age if I didn't keep the dye bottle busy, but none of it's missing. Neither one of us ever had to worry about it slipping back on the sides or falling out on the top. The one good thing the old man gave me.

Outside in the hall leading to the back door to the building the four guys I asked for are waiting. They're dressed more or less wrong, of course, but at least Vereen has made some effort at a look, so I'm satisfied more than I usually am.

Three of them look pretty much alike. Long sleeved white shirts and dark pants, little snap-on bow ties about the same color. Long-haired country boys growing bellies and mustaches. The fourth one has lost his bow tie and the top button to his white shirt. He staggers backwards in the hall when I come towards the door, and he falls against the wallboard behind him hard enough to cause it to make popping noises.

"Hey," I tell him, looking close at his eyes, "I don't want you helping me out none, hoss. You just go on back to whatever you was doing."

"What you mean?" he says. "Vereen told me I was supposed to escort tonight."

"Don't need but three of you out there this time," I says. "I'm going for a little different look."

"Well, why not me? Why don't you let one of these otherns set down?"

By this time he has straightened up to his full height and is leaning toward me while he's got himself braced with one hand against the doorfacing. His breath smells like he's been deep enough into the mezcal to eat the worm at the bottom of the bottle.

"You done lost your tie, hoss," I tell him and step on out into the hall. "These other boys got theirs on nice and tight."

As I walk past him and motion to the other three to walk out ahead of me, I feel the old boy reach up and pull at the back of my hair.

"Hey," he says. "People are waiting to see me escort you."

"Now, son," I say, "You ain't supposed to mess up Elvis's hair, especially right before he makes an appearance."

"You ain't Elvis," he says and grabs at my shoulder with the same hand he's just pulled my hair with. "Don't give me that shit."

I spin on my left foot and drop into an eastern stance facing the old boy and about three feet from him.

"Hoss," I say. "No, I ain't Elvis. And the karate I know ain't the karate Elvis played around with in Memphis, neither. It's real."

The old boy steps back, blinking, and swallows hard, while he tries to think whether or not he's gone so far he can't back up in front of his buddies.

"Just don't touch me," I say, "and everything'll be all right. Otherwise, it's going to get real strange in this hallway."

"Go sit down somewhere, Roy," says one of the other ones. "It's done time for Mr. Lee to get on stage."

We leave him blinking in the hall, and I tell the boys how I want them to arrange themselves when we go through the front door of the building.

The one in front will cue the band first, and then I'll enter with the two escorts on each side of me, walking fast and not looking to one side or the other.

This time the band nails it right on the head as I come in. The first notes of the theme from *2001* have already started, and the big drum is starting up as the spotlight hits me full in the face as I come out onto the dance floor. The old boy in front is making a beeline for the bandstand, and the other two are right beside me, their arms held way out like I told them.

We have to pass through a crowd of tables lined up at the edge of the dance floor, and of course that's where a good concentration of the edgiest ones have set themselves down. The ones like that come early, you see, and figure out where the entrance will be made so they can get close to somebody that looks alive to them.

What these folks always wanted is the same thing I see in the eyes of the women there in Vereen and Jane's in Tallahassee, leaning over from their tables with their hands stretched out toward me as I walk by them. At first, here and there a loudmouth will let out a holler, maybe something like, "Long live the King" or "Ooowee Elvis" or just a loud drawn-out scream. What he's doing is trying to find a way to handle that feeling that's come on him when he saw me come through that door. He's yelling like that to let people know he doesn't really believe that feeling and that, hell, he ain't even having that feeling anyhow. What that dude is doing is making fun of his own response to the scene so he can go on believing he's in control of himself. He knows what's what. He's no fool, he's saying.

Most of the rest of them are just real quiet when they see Lance Lee come in. They know it's not the King himself, so they don't carry on the way they always did before the big date in 1977 when they knew it was the King himself every time, no reason to doubt, no questions to raise.

But now they see me come in, Lance Lee, and they don't believe, but Jesus God, they want to. And before the show is over, they will, because I'll give them what it takes to make believers out of anybody. I'm not talking about a good imitation, you understand. I'm giving them the thing itself. Jesse Garon. The other half of the Presley twins, that dynamic duo only a few people's ever known about.

But what they don't know and what I've had to live with every damn minute of my life since the first time I realized I wasn't him is that I'm resurrecting half of myself. And that half isn't really dead now, but it was dead right up to the time the other half died. I'm alive, and the way I show it is by bringing back the dead.

When I hit the stage the drummer changes rhythm just like I taught him that afternoon, and some old boy steps up from the back of the bunch and hangs a guitar around my neck. After he's done that, I grab the mike off the stand and go into "C.C. Rider." See, I do a later Elvis. I have to, of course, because time is kicking my ass like it is everybody's. But I don't do a dying Elvis. I am *alive*, like I've been saying, in case you haven't heard.

The band is all right, there in Vereen and Jane's, a bunch

of old boys who've played together for awhile you can tell, and they rip right through "C.C. Rider," ending up with two trumpets blaring, the drummer pounding the pure dee hell out of the bass and snare, and me in that damn split-leg sideways stance that E had come to love so much. You know, left arm extended, head turned, legs split, right arm windmilling.

I do that move because I have to, if I want to put people in the same room with the later king, but I never liked the way the spraddle-legged thing looked, and I knew it was a cheat. No matter how much he claimed it was for a special "karate effect," it wasn't. I knew better, and anybody with any sense could tell it was really just a way to get out of having to get up on the toes and jerk that pelvis back in and pop it out again.

I hated it. And the reason why is that I still had that rubber band in the small of my back, and I could bring it. I could still snap that thing when Elvis was having to pose instead of move. You can tell it in some of those documentaries you see on HBO or in the discount movie houses. Whenever the sweat's flying and the fingers are popping and the hips are humping right up to the end of the act, you're looking at Jesse Garon, buddy, not at the other twin. Not the one who's O.D.'d on peanut butter and banana sandwiches and about two hundred pills a day and people sucking up to him every minute of the day.

All right. The drummer hits a last lick, and the two trumpets snap off pretty much together, and the applause starts. It's a little slow at first and scattered here and there, but like always, when I come out of the spraddle stance and face them, the clapping picks up and the women start to making those sounds. It's not exactly moaning or sobbing yet, but by the time I let loose it's going to sound like a chorus of healthy thirty-year-old housewives having a simultaneous orgasm in a heated waterbed.

"Ladies and gentlemen," I say into the microphone, "thank you very much, thank you very much." I slur it a little and mumble the words just enough to give it that sound they didn't know they were expecting but that they are glad to get, and then I go into a little rap.

"There is only one King of Rock and Roll," I say, "and I know that better than anybody in Tallahassee or in the world or in Vereen and Jane's."

Most of them are sitting forward in their seats now, and they're drinking their liquor faster and not noticing it. Several of them laugh at my little witticism, looking at each other like people will when they're in the presence of something. I give them the big grin, full into the spotlight, and let them quiet a little. Then I go on.

"His music will never die. And there'll never be another to take his place. I sing his songs in tribute and remembrance of the time he was with us." I stop and look down at the microphone stand like it was something real sacred and fascinating. Then I let my face come up and the jawline pick up the light so a shadow falls from my chin like a drape.

"And he's here with us now. While I can dream." At the last phrase the band comes in with that song, one of the worst things we ever sung, but a damn good bridge when you're cloning the King in North Florida or any damn where else, for that matter.

After that one's done and everybody's come out of the semi-trance I've put them into with it, I go into the first real hard one, the old rocker called "Hound Dog." The little drummer likes that one and rattles off the break sections like a machine gun, really getting up on his toes as he leans into the snares. I spin around and point at him after one of the best runs he does, and the crowd gives him a hand and a few loud hollers.

Elvis never liked to do that kind of thing on stage. I saw him get so pissed off at one of the girl back-up singers once in Vegas for holding a note long enough to get attention that he walked up to her and fired her right there during the performance. It looked like to the crowd that he was whispering something nice into her ear, a compliment or a little joke or something, but I know what he was really saying.

"Go find somebody else to make a fool of, sugar," he said, maybe, or, "You sing so good you gotta be on your own now." She just walked off, a smile on her face, waiting until she was out of the light before she started squalling.

He was like that. Back-up meant back-up. Support meant to be heard and not seen. If you're singing for me, you're singing for me, not for those people out there in front.

I never let that kind of thing bother me, and I figure that's one of the big problems I made for myself. I never was hard enough on people, and that left a lot of room for them to move in on me, as the old man used to always say whenever somebody was putting pressure on him. Somebody wanting rent or a car payment or especially Gladys pushing him into a tighter spot about something she wanted for her and Elvis. Moving in on him.

That's in the back of my mind there in Vereen and Jane's as the drummer hits the last lick on the "Dog" song and I end up my last move with that one, a kind of snap back jerk coming out of a long glide to my left.

Thinking about one of those looks on Vernon's face puts me in just the right mood for the next one, and I just simply sing the shit out of "Heartbreak Hotel." By the time I finish up right in time with the wailing guitar behind me, the crowd has been converted. They're yelling now, and they're baying at the moon, but it's different from the first hollers they put up when they saw me and my escorts first come through that front door. The old boys who were yelling to be able to keep that feeling at a distance have lost that little bit of control, and there's no room now at all between the way they're carrying on and the feeling that song made them have, the place I brought them to.

I have put those folks *into* Heartbreak Hotel. Big, little, old and young, man or woman, they know how the lobby looks, they have seen the bellhop and they have smelled the sorrow on the clerk's clothes. The door to one of those little rooms upstairs has opened up to them, and they have looked through that door and seen that there's nothing inside that room but a bed. And they know that they got no choice. They're going inside. Want to or not, they got it to do.

I let them stand there for a full beat, clapping for what I've done for them and looking into that dark narrow little room, and then I jerk them back with "Jailhouse Rock." Set them back up again, put a drink in their hands and a need to move in their asses, and bring them back to a honky tonk in Tallahassee watching me dance that thing like I could always do.

I have got them now. They are watching Jesse Garon work it on out, and they belong to me. And they are not just remembering a thing that did something for them a long time ago. They are seeing it now, and it's happening right in front of them, and they are more alive right now than they were before I started because they are close to something again that's more alive than anything is in their day-to-day.

You see, when you resurrect a thing you don't just remind people of how it used to be. You make it happen right now. You bring people right up against that thing that gave them that feeling in the first place, and you make them have that feeling again. When I'm rocking, when I am in the damn middle of a spasm, they ain't remembering some little scene from 1961 or thinking how it used to feel to feel that way. They are doing it right now.

Like that little blue-haired lady said to me in Pensacola last week, leaning out of her chair to grab my arm after the last show on my way out, "I don't care what you say your name is, honey. You could be Elvis Presley."

"Sugar," I said to her, "I might well be."

But I'm here to tell you I'm not. I'm the twin. This is him speaking. This is me. This is Jesse Garon Presley, and I am cloning the King.

And I still got Mama's picture with me to prove it.